# Fool, stop, Trippin'

ALSO BY TINA BROOKS MCKINNEY
*Lawd, Mo' Drama*
*All That Drama*

# TINA BROOKS MCKINNEY

SBI

STREBOR BOOKS

NEW YORK LONDON TORONTO SYDNEY

Strebor Books
P.O. Box 6505
Largo, MD 20792
http://www.streborbooks.com

ISBN-13 978-1-59309-185-9
ISBN-10     1-59309-185-0
LCCN 2007943465

Cover design: www.mariondesigns.com

First Strebor Books trade paperback edition March 2008

10   9   8   7   6   5   4   3   2   1

Manufactured in the United States of America

For information regarding special discounts for bulk purchases, please contact Simon & Schuster Special Sales at 1-800-456-6798 or business@simonandschuster.com

# Dedication

This book is dedicated to all the readers who have supported
my work and the new ones who stumble upon it.
It's not often that writers get the chance to says thanks,
but I am. Thank you.

# Acknowledgments

When I was reminded that I hadn't turned in my acknowledgments for this book, I immediately panicked. Throughout the year, I have kept a running list of all the wonderful people who touched my life and helped me along in my career but when I looked for it, I could not find it. Drats! So, I'm starting from scratch under deadline and I pray that I don't miss anyone but I know I shall. Please charge it to my head and not my heart. Nine times out of ten, you know how much you mean to me and don't have to see it in print but…here goes.

This book is dedicated to my husband, William McKinney. Without you in my corner, I don't know where I would be. Your love and support mean the world to me. The little things you do show me how much you love me and I can't thank you enough for being there. 'Cause at the end of each day, I need to see you. My children, Shannan and Estrell. I thank God for blessing me with two wonderful children. I am so proud of each of you. I wouldn't change a hair on your heads. Estrell (E), your poetry is awesome. Continue shining your light for the world to catch up with you. Visit his site at www.simplyE.net to see why I'm especially proud.

Ivor and Judy, it goes without saying that you both light up my life. When the world beats me up, I can always count on y'all to hug me through it. I love you both.

Theresa Brooks, my sister, you have been beside me supporting me from the day I started to walk. Oh, wait a minute, I forgot that you tried to take me out every chance you got (LOL) but once you got over whipping my behind, your love has shone through. Thanks so much for all you've been doing to support me on this literary journey. I appreciated every postcard, flyer, website, every picture, the youtubes. Girl, you have mad talent and it's my hope that people will see it and you the way I do. You can visit my sister who is my visionary. I tell her what I want and she makes it happen. www.preservinglastingmemories.com.

Okay, this is the hard part. Listing my friends and literary associates because this is where I'm sure I'm going to screw up. To my childhood friends, Angie Simpson, Valerie Nixon and Andrea Tanner, I don't care when I call, you always have a smile for me and a warm hug. It don't matter if we haven't spoken in months, we can pick up as if it were yesterday. How many people can proudly say they have friends since elementary school? I love you all. I also couldn't forget to mention my second mothers Ernestine Tanner and Clemetine. My cousins, Donna, Tarcia and Laura.

My Keough crew, Luana (I spelled it write), Tammy, Lessia, (if I spell this one wrong, I better not come back to Baltimore without a bodyguard), Wanda, Lois, Muriel, Donna Lee, April. Cheryl (Snoopy), Niecy, thanks for showing up and out for me and the continued support. Love ya'll too. The Godsey family, Ms. Godsey, Leslie and Allison. Diane Turner and Regena Nash, thanks for being such longtime friends. I count myself lucky to have known you both.

My reading supporters—Monique and David, Shontel, I'm about to butcher the rest of the family names so I'm going to say the whole family cause I done met them all and broke bread with them. Thanks for your support, not just of me, but the whole Strebor Family. Dee Ford, hurry up and have that baby so you can do some thangs. My road dawg, Tina Hayes, I just love you, girl. Thanks for hanging with me this year and many more to come. We've had a blast. Kathy Shewbart, I know we don't see each other as much these days but you know I love you, girl. Your insight has been missed so I got to get you reading my next book with a quickness. Muriel Broomfield, Sam Willis, Mammie Ellis, and Maceo Hayward, my DeKalb County mouthpieces. Words can't describe how you all touch my soul. Thank you. Ms. Margaret in Owings Mills, I didn't forget you! Janice from RAW, what the hell is your last name? Well, you know who you are. You are a special lady but I'm sure everybody has told you that. I love ya. The twins from Karibu—ya'll got me in trouble, LOL. Janet, where the heck you been, missy—I miss ya. Kim Floyd, Ro, Patrice, Paula Henderson, Dee-Dee, Donna Cager, Dionne McKenzie, Malcolm Craig Barnett, Donna Cooley, Angela Elam, Felicia Alston, Melonise Wheeler, Al House, Marvin Meadows, Stephanie Wilkerson, Yasmin Coleman and Lynell Washington for your edits on *Fool*.

My Strebor Family—Allison Hobbs, thanks for the late-night talks and the laughs, I'd room with you any day; Rodney Lofton, my new baby brother; Harold Turley, minus the locks that I still haven't seen; Nane Quartay (you keep me laughing), D.V. Bernard, William Fredrick Cooper, Rique Johnson (no socks), Lissa (Queen of Promotions) Woodson, Suzetta Perkins, Marsha Jenkins-Sanders (the praying one, bless your heart and thanks), Dywane Birch, man, I love you (Allison don't get mad), Sonsyrea,

Caleb, Jessica and the rest of the Strebor fam that I haven't gotten to hang with YET, I love you all.

My other writing friends, Kim Sims, Thomas Green, Gayle Sloan, all the writers in ASA, ya'll know who you are; Sylvia Hubbard, Sybil Barkley, D.L. Sparks, J.D. Mason, SHELLEY HALIMA, my co-conspirator and sista friend; Kim Robinson, Vanessa Johnson, LA Banks, oh LAWD, I can't do no mo.

My groups, RAW4ALL and its founder, Tee C. Royal, Passion4reading, Sexyebonyreaders, APOOO, ASA, Between Friends, Queens Bookclub, and GAAL Bookclub. There are others but I'm getting tired now. Charge it to the head, not the heart, cause I am suffering from CRS—can't remember shitz!

My co-workers, Talisa Clark, Gaynell McMillian, Diane Mendez, Alita Bowman, Dawn Spivey, Wayne Albert, Canettra Petty, Hassibah, Lasonji Strickland, Princella White, Kelvin Walton.

Special shouts and love to my girl Porcia Foxx—glad you are back at the V.

To everyone else I didn't mention, it's not because you don't have a special place in my heart; it is because I've run out of time to turn this in. Thanks for your support.

# *Tarcia*

"I'm telling you, Tarcia, there is something evil at work here."

"What are you talking about, Lasonji?"

"Can't you feel it?"

"Uh, no, I don't feel shit."

"Well, I can. It's like an omnipresence and it's weighing down the very air we breathe." She walks around the living room picking up my various knickknacks and dusting them off. I love my cousin dearly, but sometimes she gets on my last nerve. She is two years older than I am, but we are still thick as thieves. So when she called and said she needed a place to crash, I didn't hesitate to open my humble abode to her.

"Girl, I done told you I ain't having any of that backwoods mumbo jumbo in my house."

"I ain't brought anything to your house, heifer; this shit was already here when I got here."

"So you say. Just don't start practicing that shit up in here or I'll have to ship your ass straight back to Louisiana."

"Now see, that's some cold shit. I'm trying to help your foolish ass and you got threats."

"Not threats, promises. The first chicken bone I see lying around in a jar with dirt on it, I'm packing your shit and putting you the hell out."

Lasonji gives me a look and I cannot help but feel a tiny bit nervous. I don't want to piss her off, but I refuse to go back to living in fear of the simplest things that she would construe as evil or vengeful spirits. I moved away from Louisiana when I was fifteen and it took me a long time to get that superstitious horseshit out my mind.

"All I'm saying, Tarcia, it's some strange shit going on here and you would be a fool not to keep an open mind and hear me out."

"Girl, I ain't trying to hurt your feelings or anything but I don't believe in that crap." Lasonji bites her nails as her eyes dart from one corner of the room to the other. I can feel panic emanating from her skin, causing goosebumps to appear on my arms. *This is just the type of shit I was worried about when I told her she could stay with me until she gets herself together.*

"One day you will learn to be careful about the things that slip out your mouth."

"What's that supposed to mean?"

"If you don't know about something, you should keep your mouth shut, or you may bring unwanted events into your life."

"What did I say?"

"You know exactly what you said and I'm not about to repeat it."

"Okay, whatever." I pick up a magazine off the coffee table, pretending to read it. I flip through the pages, but the images don't register. My mind skips back to those years spent in New Orleans when we had to sprinkle salt over our shoulders to keep the devil from riding our backs. I could almost feel the prickly points of its claws on the base of my neck. *This type of shit chased me and Momma from home thirteen years ago.* I feel like a teenage girl instead of a grown woman.

"Tarcia?"

Lasonji's family has been practicing Voodoo ever since we were children. Mom and I were real careful about what we said around them as a result. As a child, they had me scared to voice my opinion, but I refuse to cow down in my own home.

"Tarcia!"

Even though I was still young, I felt relieved to be away from those old wives' tales and the strict religious taboos we were forced to follow. It was harder on Momma because she had spent her entire life in Louisiana and old habits were hard to break. But she did the best she knew how to make a normal life for us in our new home, until the day she was run over by a bus on her way to work.

"Are you listening to me?"

"Huh?" I had blanked out and didn't even know it.

"I'm not asking you to believe in Voodoo, but how do you explain all the shit that keeps happening to you?"

I don't have an immediate answer, but I am unwilling to accept the paranormal as the reason.

"What, cat got your tongue?"

"I was just thinking; that's all."

"Oh, okay. Think on, my sista."

When Lasonji goes into the kitchen, I can hear her making a cup of coffee. Even though I want one as well, I don't want her messing with anything that I have to swallow. I chuckle at my foolishness and go into the kitchen to fix my own coffee.

"I would have fixed you one too, if I had known you wanted some."

"That's alright, girl. I like to do it myself. Most people make it too weak for me anyway. I want my spoon to stand up in the cup by itself."

"Oh, you like it strong, huh?"

"Yeah, the thicker the better." We sit at the table in an uncomfortable silence. I glance through the mail, which I had brought in with me earlier, while Lasonji watches the news. I had all but forgotten our conversation of a few minutes before.

# Tarcia

"Girl, look at this; those rent-a-cops are using guns on folks like they asked for this shit to happen." Lasonji is watching the evacuation of the flooded lowlands of the Big Easy.

"Damn, this doesn't make any sense. I heard on the news this morning that black folks were taking advantage of the situation by looting."

"That is not looting; it's called survival. Tarcia, you have to see it to believe it. What else did they expect us to do when our own government left us to die?"

"If it was a bunch of white people in those areas, they would have been flown out a week before the storm hit."

"I know that's right. I'll admit there may be a few folks wading down the street with TVs, but for the most part, people are trying to get something to barter with for food and water."

"Yeah. It didn't have to come to this." I could feel her pain.

"You would not believe the conditions we were forced to stay in. I was fortunate, but my heart hurts 'cause those people are my family." Pointing at the TV with one hand, Lasonji covers her heart with the other.

"I know that's right. They wait till folks are dying, then they want to talk and ask folks to be understanding."

"So folks take matters into their own hands and now they wanna shoot them and shit. Ain't that a bitch?"

"I don't mean to sound racist but it's a double standard. Had it been a white person looting the explanation would be different; they would have said they found a box of cornflakes floating down the street."

"With a gallon of milk, eggs, and some fresh fruit for dessert, and that would be okay."

"Right. What's the damn difference? They knew those levees were not going to hold and they did nothing to help us."

"It's almost like they wanted everyone to die."

"Naw, girl, not everyone," Lasonji says. "Just the poor black folks who couldn't afford to get out. They forget that it was those same poor black folks who built that city. Don't you find it odd that most of those white communities were hardly affected by the hurricane? It's almost like they planted a bomb and blew up the levees."

"I never thought of it that way. But now that you mention it, that idea fits this destruction better than a natural disaster. It didn't have to be this bad; I blame that damn Bush. He could have made all the difference in the world."

"You ain't even lied. If he had only cared enough about the black folks it would have made a world of a difference."

"I was so glad when you called me and told me you made it out. I just hope the rest of the family was as lucky."

"Yeah, me too. We tried to stick together, but it was impossible. They were yanking children from their parents' arms and putting them on buses. This mess is going to take years to clean up." Lasonji shakes her head sadly.

"Damn, it's going to take a whole lot of time and money. Look at that house, the only thing left is the roof."

"Girl, that's my street, or it used to be." Our eyes are glued to the grim pictures showing the devastation.

"You know what I think?"

"What?"

"The blacks who do manage to make it out are not going to be able to afford to come back and whitey will come in and rebuild, making it too expensive for us to live there anymore."

"I know. That's why a lot of the old-timers tried to hang on."

Lasonji arrived in Atlanta earlier that day with a few suitcases, a cosmetic case, and a few dollars in her purse. Fortunately for her, she was able to pack her important papers such as her birth certificate and insurance policies. Others weren't so lucky.

"Now, that's what you call some evil shit," I say, pointing at the television. Lasonji looks at me as if I have lost my happy, loving mind.

"I'm going to pretend that I didn't just hear you say that."

"What?"

"Girl, are you trying to compare your life to what happened in New Orleans?"

"I'm not comparing it; I am saying that bad things happen all the time and it's not Voodoo."

"Tarcia, you may not be trying to piss me off, but you are."

"Why? 'Cause I refuse to accept that my life is being controlled by evil forces and hexes?"

"You know what, this apartment is too small to be trippin'. We will just agree to disagree. Okay?"

"Okay."

"Besides, Momma always said, 'You make your own bed; you betta know when to lie on it and when to get the hell up.'" I wait for her to say something else but she doesn't. Lasonji takes her cup of coffee, goes to her room, and shuts the door.

"What the hell is that supposed to mean?" I mumble to myself.

All of a sudden, the milk curdles in my coffee. I use my spoon to try to mix it up, but large clumps of milk float to the top. Spooked, I pour the rest of the coffee down the drain and wash away the clumps of milk that cling to the sink. Trying not to read more into the incident than is really there, I rinse my cup and leave it to dry on the drain board. *I just bought that milk yesterday, didn't I?*

Opening the refrigerator, I check the date on the milk, but I still have a week left before the expiration date. I shake the carton and it sounds okay, but for some reason I am afraid to open it.

"Girl, stop trippin'." I walk back to the sink with the milk and pour out a small amount. It looks and smells like milk.

*Now, that's weird.* Shrugging my shoulders, I put the milk back and return to my room to read a book.

# Tarcia

Alone at last, I take a quick shower and wrap my hair. It has been a long, emotional day and I cannot wait to get into bed. Foregoing my usual facial mask, I wash my face and put on my favorite nightgown. It is old as dirt, way too short, and has so many holes in it I should've been ashamed to wear it. It is more like a security blanket to me. It was the last thing Momma ever purchased for me. I also have on my trusty wool socks that come up to my knees.

Looking at my reflection, I can't help but laugh. As much as I hate sleeping alone, it is nice to let it all hang out every once in a while. I wouldn't dare dress like this if my boyfriend Kentee was spending the night. He likes to see me in thongs, teddies, or naked as the day I was born with my hair hanging freely about my shoulders, so he can play in it while we make love.

I don't mind his playing in my hair so much when we're caught up in the moment, but the morning after it's a bitch to tame. He likes to curl up behind me breathing on my neck and by morning my hair is a sweaty, tangled mess. Sometimes, when he's riding me from behind, he holds on to my hair like reins, slapping my ass. He also has a tendency to sleep on my hair, holding me hostage until he rolls over. I tried to explain to him how much trouble I go through the next day, but he insisted he didn't want to sleep next to *Aunt Jemima*.

My vain self would wake up an extra half hour early just to bump the knots out of my hair and to put on some fresh makeup. Yes, it was a pain in the ass, but I love Kentee so much, it's a small sacrifice to make.

We have been together for almost three years and although our relationship is rocky right now, I have no doubt we will get it together soon. Sooner or later he'll realize I am the only woman for him. Until then, I'll patiently bide my time. Turning away from the mirror, I get in bed and switch on the lamp.

His side of the bed looks so empty. When Kentee first bought a house, I thought we would live in it happily ever after. We even got married, but that didn't last long. Kentee came home one day mad as hell. He said Leah tricked him into believing that she had divorced him when in fact she hadn't, making our marriage null and void. He moved out shortly afterward because he said he didn't want to live with me in sin. Any other man would have said to hell with that, but Kentee isn't just any old man. Unfortunately, he had to sell his house because he could not afford to pay the mortgage, child support, and rent at his new apartment. So now I'm living in a two-bedroom apartment instead of a four-bedroom house.

Over the course of the last two years, I've nearly forgotten my own treachery. Nobody, not even Kentee, knew that I lied about being pregnant so he would marry me, and I intend to keep it that way. Soon, we will get over our rough spots and we will be back together again like it was in the beginning. Satisfied, I turn my attention to the book I have clutched to my chest, losing myself in a fictional world more interesting than my own life. I know I'm using this book as a crutch so I won't have to deal with the fact that I've lost my job but I make a promise to myself to start looking for another one…tomorrow.

I wake with a start, feeling more scared than I've ever felt in my life. My heart is beating very fast and I am cold as ice. Pulling the covers up to my neck, I try to calm down as my eyes adjust to the darkness.

"When did I turn out the light?"

*Oh great, now I am talking to myself and expecting answers.* I have to go to the bathroom, but I am afraid to leave my bed. I lie there until I can't stand it anymore. Rushing from the bed, I run into the adjoining bathroom. In my haste, I bang my toe on the edge of the footboard.

"Shit, piss, and corruption." I hop to the toilet grabbing my toe with one hand and swatting away tears with the other. Rocking back and forth, I try to rub the pain away. I'm still frightened, but I need to look at my toe to make sure the nail isn't bleeding. I hobble to the sink and turn on the light, but I can't make my eyes open. I imagine something or someone is staring back at me.

"Oh, Lawd, this is getting ridiculous." Peeping, I look at my toe first and a deep sigh escapes my lips. Slowly raising my eyes, I force myself to look in the mirror. "What were you expecting, a shrunken head or something?" My eyes are open so wide, it would be comical if I wasn't so scared. Still cold as the inside of a freezer, I am relieved to find myself alone.

Briefly, I think about crawling in bed with Lasonji like I used to do with Momma when I'd had a bad dream, but I quickly dismiss the thought. She would never let me forget it and it would open the door for more of her Voodoo shit. Nope, I will have to deal with this paranoia myself. Turning out the light, I run back to bed, this time mindful of the footboard.

I can't get warm. I light a cigarette, inhaling deeply. Smoking usually calms me but so far it's not working. I can't shake the feeling that I'm being watched.

It has to be all that talk of Voodoo and the whispers of the past that has me spooked. There is no other excuse for it. I try to remember what my dream was about, but I can't fathom what could possibly make me shake like this. I close my eyes to paint a picture of tranquility, but the canvas remains black and surreal. One thing is crystal clear; there will be no more sleeping tonight, that's for damn sure.

I roll over to look at the clock. It is after three in the morning and I'm wide awake. *I wonder what Kentee is into.* Before I can talk myself out of it, I dial his cell. *If I can engage him in some phone sex, I know I will fall back to sleep. And, if he decides to come over, that will be even better.*

"Shit." I hang up the phone. *Why the hell are his calls going directly to voice mail?* The jealous bitch in me is also awake. He only turns his phone off when he's getting busy and doesn't want to be disturbed. I try to block these unwanted thoughts from my head to no avail. Now, I'm mad, scared, and horny. Not a good place to be alone. I can't do anything about being scared, but I could ease the horniness.

I pull out my trusty rabbit and turn it on high. I put it between my legs and rest it on my clit to allow it to lubricate my pussy. Moaning softly, I close my eyes and pretend my lover is not operated by Energizer batteries. I use my free right hand to gently massage my left breast. My nipple is hard as a pebble, but this isn't enough. I pinch my nipple while moving my hips in a circular motion, pushing the rabbit between my vaginal lips. I push my nipple into my mouth, sucking gently at first and harder as the intensity of my climax builds. My clit is twitching as the walls of my pussy start to quiver. My nipple slides out as I suck my index finger, pretending it is Kentee's dick. I push the rabbit in farther, but something is still missing.

I stick my wet finger in my ass. It is tight at first, but slowly my probing finger slides inside. I'm on the verge, but I'm not ready for it to be over. I turn the vibrator to the lowest setting and lie still. My pussy clenches it freeing my hands to wander. My clit is still twitching, but not as fast. My breathing is quick and shallow. I push my finger in deeper. My asshole closes, trapping my finger inside as I rub my thumb against my clit. This feeling is so intense I have to kick the rabbit back into high gear to keep up with my own growing demands.

I don't even bother to stifle the moans that bubble out of my mouth as I match pace with my mechanical lover. My knees begin to tremble as my clit pushes against my thumb and my ass sucks my finger in deeper. I put in another finger just as I start to cum. The vibrator is warm and sticky. I cry out in relief as I turn it off. A smile replaces my earlier frown, erasing away the fear and my chills. Sleep claims me once again.

# Tarcia

Kentee and I are having a romantic dinner at Copeland's in Buckhead. I'm sippin' my second Smoking Iced Tea and he is nursing a Heineken. We stare into each other's eyes and if I didn't know better, I would swear he is about to cry.

"Baby, I love you so much."

"I love you too."

"I know things have been rough for the past few months, but I promise I am going to make things right between us 'cause I can't stand the thought of losing you."

"I'm not going anywhere, sweetheart." I place my hand on his cheek and he grabs it, kissing each of my fingers. Inside, I am melting. Kentee doesn't show this side of himself often and I want nothing to spoil the moment.

The waiter comes to ask if we need anything further and we both wave him away without taking our eyes off each other.

"Now that I am working again, we can start saving up for another house and this time, we won't let anyone else get in the way." These are the words I had been waiting to hear for the past three years as we played at being in a relationship.

"Now that my divorce is final, I don't see why we can't just start the rest of our lives right now. What do you say?"

*What does he expect me to say? Of course I'm going to say yes—I have invested too much time in this relationship to let it go now that he is finally starting to act right.*

*As much as I want to scream out my answer, I have to go to the bath-room first. The sexy black velvet jumpsuit I'm wearing takes some time to get out of and I have already waited too long as it is.*

*"Hold that thought, baby, I have to visit the little girls' room." I bolt from the table, nearly colliding with our waiter who appears to be hov-ering nearby.*

*I rush to the bathroom, grabbing at my zipper as soon as the door closes behind me. I'm bent over and hopping from foot to foot, trying not to wet myself in the process. Whoever made these outfits really should have put a zipper in between the legs for quick access in case of emergency. Finally free, I plop down on the toilet without bothering to cover the seat. Ahhh…but my relief is short lived as I feel the warm piss run down my legs instead of in the toilet…*

"What the hell?"

My eyes pop open. I'm not in Copelands. I'm still in bed and to make matters worse, I've just pissed on myself. I jump out of the bed, shaking my head in disgust, as I snatch my wet clothes off and throw them in the tub. I grab the sheets and toss them in as well.

"Shit." I don't know what is worse, finding out that the dinner with Kentee was only a dream or peeing in the bed. Is this an omen or sign from God that I'm pissing my life away with Kentee?

"Crap. It's just crap. I don't believe in mumbo jumbo." Turning on the shower I step into the stall, I try to forget both the dream and my mistake, but the dream sticks with me as I get dressed.

"I think a cup of coffee and a smoke will do me good right about now." I grab a cigarette off my nightstand and go to the kitchen to put the water on, but Lasonji has beaten me to the kitchen.

"Good morning, cuz."

"What's so good about it?"

"My, my, my. Aren't we grouchy this morning?"

"Shut up, Lasonji, you know I don't like to talk before I've had my coffee."

"Excuse me…," she mutters something else under her breath.

"What did you just call me?"

"I didn't say anything. I was just clearing my throat."

I roll my eyes at her, pretending I didn't hear her call me a bitch. I'm not used to her being in my house and I'm not adjusting fast enough. I go to retrieve my paper but it isn't outside, which adds to my frustration.

"Shit." I slam the door and start fixing my coffee. Lasonji looks up at me, but doesn't comment on my obvious bad mood. She continues to sip from her cup and read the—.

"Is that my paper?"

"Huh? Oh, yeah, I guess it is." She pushes the paper toward me with a shrug.

"How many times do I have to tell you to leave my damn paper alone until I finish with it." I slam my cup on the table, pushing the paper back toward her.

"What are you talking about? You have never said anything to me about touching your damn paper. I just got here yesterday. The last time I saw you, you were reading a magazine, not the damn paper."

"Uh…well, I'll forgive you this time, but please don't ever touch my paper until I finish with it." *That was Kentee I told to leave my paper alone, not Lasonji. Damn, should I apologize? Hell to the naw!*

"Girl, get a grip. Your ass is trippin' about a fifty-cent paper. Let me get my purse. I'll pay you for the damn paper."

"It ain't about the paper, Lasonji. It's about respecting my wishes, damn it." I smack the table for emphasis.

"Geez, it ain't that serious."

"To me, it is."

"Fine, I won't touch your damn paper no mo'. Is there anything else that's off limits to me?"

I'm being silly and I know it, but I'm not in the mood, and her back talk isn't making it any easier.

"Not at the moment, but if I think of anything, you will be the first to know." I give her my best fake plastic smile as she stalks off to her room.

"I'm not the one who peed in your coffee," she quips as she slams her bedroom door. Relieved that she has left me alone, it takes me a few moments to realize what she just said to me, causing me to stop drinking in mid-swallow.

"Pee?" I lower my cup, expecting to see large clumps of milk in my coffee again, but I don't. I swallow, but for some reason, the coffee has a bitter aftertaste that I didn't notice before. Rising from my chair, I pour the remains in the sink. The hairs on the back of my neck are standing up as I throw the milk and the remaining coffee in the trash.

"Enough of this shit, I'll pick up some more at the store later when I go out."

# Tarcia

Grabbing my paper, I start to go to my room to sulk. Lasonji has her television turned up very loud. Suppressing the urge to tell her to turn that shit down, I am struck with a blinding vision of clarity.

*Why am I mad at her? She didn't do anything.* I pause outside her door. Hesitating, I knock twice, but she doesn't answer. I knock a third time and she turns down the television.

"I'm sorry." I wait outside the door, unsure whether she is going to accept my apology. She makes me wait for a few more seconds before she opens her door. I raise my arms for a hug, but she ignores me and sits on her bed. I take this as an invitation to come in. She doesn't say anything and for a minute I don't either.

"So what are your plans for today?"

She keeps changing channels as if she doesn't hear me.

"I said I was sorry."

"And that's supposed to make it okay?"

"What do you want from me? Do I have to get on my knees and kiss your feet?" I sit down on the foot of her bed staring at her feet.

"Ain't nobody asked you to kiss my feet, but I'm kinda liking that on-your-knees part." Unsure whether she is joking, I toy with the idea for a hot second before deciding it isn't worth the effort. I get up to leave with a big knot in my throat.

"Just kidding," she says. Relieved, I sink back down.

"I am sorry. I've been depressed since I lost my job and I lashed out at you."

"So are you ready to talk about why you lost your job?"

I shrug my shoulders, unsure where and how to begin and how much of the story I am ready to tell. I stare at the television as I think about why I'd lost the job I'd been working for the past five years.

"I got into a fight," I mumble.

"A fight? You mean like fisticuffs?"

"It was a verbal fight, but if my supervisor hadn't been there, I would have snatched the hair right off that heifer's head."

"You got into a fight with another woman? Why?"

"That bitch ain't no woman."

"Huh? You ain't making sense."

"I got into a fight with my co-worker. It had been brewing from day one, and one day I lost it."

"Humph. You don't let anybody come between you and your money."

"I know. It was stupid, now that I think about it, but at the time I wasn't thinking. I was reacting."

"And they fired you on the spot? What about the other girl?"

"They didn't fire me right away. We were both sent home and told that they would notify us of their decision."

"And?"

"They sent me a letter the day before yesterday telling me I was terminated."

"That's cold; they didn't even tell you to your face."

"Yeah, that's what I was thinking. I worked for them for five years and they let me go just like that."

"Who was she?"

"My boyfriend Kentee's ex-wife."

"Oh, this keeps on getting better and better. You worked with Kentee's ex?"

"I was there first. She should have left when she found out who I was."

"Why would she do that? In case you don't know, the job market is tough. What does Kentee have to say about this?"

"I haven't told him yet."

"Why, you mad at him too?" I am getting annoyed. Lasonji's tone is condescending, so I get defensive.

"No, I ain't mad at him; it ain't his fault. It's that bitch's fault." I jump up and pace around the room. Walking from one corner of the room to the other, I feel the walls closing in on me.

"Sit down, girl. Let's talk about this like adults 'cause you can't go around with all this anger pent up inside." Lasonji leaves the room and comes back with two coffee mugs. I eye the cups suspiciously since I'd just thrown away all the coffee.

"What's this?"

"Mint tea. It cleanses the spirit and gives clarity to your thoughts."

"Oh, Lawd, here we go."

"What? Wait, you're just trying to change the subject. Take the damn tea, girl." I take the cup, but I don't sip it until I see her drinking hers.

"Mmm, this isn't bad." I can't remember the last time I drank anything warm other than coffee.

"Stop stalling and get back to the story."

"She started working there while I was on my honeymoon. I didn't know who she was at the time, but I didn't like her ass right from the beginning."

"Why is that?"

"'Cause she's one of them high-yella girls that acts like her shit smells like peppermint."

"Umph."

"What's that supposed to mean?"

"Oh, nothing, I was just clearing my throat."

"Yeah, whateva. Anyway, it was clear from the first day she didn't like me and I didn't like her. My boss started giving her all the assignments I used to do and before I knew it, she was transferred into my department and I was out."

"Out? What does that mean?"

"Originally they hired her as a floater. She went from desk to desk. I worked in word processing. She got my job and I got hers."

"Did they cut your salary?"

"No."

"So at least you had a job. Did it ever occur to you that she might have been better at it than you were?"

"Whose side are you on?"

"I ain't on anybody's side. I don't know this chick from Adam."

"Well, I must have been doing something right, or they wouldn't have kept me so long."

"True dat."

I drain my cup with a few fast swallows, causing my mouth to tingle.

"You got any more of this tea?"

"Oh, you like it, huh?"

"It's alright. I'm just thirsty." She leaves the room and I look in the bottom of the cup to make sure there isn't anything floating in there that doesn't belong. The bottom of the cup is clear, so I follow her into the kitchen to watch her make it. Lasonji is just putting the tea back as I enter the room.

The tea did not come in a box. She had it wrapped in plastic wrapper with no name on it. All of a sudden, I don't want any more tea.

"Uh, I changed my mind. I think I will have a glass of water."

"Suit yourself." Lasonji pours water into her cup once again, ignoring me. She wraps plastic wrap around the other cup—for later, I guess—and sits down at the table. I get a glass from the dishwasher and fill it with ice and water from the refrigerator, then I sit across from her.

"At first, I was mad about the transfer and I admit it showed in my performance and on my face. It wasn't until my former supervisor sat me down for a long talk that I had an attitude adjustment."

"What did she say to you?"

"Basically that I had two choices: quit or get over it."

"Damn, straight to the point. I like that."

"Yeah, she was. It was something I needed to hear. So I let it go and I started to enjoy my job. I realized I was burnt out in my old job and moving around was better for me."

"How so?"

"I don't deal with women all that well, but I had to while working in those close quarters. Floating around was like being my own boss. When I finished my work, they didn't care if I read a book or did crossword puzzles as long as I was at my desk and answered the phones."

"Sounds like the bitch did you a favor. Does this bitch have a name?"

*She is really pissing me off.*

"Her name is Leah." Just saying her name grates on my nerves. Refilling my water glass, I quickly drain it and fill it again. I wait for another smart comment and when it doesn't come, I continue.

"When I accepted my position, I was happy. Leah stayed out of my way and I stayed out of hers."

"So what happened?"

I shift in my seat. I don't want to tell the rest of the story, but I have come too far to stop. "I did my job and got in a lot of extra reading on the side. I was loving it."

"Stop being evasive and answer the question. You know what I'm talking about."

"With Leah?"

"Yes, with Leah. Who else were we talking about?" *What's up with all this sarcasm?*

"She was in the break room talking all this noise about Kentee and it pissed me off."

"What was she saying? Did she say they were still talking or something?"

"No, she's old news to him, he loves me."

"Oh yeah, that's right. I forgot."

"Why do you do that?"

"Do what?"

"Say shit like that. You sound like you are judging me."

"Fool, you betta stop trippin'. I'm just trying to wrap my mind around what you are telling me."

"She brought in this cake to celebrate her divorce and had the nerve to offer me a piece."

"Huh?"

"Huh what?"

"That made you mad? I would've thought that would have made you happy because that would mean you and Kentee could get married, right?"

"It was the way she said it that pissed me off. I guess it's something you had to hear for yourself to really understand. I mean, why in the hell would I take a piece of cake from her when I don't even like her ass?"

"Well, I don't see it as a reason to get into a fight with somebody. You could have just said, 'no thanks' and walked away."

"I guess I didn't explain that well. Let me back up. When Kentee and I got married, he told me Leah divorced him while he was in jail. I believed him, but she lied."

"How do you know she lied? Did she tell you that?"

"Hell no, she didn't tell me that, Kentee did." Lasonji gets up and begins pulling food out of the refrigerator.

"See, that's your problem. Want some breakfast?"

"No, I don't want any breakfast. I wanna know why you think I'm the one with the problem. I thought you wanted to hear what happened."

"I heard. The problem is I don't think you heard yourself."

"What's that supposed to mean? How come you just can't speak in plain English so I can understand what you're trying to say?"

She bangs down the frying pan she is holding and whirls around to face me. Rushing forward, she gets all up in my face, causing me to recoil away from her.

"Stop me if I am wrong. You develop this hate relationship with a woman you don't even know based on what some negro done told you. You gave him every benefit of the doubt and never once did you consider there might be two sides to this story. But because the nigga was laying the pipe you believed him."

*This bitch has gone too far now. I don't have to stand here and take this shit; I'm going to my room. Fuck her and the white horse that she rode up in here on.* I get up to leave.

"Oh, so you done talking now that I called you out?"

"You are not my mother and I don't appreciate your getting all up in my face."

"I ain't trying to be your mother. I'm trying to talk some sense into you."

"Why you jumping all over my man? You don't even know him and you putting him down."

"Putting him down? When? What did I say to put him down?"

"Well...you called him a negro."

"Oh, my bad. With a name like Kentee, I assumed he was black." Turning again, she puts some bacon in the pan to fry. *Damn, she really didn't put Kentee down. It was just me getting all defensive again. I am really trippin'. I was ready to beat her down simply because I thought she wouldn't approve of him. Maybe if things were better between Kentee and me, I wouldn't have reacted the same way, but he has me on an emotional roller coaster and I can't get off. But she still didn't have to get all up in my face and shit. That wasn't right and if I would have hit her ass we would have been up in here tearing shit up.*

"Tarcia, this is what I heard you say, so please stop me if I am wrong 'cause I'd sure hate to jump to the wrong conclusion, especially since you lost your job behind this shit." *There is the sarcastic voice again, I hate that shit.*

"You got involved with a man you later found out was married. He told you he was divorced and you were pregnant, so you got married. You later found out he was never divorced and you blamed Leah for deceiving you. Am I getting it right so far?"

"Uh..." *I ain't about to admit that I wasn't pregnant to begin with 'cause her ass would really start trippin' on me.*

"I thought so. Then Leah comes to work at your job and you get a case of the ass with her 'cause she's married to him and you're not. Sounds like Kentee's the root of this evil to me."

"How can you say that? You don't even know Kentee. Hell you siding with that bitch instead of your own flesh and blood. What's up with that?"

Lasonji turns off the flames and calmly puts the food back. She places the used dishes in the dishwasher and when she is done she turns to me. Her breathing is heavy and her eyes hold a warning that I am treading on dangerous grounds.

"I'm going out. I don't like the vibes I am feeling from you right now and I don't trust myself around you. I want you to really think about what I said, but more importantly, I want you to think about what I didn't say. When you are ready to discuss it, let me know. Until then, this subject is closed. I will not ruin our relationship over some bullshit."

"You...you can't talk to me like that. Hell, you are living in my house. You owe me!"

"Owe you? Bitch, please. I'm thirty years old and you're my family. I also love you, but that does not make me a fool. I know bullshit when I hear it and I will not compromise my beliefs because you're stuck on stupid."

"Who the hell are you calling stupid." I jump up ready to fight, cousin or not. "No one calls me stupid. That's what started the fight between me and Leah."

"Oh, so now you wanna hit me? Why, 'cause I didn't co-sign your story? Things happen for a reason. I'm here because a force greater than me pulled me. I'm not a charity case because I can afford a hotel, but I'm not fighting my Karma."

"Karma! Karma? What the hell does this have to do with Karma? You survived a fucking hurricane and lost everything, that's why you are here."

"I didn't lose everything. I'm alive and that means more to me than some material possessions. Plus, come Monday morning, I'm gonna have me a job. Can you say the same?" She showed me the back of her ass as she sashayed out the room, slamming the door to her bedroom again. *This is not going at all like I planned. We should be having a big old slumber party and all we are doing is fighting. I don't really believe that she can cast a spell on me that would make me walk in front of a Mack truck or anything, but there is no sense tempting my fate when my life is already in the toilet.* The slamming of the front door startles me. I didn't hear Lasonji leaving her room so I'm curious as to where she's going but it immediately reopens. She struts back into the room and I'm ready to kiss and make up.

"One quick question and I'm out. Does he do you like you do you?"

I don't immediately catch where she is coming from, but when I do, I am mortified. She must have heard me going at it last night. I don't even bother to answer. In fact, I can't because I'm so embarrassed.

"I thought so." She spins around and goes back out the door.

"Well, I'll be damned."

# Tarcia

Lasonji was right about one thing; she will have a job come Monday morning and I, on the other hand, still have to find one. She got a job at MARTA as a bus driver, over the phone, without even having to go through the interview process. Lasonji has been driving buses since graduating from high school and Georgia always has a need for them. Our city is growing by leaps and bounds and traffic is a nightmare. People are opting to take public transportation to avoid gridlock and the high price of gas.

Reality has cold-cocked me. It isn't Lasonji who needs me, it's the other way around. Unless Kentee steps up to the plate to help me out, I'm going to start feeling the pinch of unemployment sooner than later. The bottom line is I need a job with a quickness because I hate depending on folks.

Lasonji and I have always been close, but we were raised differently. She is pretty, but she refuses to flaunt her good looks to get what she wants out of life. Momma taught me to use what I have to get what I want. Lasonji didn't wear makeup or do the things that most women do to attract a man. She is more comfortable wearing her hair in a ponytail than sporting a head full of curls. She reminds me of an actress who played in the movie

*Set It Off*, Kimberly something or other. Her most striking feature is her eyes. They make me uncomfortable sometimes because I feel like she is staring straight into my soul while giving me that "are you a fool" look that she has perfected over the years.

Lasonji dumped her husband of five years and is starting all over on the dating scene. I personally think she is bitter, but she claims a man doesn't define her. I honestly don't know what that means.

"I know that's why she sweating me and Kentee. She ain't got a man, so she wanna stir up some shit with me and mines." I march back into my room, miffed and slightly puzzled at the same time.

*I ain't heard from Kentee this weekend. Matter of fact, I haven't heard from him since last week. What's up with that?* I dial his number, expecting to leave a voice message, but he surprises me when he answers.

"Speak."

"Speak? That ain't no way to be answering your phone." His voice is sounding so sexy I want to cum right through the phone.

"Aw girl, you know how I do. Why you trying to trip on a brotha?"

"I ain't trippin', boo. I just miss you. You ain't come by and gave your baby some love in a minute. What's up with that?"

"Uh, you know I've been working a lot of overtime and shit, trying to handle my business."

"And what does that have to do with it? You always worked overtime before, but still had time to spend with me."

"Tarcia, I'm trying to get back on my feet. Just bear with me for a minute. We will be together soon." *He ain't said nothing about his divorce being final, I wonder why?*

"I called you last night because I had a bad dream. How come you didn't answer your phone?" I'm pouting and his nonchalant attitude is not helping.

"Er, I was probably 'sleep. What time was it?"

"I don't know."

"Look here, I got my kids today, but I might be able to swing through tonight after I drop them off." This was not the type of response I was looking for, but it would have to do.

"Oh, by the way, my cousin is staying with me for a while until she can find herself an apartment."

"Your cousin? What's up with that?"

"She's from New Orleans."

"Oh, is she one of the refugees?"

"No, she ain't no refugee, she's an evacuee."

"Refugee or evacuee, what difference does it make? She here, ain't she?"

"A refugee is coming from another country. My cousin lives in this country, so that's the difference."

"Oh, excuse me, now you want to be politically correct and shit." Kentee chuckles as if he has told a good joke.

"Whateva. I only told you because I didn't want you keeping me waiting up all night iffin you ain't coming by."

"Yo, I told you I'd see you later, now 'bye." *I hate when he hangs up on me even if it's his signature good-bye. I could've had something else to say and he wouldn't know. It's just rude and one of these days, I'm gonna tell him.*

In the meantime, I've got some work to do. Glancing at the clock, I notice that it's already after one o'clock and I haven't made my bed. I don't really need a shower since I had taken one earlier this morning after my unexpected accident. *Kentee didn't even ask me what my dream was about. Now that's unusual because he*

*used to use my dreams to play his numbers. He must be really busy trying
to make that money. One time he used one of my dreams and he hit the
number for over five thousand dollars. If he gets here before the drawing,
I'll mention it to him and maybe there will still be enough time to play.
I could use all the cash I can get my hands on.*

I make the bed and decide to cook some dinner for us. I'm not
the best cook in the world, but I do know my way around the
kitchen a little bit. I open the refrigerator, but nothing appealing
pops out at me. Then it hits me. As a peace offering to Lasonji, I
will make red beans and rice and some cornbread. It'll be inex-
pensive to make and remind her of home. If Lasonji comes back
in time, she'll get to meet Kentee and see how good he is for me.
I'm confident that once she meets him, she'll see how deeply in
love we are and lay up off him. Realizing that I don't have any of
the ingredients I need, I rush into the bathroom to change my
clothes and brush my hair. I don't have time to fool with makeup
right now and pray I won't see anyone I know at the store. I grab
my keys from the dresser and my purse, checking first to make
sure I have my checkbook, since I rarely carry it, and then I head
to the store.

While driving, I cannot get my cousin out of my mind. I keep
hearing her say I was stupid, but I'm not getting mad this time.
I am trying to understand how she came to her conclusions without even knowing the principal players. Fighting with Lasonji
was the last thing I wanted to do, not only because she might put
a mojo on me or make my hair fall out overnight, but because
she's the only family member I have left who gives a damn whether
I live or die. When Momma and I ran away, we cut ties with
everyone, including her own mother. They probably would have
respected us more if we had announced our intentions to leave,

but Momma was afraid that they would bury our drawers in the backyard, making it impossible for us to leave the front porch. So we had to wait until everyone in the house was asleep before we could leave.

Momma didn't stop looking over her shoulder until she saw the sign from the window of the bus that said, WELCOME TO GEORGIA. My aunts and uncles still blame Momma for my grandmother's death because they said she died right after we left. I didn't find this out until I called Lasonji to tell her that Momma had gotten run over by a bus. So keeping Lasonji in my corner is very important to me.

Lasonji has me thinking about Kentee and the half-assed treatment I'd been receiving. I hadn't really noticed that he hadn't been around, or called for that matter, until last night. I was so busy feeling sorry for myself about my job that his absence didn't even faze me. Automatically, I want to blame Kentee's lack of attention on Leah and his damn kids, but if I am honest, that only explained this past weekend. It doesn't explain the other days that he hadn't come through to check on me.

After nearly sideswiping a parked car, I decide to concentrate on driving and leave all that deep thinking for another time when I can fully concentrate. I fly through the grocery store like a woman wearing gasoline drawers, tossing everything into the cart as quickly as I can, rushing to the checkout line while barely avoiding another cart trying to get into the express line before me. I don't realize my wallet is missing until after the cashier finishes ringing me up. *Now I know damn well I saw my wallet when I was checking to make sure I had my checkbook. Where the hell could it be?*

"Uh, will you take a check?"

"This is the express line, ten items or less and cash only. I can let you slide with your twelve items, but I cannot take a check. I have a void," she yells to the manager in the booth.

*What da hell? I can't even take my items to the longer line because they won't take my check without my identification, which is in my damn wallet. This shit is crazy because I know it was there before I left the house.* Pissed, I leave the shit right on the belt.

I check in between and under the car seats, but my wallet isn't there. I have no choice but to drive home empty-handed.

# Leah

With one eye squinted open, I test the brightness of the morning sun. Warming rays pierce my eyes as I quickly close them again. I'm not ready to get up and face my day because this bed is feeling so comfortable. But I fight the desire to snuggle deep in the sheets and catch a few more winks. It's Saturday and it's Kentee's weekend to watch the kids, which is all the motivation I need to get my behind up and outta the bed. Normally, he picks up the children at ten and when they're gone, I have the next thirty-two hours to please myself. The very thought of freedom is enough to wipe all the weariness from my brain as I embrace the sun.

I dance around the bedroom as I pick out my clothes and make up my bed. It has been a long and tiring week and I'm looking forward to a relaxing couple of days with Craig. I start singing while I pack my children's bags 'cause in just under forty-five minutes, I'll be taking off the Mommy hat for the weekend. It's a wonderful feeling.

I never dreamed motherhood would be such a full-time job. I also never envisioned myself being a single mother of three children, but shit happens. As a child, I never wanted children. I envisioned a loving and supportive husband who would make me the center of his world. I even fantasized about the life we would live, both of us successful in our careers and jet-setting around the world. Children were never part of these fantasies. Unfortunately, life has a way of changing both your expectations and dreams, oftentimes all in the same sucker punch.

When I married Kentee, I thought I'd met the yin to my yang, my soul mate and life partner. It was like that in the beginning. He showered me with attention and affection. Our relationship was spontaneous and full of fire. This all changed in the twinkling of an eye when I peed on a test strip, marking the end of our love affair with ourselves. From that moment, we had to be responsible parents; something neither of us was prepared for.

Feeling morose, I try to rid myself of those painful memories. Kentee and I have been over and done with for a few years and I am finally happy about it. No longer am I holding on to false hope that he will return. It still feels weird seeing him when he comes to pick up the children. It's like he wants something from me and I cannot figure out what it is. I am content with our relationship as it is. I know that he doesn't approve of my growing relationship with Craig, but that's his problem, not mine. Kentee moved on without my permission, and now I'm moving on too.

I'm just waiting for him to mention the fight I had with his hoodrat girlfriend that almost put my job in jeopardy. So far he hasn't said anything but I know it's coming soon.

Yesterday, I finally received word that I wouldn't lose my job as a result of the altercation. According to my supervisor, they let Tarcia go. Although I was happy not to lose my job, I don't like the fact that she got fired. It's rough out there and even though she did me dirty, she didn't act alone. My ex played a part in the whole thing, a very big part, and if I was really going to get mad at someone, it would be him.

I had been avoiding Tarcia like the plague ever since I found out she was the woman my husband left me for. Maintaining my cool wasn't easy, because I really wanted to yank every hair out her head and punch the pure taste out of her mouth at the same time. It was only by the grace of God that I hadn't put my foot up her ass prior to the argument. God handles things in His time and not mine.

The fact that they chose me over her has to be an indication of the good job I am doing. More importantly, I love my job and when it comes down to it, better her than me. *Shoot, she didn't give a rat's ass about me when she was sleeping with my husband. Why should I care about her ass?*

Rushing to the bathroom, I stare at my reflection, pleased at what I see. I have come a long way from the emotional wreck I was when Kentee first left me broke and practically homeless.

A few short years ago, I was about to be homeless, with three small children. I was so despondent, I even contemplated killing myself and my children. God delivered me from my darkest despair.

Today I'm living in a beautiful house, and I have a great job and a new man who cares about me and my children. *God you are good. Oh Lord…if you would bless me with the skills…I will write a book about how you delivered me from evil. How you picked up my broken-down body and forced life into my bones. And Lord, how you gave me hope and made my life better than I've ever imagined it could be. I just want to thank you, Lord. And can I say an amen, Lord for sending me a real man who knows how to handle his business and for showing me that I needed to make a choice, Lord. Oh, Lord, thank you.*

I dance around the bathroom as if I am really in church. Even though I am joking around I mean every word I say. Kentee thought he was working his way back into my good graces, but I had news for his behind, it was not gonna happen.

"Damn." My happy feeling has evaporated. Dealing with Kentee depresses me. He makes me feel like he is doing me a favor by watching his own kids. As much as I want this weekend of freedom, I wish he would agree to pick up the children from my mother's house so I would not even have to look at his ass. But he ain't trying to hear that. He thinks he is going to work his way back into these panties. Little does he know, I'm so over his shit, it ain't even funny. The only way he will ever see my panties again is if he checks the washing machine. Fool me once, shame on you; fool me twice, shame on me. That motherfucker fooled me a whole bunch of times, but it is over now. I am going to send him on his way with a quickness so I can enjoy the rest of my weekend. I've spent enough time thinking about his dumb ass.

I know how Kentee's mind works. He's trying to show he's worthy of a second chance. I haven't discouraged him yet, but I haven't encouraged him either. I don't think he deserves the advance notice since he didn't tell me he was having an affair with Tarcia after the twins were born. "What's good for the goose is good for the gander," Momma always said. If I have to pretend to still have feelings for him in order for him to do right by his kids, then so be it. I need my downtime for the children's sake, without being a burden to my mother all the time who is suffering from her own health issues. Nagging thoughts invade my peace as I hold a conversation with the mirror.

*How much longer do you think you are going to be able to string him along?*

*As far as I am concerned, I ain't never gonna tell him the truth. He never told me the truth so why should I be so forthcoming?*

*I'm not saying that you have to blab your mouth about Craig, but you will have to stop letting Kentee think you are considering his games. Why did you tell him that you would ask your mom to watch the kids next week, so ya'll can go out on a date?*

*How stupid is this? I am arguing with myself.*

Disgusted, I turn away from the mirror and start getting dressed. Yes, I am playing with fire but I'm not ready to end my weekend retreats. The reality is that if Kentee knew the extent of my feelings toward Craig, he would never see his children again. I brush my hair as I try to convince myself that I am doing the right thang. The phone interrupts my private conversation.

"Hello."

"Hey, baby, it's me." The words grate on my nerves. I haven't been his baby in a long time.

"Hello, Kentee. Is something wrong?"

"No, I'm on the way. I was just wondering if you want to hang with me and the kids today."

"Kentee, I hang with the kids every day. So no, I will pass."

"What about the hanging with me part?" *Ew, does donkey shit stink? How do I tell him that I would rather be run over by an eighteen-wheeler than go anywhere with him?* For now, I choose to play his game, so I stall.

"Uh…Kentee, I have to work today. They are depending on me to finish up this brief I was working on before I left."

"Damn, that job is really taking advantage of you. That's why I never let you work when we were together. We are going to have to see about your getting back to the full-time mom status, aren't we?" Kentee is laughing, but I cannot force myself to pretend that I found that even remotely funny. Kentee wants to keep me barefoot, pregnant, and dependent so he can control me. That shit is not happening to me ever again, even if Craig and I do decide to take our relationship further.

I will never ever be in the position where I'm totally dependent on a man. I will always have my own money and if the fool wants to act an ass, it won't have any financial effect on me. That was a life lesson Kentee taught me well and I refuse to ever forget it.

"Maybe I can join you some other time. Are you still going to be here at ten?"

"Yeah, I'm leaving the house now." I can tell he is pouting.

"Okay, I'll have them ready because I really need to get to work."

"Alright, then, see ya later."

I stop by Kayla's room first. She's about to turn eight and is the spitting image of me when I was her age. She pretends to be asleep, but I can tell she isn't. Her lips are holding a trace of a smile. I play along with her charade, acting like I'm going to leave the room, but she giggles.

"I'm just playing, Mommy."

"Oh, you're trying to trick me, huh?" I approach her with my fingers splayed and ready to tickle. She laughs before I even touch her.

"Mommy, stop, I have to pee." She has a point. If I tickle her now, she will wet the bed and I don't feel like adding linen changes to my list of chores I need to do before Craig gets here.

"Okay, you win. Hurry up and get dressed. Your dad will be here soon and you know how he hates to wait." She throws back the covers and leaps from the bed.

"I love you, Mommy."

"I love you too, Pumpkinhead."

"What are you going to do while we're gone, Mommy?"

"Oh, I don't know. I think I might go to a movie with Mr. Craig."

"Good, I don't want you to be lonely. Ask him to take you to see an adult movie for a change, not that baby stuff Malik and Mya wanna see."

"What do you know about adult movies?"

"Mom, everyone knows adult movies are rated 'R.' It even says it on commercials, that children under seventeen are not allowed."

"Well, excuse me." I pinch her nose as I turn to leave the room. "I'll make sure I ask him. Now get dressed." I close the door behind me. I'm shocked that Kayla is finally able to look past herself and care about what I'm feeling. This is one of the biggest problems I have with raising children; they focus only on themselves and not the family as a whole. My oldest is growing up.

Next, I check on Malik. Much to my surprise he's already dressed. He was so quiet I didn't hear him moving around the room he shares with his sister Mya. Although he's too old to share a room with his sister, he's very protective of her and wants to look after her. Mya and Malik are twins, but they are as different as night and day.

Malik will be in second grade next year and he finds it difficult to be away from his twin during the school term. Mya has autism and she'll continue to receive full-time care at the daycare center she attends while her brother and older sister go off to school.

"Hey, little man, how long you been up?"

"Hi, Mommy. Mya kept making noises so I got up and got dressed."

"Why didn't you come and get me?" I ask, stooping down to check Mya's head for a fever. Mya sleeps on the floor. She kept hurting herself when she rolled out of the bed, so I decided it was safer for her to remain on the floor.

"They weren't sick noises, she was making sleep noises."

"She was snoring?"

"Yeah, that's what she was doing, snoring."

"Oh, okay. Are you ready to spend the weekend with your dad?"

"I guess." He doesn't appear to be excited, but in all honesty I didn't expect him to be. He's not one to be easily fooled by the okie-doke and his father is full of that.

"Do you need me to help pack your bag?"

"No, I did it myself."

"Good. Did you put in some clean underwear?"

"Yes."

"Then why don't you go downstairs and watch television while I get your sister dressed."

"Okay." He hops off the bed without further ado and races down the stairs. If he is trying to beat his older sister, he will still be in luck because I could still hear her puttering around in her room.

"Come back here, young man, and make your bed."

"Sorry, Mom." He made his bed quickly by pulling the covers up without bothering to smooth out the wrinkles in the sheet under his comforter.

"I'll fix it later, go 'head and claim your spot."

I tap Mya on the shoulder as she rolls over. I sign to her that it's time to get up and surprisingly she signs back. She gets up and proceeds to make her bed. This is another small shock. Some days Mya's full of cooperation but I have learned not to expect it. I kiss her gently on her forehead and remove her suitcase from the closet.

Mya has been using sign language to communicate ever since she turned three. Craig, her teacher, discovered her hearing problems when she started at the daycare center, then he started teaching our whole family how to communicate with her. Mya used to get so frustrated because she couldn't communicate with her brother and sister, so signing helps us all.

I hold up several outfits for Mya's inspection. Over the last few years, I learned I would get better results from Mya if I allowed her to make some of her own choices. She points to a pretty dress that she wants to take with her, and I smile at her selection. I ask if she wants to wear a different dress today and she nods yes. I place the outfit on her bed and finish putting the other dress in the suitcase along with clean underwear and socks. The doorbell rings as I'm tying Mya's shoes. I can hear Kayla running down the hallway before I can get out the door.

"Don't forget to ask who it is before you open the door, Kayla," I shout down the stairs.

"Okay." I look over the banister, but I can't see who is there.

"Who's at the door, Kayla?"

"The mailman."

"Oh, okay, just put it on the coffee table."

"I did already."

Why the hell was the mailman ringing the doorbell? I turn my attention to my own appearance. Although I don't give a rat's ass what Kentee thinks of me anymore, I refuse to look haggardly. I comb my hair into some semblance of order and go to fix breakfast. I turn down the television because Kayla has it up loud enough to wake the dead.

"Aw, Mom," Kayla whines.

"Aw, Mom, 'nothing, I'm protecting your hearing and mine too." A glance at my watch tells me that I don't have time to fix breakfast after all. *Let him feed them!*

I bring their bags to the door so Kentee can be in and out. I don't do this for him, I do it for me. I'm anxious to get my weekend started as well. Craig didn't tell me what we are going to do, but I'm ready for some adult fun!

# Leah

"Hi," Kentee says when I answer the door.

"Hey." I waste no further time with pleasantries. I start handing him bags before he can get both feet in the doorway. I develop an attitude just seeing him looking so good in his jeans and his black muscle shirt. I look away as I start to remember the good times and remind myself of the bad.

"Damn, don't I get to come in?"

"Why? The kids are ready." I'm not trying to be rude; I just don't see the need for chitchat.

"I just want to come in for a second to catch up and see how you are doing."

"I'm fine. I told you on the phone I have to work. Please be sure to have the children back by six tomorrow night. I have to make sure that Kayla is ready for school in the morning. She has a tendency to lose her homework assignment until Sunday nights."

"Damn, Leah, you don't have to be so cold. Hell, you weren't all mean when I spoke to you a few minutes ago. So why the attitude?" *'Cause I'm still sexually attracted to your dumb ass and it's easier for me if you get the fuck out before I do something I will regret for the rest of my life.* I pause, placing my hands on my hips while looking him up and down as if he has lost his ever-loving mind.

*Is a weekend reprieve worth all of this? Hell to the yes, but I don't feel like faking it anymore. It's wearing on my nerves.*

"Kentee, we are not friends. We will never be friends after what you did to me and the children. You are my babies' daddy, that's it." He starts to speak, but I cut him off with a wave of my hand.

"I have agreed to be civil with you for the sake of the children, but it doesn't mean I have to invite you into my home or entertain you. Now if this means that you are not going to take the kids with you, fine."

"Whoa, baby, hold on. Let's not go back to where we were. I was trying to make conversation, that's all. They are my kids and I want to spend time with them."

Turning before he could utter another word, I announce his presence.

"Daddy's here." Kayla comes running. I could tell she was listening because she came much too quickly. Normally, she would be so engrossed in cartoons I would have to call her at least three times before she hears me. Malik is slower to move, but he comes as well with Mya bringing up the rear.

"Kentee, don't have my babies around none of your women! Do I make myself clear?"

"I am not one of the children."

"Could've fooled me."

"Ya'll give Momma a kiss." Six arms come at me at once and we have a group hug. One by one they let go and follow their father. Kentee leaves without saying another word.

"Be good." I close the door. "Yes!" I still can't believe that Kentee is taking the kids on a regular basis and paying child support. I don't know what happened to him while he was in jail a few years ago, but whatever it was, I'm thankful. Since Kentee started picking up the kids, I rarely bother Momma to babysit.

She only takes the kids when she wants them and I feel better about that. I get the much-needed break from them to enjoy my life and take care of my needs.

I dance into the bedroom to the imaginary music I hear playing in my head. I stop to call Craig and let him know the coast is clear.

"Hey." My voice is sultry, sexy, and suggestive.

"Hey, yourself. Did he come?"

"Yep, he sure did." I'm sure he could hear the smile in my voice.

"So we can begin our date now?"

"Absolutely, the clock is ticking."

"I'm on my way."

"Wait, what should I wear?"

"I thought we would bum around the mall, catch a movie, maybe, and play the rest of the day by ear. Does that sound okay, or do you have something else in mind?"

"Oh, that's cool with me. You know I never turn down an opportunity to shop."

"I know that's right. I'll be there in about twenty minutes."

"I'll be ready." Realizing that I have no time for the long bath I was anticipating, I quickly jump into the shower. Humming a ditty, I want to shout for joy. Craig makes me so happy. I don't have to pretend with him and this is so important to me. He knows all of my secrets and accepts me as I am. We have been dating for about two years and I find myself falling deeper in love with him with each passing day. I enjoy our time together so much. It doesn't matter what we do, as long as we're in the same place.

With my shower finished, I spray my favorite perfume on all my pressure points. Naked as the day I was born, I rustle through my closet searching for yet another outfit. Since we're going shopping, I decide on a pair of low-riding jeans and a tight tee. I complete the outfit with a pink shawl tied around my waist, accenting my butt. I lightly dust my face with makeup and am back in the living room in fifteen minutes. I can't wait to get our date started. And by the grace of God, I didn't wait lon. Craig blows the horn and I practically skip to the car!

"Hey, you sexy thang."

"I beg your pardon. You give a whole new meaning to the word *sexy*." Craig could easily pose for *Esquire* magazine and put those young boys to shame. He's my six-foot chocolate bar with the most intense eyes I'd ever seen. He wears his hair close to his head with long sideburns that connect with his neatly trimmed beard.

"I hope you don't mind, but I decided against shopping today," he said.

"No, baby, I don't mind at all. Come on in and we can talk about what we will do for the next thirty-two hours. I do get all thirty-two hours, don't I?"

"Without a doubt I want to make every second count, but you are going to have to trust me. Can you do that?" His voice is very seductive, causing my panties to cling to my moist clit.

"You already know I have trusted you with my most valuable possessions, my children and my heart." I pull him toward me and plant wet kisses on his forehead, eyebrows and last, but certainly not least, his succulent lips. He sucks my tongue into his mouth as I try to trace his lips. A moan escapes, but I can't tell who it came from, him or me. Gently, but firmly, he pushes me away.

"You keep that up and we will never leave the house."

"And the problem with that would be?"

"Let's go." Confused at his sudden desire to leave just when things are starting to heat up, I stare at him.

"Go, where are we going?"

"Trust me. Get your purse." I grab my purse and follow behind Craig. His familiar Polo Black scent captivates my mind, body, and spirit. The route we are taking is familiar; we're going to his house, a palace compared to mine. He has every modern piece of technology, including a stereo that plays all through the house at the click of a button on the remote control. Luther Vandross is playing as we enter.

Candles are lit throughout the living room and leading up the steps. Rose petals align the steps as he gently pulls me toward his bedroom. I'm not disappointed with this change in plans and don't mind one bit if he decides to spend the next thirty-one hours in bed with me.

His bedroom is also lit with rose-scented candles. It smells romantic and intoxicating. Releasing my hand, he kisses my nose. He begins his seduction by lifting my shirt over my head. He keeps my face covered as he spends time licking and sucking my nipples, now exposed since I didn't bother with a bra today.

"My, my my, what have we here?" He slurps around my nipples causing them to become erect raisins. I want him to pull the shirt from my face so I can see his face as he sucks my titties, but I let him lead this dance.

"Do you trust me?" he whispers.

"Yes." He pulls the shirt from my face and kisses me deeply. I wrap my arms around his neck, bringing him closer. He pushes me away. He unbuckles my pants and pulls them down around my ankles. With my feet trapped, I can't move but I don't have to. He lifts me up and places me on the bed. I lay limp on the bed as he pays attention to my hips, waist, and thighs.

"I'll be right back." My breasts are cold and in need of attention.

I cover them with my hands, trying to keep them warm. My feet are still tangled in my jeans and I resist the urge to free them. Craig is running this train and I'm a willing passenger. His foreplay is creative, but he didn't need to do all this to get me excited; I get excited just by looking at him.

Craig comes back in the room totally naked, his dick pointing at me. My eyes grow wide as I look at his massive shoulders, tight abs, and his thunderous thighs. Made in America should be stamped on his chest. He is beautiful.

"See something you like?" He strokes his dick and massages his balls.

"I do indeed. Can I have some of that?"

"Trust me, in due time." He pulls my jeans from my feet as I prepare for him to enter me. My hands reach out to grab his dick, but he pushes them away. He lifts me from the bed and carries me to the bathroom. The fragrant smell of roses from the bath water overwhelms me. He gently lowers me into the warm water, even though I'm still wearing my thong. Bubbles rise over the top and water slops over the sides, but he doesn't stop to wipe it up.

He climbs in the tub behind me, causing more water to spill, and pulls my body back against his chest. I can't suppress the low moan that escapes my lips. His body feels so good. His hands move up and down my arms, gently massaging them.

"I've been waiting to do this all week. Do you have any idea how hard it is for me to keep my hands off you when I see you? I just want to grab you and eat you up."

"I know, baby, I feel the same way. I don't want your co-workers all up in our business, but I wanna kiss you and hold you every time I see you." Craig starts washing my body with some rose-scented soap. He washes my arms and my chest, but he is in no hurry. The water bubbling from the jet spouts is designed to maintain the temperature, but those jet streams have nothing to do with the rising temperature in the tub. Cupping his hands, he pours water on my head. Shock prevents me from turning around and slapping the shit out of him as water drips into my eyes. I can't believe he would ruin my hairdo. I just got it done a few days ago.

"Trust me," he whispers into my ear, taking the fight out of me. He washes my hair, conditions it, and finger combs it. Lawd only knows what I'll do with it after the bath, but I don't care. His fingers are so relaxing. I've never had a man wash my hair before.

"Sit facing me," Craig instructs. I rise from the water, turning to face him. Water is still dripping in my face, so he hands me a hand towel to wipe it off.

He washes my feet with a foot brush and removes the polish from my toes, filing my nails into perfectly round arches. He scrapes away the dead skin from the bottom of each foot and when he's through, he licks my toes. He uses a small razor to rid my legs of the new growth I hadn't had a chance to get to today in my quick shower.

"Ummmm."

"You like?"

"Oh, hell yeah." I rest my toes against his dick. It's hard and throbbing. I want to reach out and touch it but I can tell from Craig's body movements, he isn't finished with me yet. He continues washing my body in his slow and deliberate manner.

"Stand up," he commands. I stand and he uses his hands to turn me around. He washes my butt like it's fine china. He pays attention to each cheek and spreads them to wash the crevice.

"Bend over, baby." He uses the friction of my thong to excite me until he slides it down my legs and discards the thong on the floor. From clit to crack, he rubs the washcloth in rapid motion, creating just the friction I need to cum. I scream as I near release.

"Oh, damn, baby, I'm cumin'." He removes the washcloth and pulls me toward his mouth. He sucks all of my juices, leaving me weak at the knees. I struggle to stay standing as Craig washes my pussy clean with his tongue. From ear to ear, he's all smiles. He rises from the tub. His massive dick points at me, mocks me, because I'm ready to back that thang up, but he has other plans.

"Not now, baby, we have to set your hair."

What the hell is he talking about? I don't know how to set my hair without looking like a Chi a Pet, which is why I wear it in a ponytail in between hairdresser appointments. I start to get upset until he utters the same two words he has been saying all day: "Trust me."

I sag against the towel he holds in his arms as he dries me off. He pushes me toward the vanity chair in his bathroom. I notice the bags from Sally's Beauty Supply. In the mirror, I watch Craig dry off and pull on his boxers. His body is magnificent and his dick is still erect.

Craig arranges the items inside the bag that he is going to use. First, he massages my scalp and roller sets my hair better than my hairdresser has ever done. The rollers aren't flopping around on my head when I touch 'em. I'm so impressed with his skills.

He takes my hand, removes the polish from my fingertips as well, and then he applies a fresh coat to my fingers and toes, a fire-engine red that he also has in the bag. I assume Craig's through, but he has more surprises for me in that Sally's bag.

He carries me from the vanity bench to the bed so my toes will not get messed up. He lays me on my back and uses Orange Chocolate Shea Butter to massage my feet, legs, thighs, stomach, and arms. The aroma is heavenly. My legs feel like jelly and I'm so relaxed, I can't stand up.

"How's that feel?"

"Sweet. Thank you, baby. How did you know I needed this?"

"This is for me as much as it is for you. I just want to pamper you today. Now get your clothes on and let's go."

"Where are we going?" I thought we were going to spend the afternoon in bed, but it's obvious he has other plans.

"Just put your clothes on, woman." His voice is stern, but he is smiling. I slither out of the bed, still feeling loose and relaxed.

"My hair is still wet."

"We won't be out there long, come on."

It's warm enough outside that my hair will dry soon, so I'm not worried about catching a cold. I don't like going out of the house with rollers in my hair, but I'm anticipating what else Craig has in store for me.

"Let me take care of this, please. Just put some clothes on that fine ass before I change my mind." I debate calling his bluff, but I'm curious. I scramble into my clothes as he gets dressed. He grabs me by the hand and leads me to his car. We drive a few short blocks to a day spa. Without saying a word, I follow him into the spa. Craig speaks with the woman behind the desk and he turns to me.

"I'll be back in about a couple of hours." He walks out the door and I'm standing there with my mouth open.

"Come this way," the lady instructs. I'm led into a small, dimly lit room where I am given a facial. With the mask still on my face, they place me under a dryer and give me an *Essence* magazine to read. I'm floored by all the planning Craig has done to make this day special for me. I want to cry at his thoughtfulness, but my face is too tight from the mask.

I'd never been to a spa before so I don't know what to expect. Much to my surprise, it's very private and I only see other people when I'm moved from treatment to treatment.

"Would you care for a cup of apple cider?"

"Yes, thank you." I take my first sip and it's delicious. I finish my cider and the technician washes my face clean of the mask. My pores are tingling. When my hair is dry, they style it for me. I'm feeling like a million bucks.

"We are going to give you a makeover. Do you mind if we arch your eyebrows?"

"Wow, a makeover too?" Overwhelmed, I can't speak anymore, so I nod my head. She wheels over a small cart and brushes my eyebrows in the desired shape. She applies the wax and I brace myself for the sting, but shockingly there is little or no pain.

"Your pores are open from the facial, so the hairs come out easier."

"I never knew that." She smiles at me. We don't speak again as she busies herself applying makeup. When she finishes, she spins me around to look in the mirror. The results please me. I never knew I could look this good. This has been a truly amazing day.

"Do you like?"

"Oh, yes, I do. I've never worn these colors before. I normally use a green shadow on my eyes and that's it. Can you write down what you used so I can buy it?"

"Your husband has already taken care of that." Husband, did she call Craig my *husband*? I start to correct her, but change my mind.

"Wow." I beam at my reflection, hardly able to believe the beauty staring back at me.

"He has another surprise for you." She hands me a white plastic garment bag and another bag.

"You can change in here, you won't be disturbed." She quickly leaves the room, closing the door behind her. I unzip the bag, anxious to see what Craig got me. Never in my life has a man gone shopping for me. I fight back tears that will surely mess up my makeup.

"Oh, my God." I hold a denim Phat Farm jumpsuit with red pockets and trim around the collar in my hands. It's the same outfit I'd seen in an *Essence* magazine last week. I grab the bag and the boots are there as well. *How did he know?* Squealing with joy, I pull off my clothes. I hold my breath as I slip my legs into the jumpsuit. After it passes over my ample hips, I allow my breathing to resume. It's a perfect fit. I slip on the boots, anxious to find a full-length mirror so I can see how it looks. I open the door and step out. Craig is there holding two dozen red roses in his arms and wearing a bright smile on his face. Who needs a mirror? His eyes and smile tell me all I need to know.

I start to run forward, but I catch myself. Instead, I strut around, letting him get the full picture. I don't feel like a mother at this moment. I feel sexy and desirable. Craig hands me the flowers and kisses me on my nose.

"I don't want to mess up your makeup." His voice is husky and I can see the imprint of his dick in his jeans.

"Thank you, baby. This is so sweet and the nicest thing anyone has ever done for me. How did you know that I needed this?"

"Didn't I tell you to trust me?"

"That you did. That you did."

# Kentee

I'm still trying to get used to being a father. Sure, it was easy to claim it when you had a wife doing the majority of the work. It becomes a whole different ballgame when you're left to do the work alone. Don't get me wrong, I love my kids and all, but these weekend visits are draining me both financially and mentally. The bottom line is I want my wife back.

When I got out of jail, I made a decision to do everything in my power to win Leah back, but so far she's been resisting my advances. If I could get her to spend a little time with me, I know I could get her back.

"Where we going, Daddy?"

"How about we go over to your cousins' house?"

"Yea!" I knew this would be a hit with Kayla and Malik. The weekends are the only time that they get to spend with their family. I called my sister earlier and she agreed to let me take the kids out for some pizza at the skating rink. She would keep Mya while we skated. Four kids at a skating rink is not an easy thang, but I found out that a lot of single mothers bring their children to the rink on Sundays and they are normally more than happy to help out a nice-looking brother like myself.

If I'm lucky, I might pick up a new flava of the week to occupy my time until I can convince Leah that I've changed.

Kayla and Malik take skating lessons twice a week. They can roller skate and ice skate. I'm more a work in progress, but I can manage my way around without falling most of the time as long as one of those kids don't push me. My sister's kids have little skills on skates. They tend to hold my hand and allow me to lead them around the rink. This makes me a pure chick magnet.

"Kayla, watch out for your brother, okay?"

"Yes, sir." Kayla's very respectful to the point that I often look at her in amazement. I can't help but to attribute their manners to Leah, 'cause Lawd knows I wasn't around long enough to make a difference in their lives. This hurts me deeply. I can't change my past, but I have every intention of changing my future. Despite all my moaning, groaning, bitching, and complaining, I'm happy to spend time with my kids. Child support, however, is kicking my ass. I would rather spend time with my wife and kids so we all could benefit. I would get some of her good loving and maybe, just maybe, I could stop the automatic garnishments of my check.

I spot a honey in pink at twelve o'clock before she can enter the rink. She's holding hands with a child who I assume is at least two. I speed up so I can meet her at the first turn. She is clearly anxious and I put on my best smile so she will feel comfortable. Without thinking, I shake loose my sister's children and focus on my prey. I learned later that if I had looked back, I would have seen my niece and nephew sprawled out on the floor.

"Hey there." I glide by as if I'm a pro and don't even bother to wait to hear her response. I ain't trying to let her know I'm sweating her. She'll need me before I need her, judging by the way she is flailing her arms.

When we go around the bend, Keira and Sean reach for me

again and I steady them, but set them free as we get on a straight path. Speed skating, I catch up with the lady in pink again.

"First time, huh?"

"Am I that obvious?"

"I was speaking about your child. You look like a pro," I lied. I sail past her as if she is standing still and allow my praise to sink in. I can actually feel her checking out my ass and I clench it to give her a better look. I don't care what those ladies' magazines say; women check out men the same way we look at them.

She's young, much younger than I like, but she is fine as hell. So I can make an exception to my old rule of keeping my dates over the age of twenty-five. I quickly skate back to her because I don't want anyone else to scoop her up before I make my move. She is still flailing about, but this doesn't deter me from pursuing her.

"Is this your little girl?" I ask as I circle around for the fourth time. I don't wait for an answer and keep going. The next time, I don't say anything. On the sixth circuit, she yells to me.

"I don't have any kids. This is my goddaughter."

Bingo, she took the bait. The picture I was playing in my mind has gotten clearer. The last thing I need in my life is another woman with a child. But I have to face reality. In Atlanta, finding a woman without a child is rare and if you do, she has an "ugly" stamp on her forehead. Despite the warning signals flashing in my head, I decide to push the envelope.

I circle behind her several times debating on how to make my move and when I'm comfortable, I approach her. To aid her in her decision, I have Kayla with me.

"Forgive me for being so presumptuous, but we old folks can't teach our young ones. First of all, the kids don't trust us 'cause we're liable to fall at the drop of a hat. The only way to teach the young ones is to let another young one do it. They can afford to break a bone. Do you feel me?"

The lady in pink is looking at me as if I am smoking bat shit pretending it's crack, but she's thinking about it.

"Sure you right."

I want her to proceed into the no-skating zone before I fall but she keeps right on skating. So I have no choice but to follow her if I want to continue the conversation. This scares the shit out of me because I can only handle myself on skates in the best of circumstances. The good Lawd knows I can't handle another person in the mix, especially someone with limited skills. We will both wind up looking like Boo-Boo the fool.

Acting more brazen than I feel, I grab her elbow and lead her off the floor. She doesn't resist, despite the fact that she don't know me from Adam. I tear my eyes away from the floor long enough to see if she's going to hit me, but since she's smiling, I take this as a good sign. She ain't even concerned about where her god daughter went when Kayla took her hand. This is my first warning sign, but as usual, I ignore the shit and think with my other head. In my mind we are already buck naked and getting it on.

"Are you always this aggressive?"

"Only when I see something I want."

"And what do you see?" She's fishing for a compliment that I'm not going to give.

"I don't want you to get hurt, and if I leave you alone much longer, you're cruising for a bruising."

"I suck, don't I?"

"I wouldn't put it like that." Laughing, we proceed into the no-skating zone and find a table. I wipe the table, clearing it of crumbs left on it from a previous snack.

"You want a Coke or something?"

"Yeah, that would be nice. Thank you." I order the drinks and some fries. Dag, I'm moving so fast even for me, I don't even know the lady's name. To keep the gold diggers in line, I usually don't like to set the precedent that I'm paying for shit. I drop off the drinks first, while the fries are cooking.

"Dang, baby, I don't even know your name." She takes a sip before she answers.

"It's Meeka."

"Wow, that's different. Kinda makes you want to purr after you say it." The thought is so intense. I have a mini commercial playing in my head, and all of it is X-rated.

"Are you always so easily amused?" She's laughing too, but I don't know if she's laughing with me or at me. If she's laughing at me, I'm playing this all wrong. After getting the fries, I return to the table.

"So are you going to tell me your name or do I need to guess?"

"Guess, naw, I don't think so. You would never get it anyway. My mother was as creative as yours when it came to naming her children."

"Kentee."

"How the hell did you know?" Suddenly, I feel afraid. The last thing that I need in my life right now is a stupid bitch stalker or a straight-up nut. Nervously, I pluck at my collarless shirt. I begin to run through a list of folks who stalk me. Tarcia's my number one suspect. That heifer is crazy and I'm trying to distance myself from her. But I am not ready to cut her off yet because the girl has some mad skills in the bedroom and is always willing to come through when my finances get shaky.

"Earth to you," Meeka said.

"I'm sorry, baby, I did zone out on you, I guess. So how do you know my name?"

"Your daughter told me." Whew, what a relief. I thought I was going to have to excuse myself to the bathroom and make a run for it.

"Tell me about yourself. I know you fine, so you can skip that part." Her face immediately lights up like a Christmas tree right before the holiday.

"I'm single, and looking for love." If I were thinking with my right mind, I would leave her ass right here. I ain't looking for love from anyone other than Leah, but my dumb ass stays.

"Uh...damn, baby, you don't mince your words, do you?"

"Why, we both adults. Why should I pretend? That's just wasting time."

"I know that's right. So tell me more about you. Is that really your goddaughter?"

"Yeah, she is my friend's baby. When she gets tired of being a mom, I step in so she can have some downtime."

"Wow. That's what I call a friend." She smiles at me. But something in her eyes does not look right. She left the child without blinking an eye and she hasn't once looked to see if she is okay. All of a sudden I don't want to be around this chick anymore. I keep getting flashbacks of Tarcia's crazy ass and I don't need no mo' drama in my life.

"Look, I ain't trying to block you in your search for love, so I'm gonna leave you now."

"So you running scared?" She folds her arms across her pert chest, clearing a path for attitude.

"Naw, I ain't running scared. But to be honest, I ain't looking for love right about now. I wouldn't mind a friend with benefits, but that is as far as I want to go."

"Humph, you sound scared to me." Her voice is rising and I feel the beginnings of a scene. I don't need this with my kids around. All I need is for Kayla to go back and tell her mother some other woman started acting an ass on me, especially since she warned me not to take the kids around any women.

"Look, Meeka, it was really nice meeting you, but I got to get back with the kids."

"So you don't want my number or something?"

"Uh, sure. Put it on this." I pull a worn business card from my wallet and give it to her.

"I'm not writing my number on the back of that shit. It looks like something you need to throw away anyway." She pulls a new card out of her wallet and hands it to me.

"Use it when you grow some balls." She jumps up and skates away like she was born with blades under her feet. Gone is the clumsiness that attracted me to her in the first place.

"That bitch just played me." Stunned, I can't believe the game she ran. Thankfully, I saw through her. But I still wondered how she knew my name. She didn't have time to talk to Kayla. Needless to say, I know this won't be the last that I hear from Meeka.

It's way past time to go. I skate back out on the rink and snatch up my children. I have a deep burning need to get far away from this rink as fast as possible. I all but drag both kids to the booth to trade in their skates for shoes, and then hustle them to the car.

"Daddy, why we got to leave now?" Kayla asks.

"I don't want to leave Mya alone for so long." In the backseat, Malik is silently crying.

"What you crying for, boy?"

"You left Kiera and Sean. How are they going to get home?" Shit, I had forgotten all about them. I turn the car around in the middle of the street. My sister would have my ass if she found out I left her children, but that's how shaken up I am.

"I'm just testing ya'll to see if you care about your cousins." I turn to look at my children. If they bought my lie, their faces do not reveal it. They know, like I do, that I'd forgotten them. All I can do now is pray Kiera didn't see us leave.

I stop in front of two cars since I'm going to run in and out and I jump out of the car, leaving Kayla and Malik inside. If I was thinking about anybody but myself, I wouldn't have left the car running, but as it is, my mind is still focused on getting away from Meeka. Something about that chick was not right and only time and space would make me feel better about the entire encounter. I didn't anticipate the problems I would have finding my niece and nephew or the long lines at the skate rental window. I also didn't anticipate anyone else coming to the rink in the middle of an open session or leaving at the same time as I am. But luck has never been one of my friends. Someone wanted to get out, so Kayla decides to move the car for him. But instead of putting the car in drive, she puts it in reverse and slams into the car of a woman who is just arriving at the rink. I witness this as I exit the skating rink and my heart sinks into my shoes.

The lady's pissed as she jumps out of her car to inspect the damage. Her intentions of snatching my daughter out of the car and beating the shit out of her is written all over her face. I'm distracted from my daughter's precarious situation by the woman's beauty, and I allow my dick to consider this until she reaches the driver's side of my car. Shoving my niece and nephew forward, I try to diffuse the situation.

"Whoa, hold up. I saw the whole thing." I open up the back door so my sister's kids can get in. I can't close my mouth as I gaze at her. She's about five feet four inches tall and may weigh about 130, give or take a pound. Her waist is tiny but her breasts are huge, probably a 34DD. Her hair or lack thereof, is what causes my heart to skip a beat. Normally, I prefer a woman with long hair but this woman's head is shaven clean and it has my dick's attention. *She looks like an African goddess, so regal and majestic. I just want to massage her head and lay my face between her breasts.* I wonder how she even stands up without tipping over. Her eyes burn me with their concentration. *Dayum, this bitch is fine.* The fact that she's red-hot mad doesn't take away from her beauty, even when she starts spewing obscenities at me.

"Don't just stand there gaping like a blithering idiot. Do you see what she did? Is this your child?" *Do I lie and say they are my sister's kids, so she will think I'm unattached and available? Or do I fess up and take my chances?* I mentally flip through the Player's Handbook and decide to tell the truth. Normally a no-no in the book, but I hope a maternal instinct will make her considerate of my children's feelings, especially if I tell her that they just lost their mother last week.

While she is pacing back and forth in front of her car and cussing up a blue streak, she whips out her cell phone from her hip. She spins around and glares at me. It's moments like this that make me hate the asshole who invented this tattle-tale device. It has its good points, but this is one of the bad ones. A cell phone means police, child welfare authorities, increased insurance payments, and the wrath of Leah. And I really cannot afford to deal with any of these issues.

"Aren't you going to say anything? Cat got your fucking tongue?" My feet begin to move in her direction. I try a smooth playa move to get her to put away her cell but she's clearly not in the mood. Meanwhile, a crowd is beginning to form. I look around for Meeka, but thankfully I don't see her.

"Hey, hey, hold up, shorty. Can we talk?"

"This child just backed right into my car."

"Baby, hold on. I saw the whole thing and I agree with you." I have my hands raised to ward off a sudden attack because girlfriend looks like she's about to beat my head in.

"'Baby,' my ass, look at my car."

"Look, it was a mistake. She didn't mean it."

"I don't give a rat's ass if she meant it or not. That ain't gonna get my car fixed."

"Wait. Come on now, sis, we can handle this without bringing in the po-po."

"The who?"

"Po-po, five-O, the police." It's obvious she's not familiar with street slang.

"First of all, I ain't your baby and I damn sure ain't your sis. I'm a pissed-off woman with a banged-up fender and I want to know what you are going to do about it." Her finger is poised over the send button. Kayla chooses this moment to start crying and Malik, not to be outdone, joins her.

My head turns back and forth, not sure which situation demands my attention first. It's obvious my attempt to woo the woman isn't working, so I cut the bullshit. With my hands still up in the air, I give her my full attention.

"Please bear with me a second." I scoop Kayla up in my arms and give her a big kiss on her plump cheeks. "Baby, hush. It's going to be alright, but Daddy needs you to be a big girl right now so I can handle this. Can you do this for Daddy?"

"Yes…sir." She is blowing snot bubbles and her lips are quivering with the effort not to cry anymore. I place her back into the car and fasten her seatbelt.

"It's okay, big guy, stop cryin'. Okay?" Malik nods his head while wiping his face.

"Are you guys hurt?"

"No," they chorus. Relieved, I shut the door and give the lady my attention. She still has her finger poised over the send button. I turn to the crowd. "It's all over folks. There is nothing left to see." The crowd starts to disperse, but they don't leave. They go inside the skating rink and gawk at us through the glass doors.

"Nosy bastards." I shake my head in disgust. Taking a deep breath, I approach the lady, pulling out my wallet as I do.

"My name is Kentee Simmons and I really do apologize. I only meant to run in and out, and I swear to God I don't know what possessed my daughter to move the car. She has never done anything remotely like this before."

"That doesn't change a thing, Mr. Simmons. The fact remains I got a jacked-up car."

"I know this and I accept full responsibility."

"You damn right, you do."

"Hey, you don't have to cuss at me. I already said that I was sorry and I understand you are pissed. Hell, you have every right to be, but this attitude isn't helping."

She taps her foot against the ground in irritation, but she lowers the arm holding the phone. She doesn't flip it shut but at least she hasn't hit send. Once you dial 9-1-1 it doesn't matter whether you hang up or not; they are calling you back to find out what the problem is. I speak quickly before she can change her mind about listening to what I am saying to her.

"My cousin owns a body shop a few miles from here. It's fully certified and I would like to take your car there to have it assessed, and if you approve of his operation, let my cousin make the repairs."

"If you think that I'm going to take my 2006 Lexus LE to some backyard punk, clearly you have bumped your head."

"Damn, baby…he's not some backyard punk. He has been in the body business for over twenty years and is highly respected in his trade." Her eyebrow shoots up as she considers my request.

"I have already told you that I am not your baby, so please stop calling me that."

"Uh…my bad. Sorry, but I don't know what else to call you. You didn't give me your name."

"Amber."

"Amber, you don't have to do this as a favor to me, but I would appreciate it if you do. If you call the police, the insurance companies will get involved and not only will my rates increase, yours will too. Just because it's my fault don't you believe for a minute that your insurance company won't find a way to increase your premium as well." She doesn't say anything, so I continue.

"Plus, if you call the cops, I could lose my kids and that would be the worst tragedy of this whole unfortunate incident. I'm a single father trying to do the right thing." I walk toward Amber, trying to turn her around so the kids can't hear what I am saying. She allows me to turn her.

"Their mother is dead. I'm all they got. If they cite me for neglect for leaving the kids in the car, they'll wind up in foster care. Do you want that on your conscience?" She still doesn't say anything and I'm unsure whether she is thinking about it or playing with me. I can't read the expression on her face. I'm pouring it on thick and the sista is doing her best to be a hard ass.

I hand her my license. She looks from me to the four children who have their faces pushed up against the window looking pitiful. *They all deserve ice cream cones for this!*

"You ain't trying to shaft me, are you?"

"Naw, sis…uh…Amber. I ain't trying to shaft you, honest."

"Where is his body shop?"

"It's about five blocks from here. All I need to do is drop by my sister's and ask her to watch the kids and I will ride with you to my cousin's shop. I don't want to take the kids with us because a body shop ain't a place for children." I can see the conflict in Amber's eyes. I pray that she'll come to the right decision.

"Okay, let's go."

"Cool, I'll lead the way."

"Don't try to rush off and lose me."

"Keep my license. You'll be able to find me if I try to run, but I promise I will go as slow as I need to for you to keep up. If I get too fast for you, beep your horn and I will slow down. Okay?"

"Okay."

We get in our respective cars and I gently rock our cars apart. Kayla had really jammed our cars together good. *Lawd, please don't let her whole front end fall off when I get us apart.* Finally, we are separated. I slowly pull out of the parking lot with Amber close on my tail.

I look in the rearview mirror at the solemn eyes of the four children. Clearing my throat, I start to caution the children against running their mouths about the accident, but they beat me to it. In unison, the children quip, "Not a word of this to your mother."

I laugh because something always seems to happen that forces me to swear them to secrecy.

# *Tarcia*

"Hello."

"Hey, Tarcia, it's Meeka. How you doing?"

"I can't complain." *What's this bitch want? She hasn't spoken to me in two years.*

"Are you and Kentee still dating?"

"Yeah." *She doesn't need to know that things aren't going so good at the moment. In fact, the less I say to her about Kentee the better, 'cause that was the reason we fell out in the first place.*

"Oh. I just saw him, so I thought I would ask."

"Where did you see Kentee?" *She better not start some shit with me about Kentee because I will go over there and kick her troll-looking ass.*

"At the skating rink. I've been going there on the weekends to get my exercise in. A girl has got to stay in shape, you know."

"Yeah, that makes sense. He is with his kids today, so it would make sense for him to be at the skating rink."

"I didn't see his kids. He acted like he was there by himself."

"'Acted like'? What's that supposed to mean?"

"Uh…I mean…I just didn't see his kids. I guess they were there somewhere in the rink and I probably didn't recognize them. After all, it's been almost two years since I saw pictures of them and now that I think about it, there were a lot of children there.

So yeah, they could have been there." She's rambling, and normally when a person starts to babble they're lying or trying to hide something.

"Cut the shit, Meeka. What did you really call to tell me?"

"Well, I wasn't going to say anything, but Kentee was all up in my face asking for my phone number and I wanted to know if you two were still kicking it before I let him holla at me."

"Let him holla at you? Girl, I can't believe you would even twist your lips to say that to me. Even if we weren't together, which we are, why would you want my sloppy seconds? Don't you know that boyfriends, either current or past, are off-limits to friends?"

"Well, Tarcia, since you want to get all stank with me, we ain't been friends in a long time. I was giving you a courtesy call before I accept his invitation to dinner." *Oh, hell naw.* Now I know she's lying. Kentee might have tried to get into her panties, but his cheap ass is not springing for no meal unless she gives up the ass first, he gets hungry, and he can't get rid of her. He might take her to McDonald's for a Happy Meal, but that is it. I know that much about Kentee.

"Meeka, you're a lying ass. You might have seen Kentee, but as far as him asking you out to dinner I won't believe that even if I see it with my own eyes. First of all, you are not his type. Secondly, he knows you and I used to be friends."

"Well, obviously he forgot because he did push up on me. When I wouldn't give him my number, he gave me his."

"So what's his number?"

"Uh…"

"I thought so. Bitch, don't call my house no damn mo'."

# Kentee

eaving the kids with my sister, I'm free to handle our business. I am ready to get this shit behind me and go for a stiff drink, a hot meal, and hot sex, in that order. It doesn't matter where I get it from as long as it is good.

"Do you want to follow me or can I ride with you?"

"Ride with me. That way I'll know you are on the up and up."

"Are you going to bring me back to pick up my car?"

"That depends on your cousin's shop. If you lied to me, the 'po-po' will allow you one phone call to be picked up."

*Damn, what a bitch.* I park my car and get in the car with Amber.

"Dag, you don't give a brotha any slack, do you?"

"Why should I? Momma didn't raise a fool."

"Oh, okay. But if you allow yourself to get to know me, you will find out that I am one of the nice guys."

"So you say." I laugh because of the emotion she puts into her words. After a few seconds, she laughs too, slicing the tension that is riding in the car with us.

"I just want to thank you for not involving DeKalb County in all of this."

"You ain't out the woods yet. If I suspect any shady business at your cousin's shop, I'm not only gonna call DeKalb County, I'm gonna call all my kinfolk too. I ain't trying to get all caught up in some chop-shop type of shit."

"Oh, Lawd, not the kinfolk. You wanna make sure I get the beat down. Well, I ain't even trying to go there. This face is too pretty to mess up."

"Umph."

"What? You don't think this face is cute?" I turn left and right, giving her both sides of my profile.

"I think you're your biggest fan."

"Ouch. You didn't have to go there."

"Just callin' it like I see it."

"Hey, I love myself, but there is enough to go around."

"I'll bet you do." A witty retort escapes me, so instead of floundering awkwardly, I compliment her.

"You are one fine woman." I must have shocked her 'cause she took her foot off the gas momentarily.

"Which way?"

"Turn left at the next light." Silence fills the car once again. I really don't mind the silence 'cause at least she ain't cussing at me and giving me more grief, but I'm beginning to get a little ticked because this is cutting into my time. I should have dropped the children off a half hour ago and I really don't feel like hearing Leah's mouth when I get there. I'm surprised that she isn't blowing up my phone. I still have to go back and get them and drive halfway across town, which will make me late for Tarcia's house, and when that girl gets a hold on attitude, she doesn't let it go easily.

If my money wasn't funny, I would drop off the kids and have me a few drinks and some supper at Hooters. Since my pockets are light, I will have to settle for Tarcia. Hopefully, since her cousin is there, she won't clown on my ass in front of her. The reality is I'm damn near broke and payday ain't until next week. I hope Tarcia will let me hold a few dollars to tide me over. I allow my irritation to manifest into attitude toward this haughty-ass bitch sitting next to me. She acts like I have to kiss her ass just 'cause of a little fender bender. Well, she can kiss my black ass if she thinks I'm going to keep taking this shit from her.

"Am I still going right?"

"Yeah, turn right at the second light. The shop is on the left-hand side." I fold my arms across my chest, trying my best not to look at her long slender legs peeking out from under her short skirt. The fragrance she is wearing is tickling my nose and I can't help but to gulp in deep breaths of her essence. My dick has gotten hard just smelling her and I have to fold my hands in my lap to keep her from seeing it trying to get out of my pants.

"What's the name of the perfume that you are wearing?" Amber acts as if she doesn't want to tell me, but finally relents.

"Clinique Happy."

"It suits you."

"Thanks." She parks the car and I bounce out to go speak to my cousin.

"Be right back." I don't wait for her to respond as I trot to the shop. I fill in my cousin on the details and he agrees to help me out.

"So what did your cousin say?"

"He'll be right out to give me the estimate and describe what he will do to your car. I told him you are my girlfriend."

"You wish." She's right, for a nanosecond I do. There's something about this little fireball that makes me want to get to know her better. She's obviously one of those serious chicks always thinking of ways to come up. She is just the type of woman that I need in my life if I am doing the right thing. She's such a tease with a bite, but I'm gonna have to cut her down to bite size if I don't want to choke on her.

"Look, girl, you fyne and all that, but I ain't sweating you like that. I just want him to fix your car so I can go on with my life."

"Oh, am I detecting an attitude? Because I can get mines back; it ain't a thang but a chicken wing."

"Naw, I'm just trying to tell you I ain't sweating you." She huffs and puffs, folding her arms under her beautiful breasts. As hard as I am, it's difficult to ignore her perky nipples, but I'm trying. Our verbal sparring ends when my cousin comes out, and not a minute too soon 'cause I was about to put my hands around this pretty heifer's neck.

"Don't you want to know what my cousin thinks?" *Bitch, get out of the car and talk to the man. Damn, I thought you were smart.*

"I was waiting on you." Pissed, I exit the car. I'm probably going to have to ask my cousin to drive me back to my car 'cause me and this bitch aren't gonna make it without me having to slap her ass. I'm amazed that someone who comes in such a cute package could be such a fucking bitch.

My cousin gives her a date to bring the car in and Amber and I exchange numbers. She gives me back my license after copying down my information. She gets back in her car, but doesn't start it right away.

"Don't you want a lift to your car?"

"Naw, I'm straight, my cousin will drop me off." My cousin gives me the "oh hell I ain't" look, but doesn't dispute me.

"Whateva." She backs up the car, flips me the bird, and is gone. Twice in one day I have escaped a she-devil in disguise. *Maybe I really do need to slow my roll. Naw, I think not!*

# Tarcia

When I open the door the most marvelous aroma greets me. I place my purse on the coffee table and go into the kitchen to see what's up.

Lasonji is stirring a large pot. Her back's to me so I can't tell if she still has an attitude.

"Whatcha cookin'?"

"Red beans and rice." I do a double-take. How did she know I was going to cook the very same thing tonight? My knees buckle and I clutch the countertop to keep from falling. Premonition? Psychic ability? Voodoo?

"Smells good." I try to mask my fear as I turn to go back to my room.

"You still like it, don't you?"

"Uh, yeah, but I guess it spooked me that I just went to the store to get some ingredients to make it, only to find out that I didn't have my wallet."

"So where is your wallet?"

"Beats the shit out of me." I back out of the kitchen, unwilling to turn my back on my cousin. I'm afraid of my own flesh and blood. Regardless of how good it smells, I doubt that I will be able to eat any dinner tonight.

I put my purse on my bed and begin searching my room, but my wallet has disappeared. Locking the door, I decide to take a shower while I'm in the room. I want to be dressed when Kentee shows up because I don't want him spending any time alone with Lasonji. I can't trust the things that come out of her mouth because she is very opinionated.

I finish my shower and put lotion all over my body. Sliding into my clothes, I cannot get these coincidences out of my mind. I believe in déjà vu because I've experienced these feelings before but never in my life do I recall so many incidents occurring at the same time. In fact, all this weird shit started happening when Lasonji arrived. Unexpectedly frightened about what else she could be putting in the dinner pot, I return to the kitchen.

"You find it?"

"No. It has to be here somewhere 'cause I haven't been anywhere in days."

"Yeah, as soon as you stop looking for something it usually shows up."

"So what made you pick this meal to cook?"

"I don't know, I woke up with red beans on the brain."

"Wow, so did I. Oh, by the way, Kentee said that he is going to come through tonight. Do you mind if we have one more for supper? It looks like you made enough." I scan the counter for her ingredients but she apparently cleans as she cooks. I even try to peek in the trash can, but that would be too obvious. I will have to wait until she either goes in her room or retires for the night.

"Sure, I'm anxious to meet the brotha who has got your nose all wide open."

"My nose is not wide open."

"Oh, my bad."

"Do you want to invite any of your friends to dinner?"

"Very funny. There will be a day when I have friends in Atlanta and I might take you up on that offer." Rather than stay and trade barbs with Lasonji I decide to return to my room to put on my makeup.

"Do you need me to do anything to help you?"

"Naw, I got this."

"Fine, I'm gonna do my makeup and perhaps read a little before he gets here. I'm not sure what time he is coming."

"Figures."

"Excuse me?"

"I didn't say anything." I want to call her a liar so bad it actually hurts, but I refuse to take the bait. I return to my room, taking care not to slam the door like I really feel like doing. This day had been weird all the way around, beginning with the nightmare I had last night and including the aborted argument that I had with my cousin. I hope that some serious fucking will stop the creepy crawlies from tramping down my back.

I spray my pressure points with musk oil. Kentee doesn't go for those expensive perfumes. He says a woman's natural scent does it for him. I twist my hair in a bun and lightly apply my makeup. My lip gloss is missing from the bathroom countertop, so I check my purse. The fact that my wallet is in my purse doesn't strike me until I return to the bathroom. Rushing back to look again, my mouth just hangs open in shock.

"What the fuck?" I know that wallet wasn't in my purse the whole time, but I have no other explanation as to how it is there now and not when I was in the market. There was no way that I missed it since I damn near emptied my purse looking for it.

Lasonji? That is impossible because my door's locked and I keep the bathroom door open as I shower. There is no way she could have gotten into my room to replace the wallet without my either seeing or hearing her. So how the hell else did it get there?

Picking up my wallet, I go through it to make sure that everything is still in place. "Damn, first I lose my job and now I am losing my mind."

Despondent, I shuffle back to the kitchen barely picking up my feet. Lasonji is reading the paper and sipping on a cup of tea. My body slumps to the nearest chair as I wait for her to ask me what is wrong. When she doesn't ask quick enough, I sigh loudly. Folding the paper, she just stares at me.

"What's the problem now? I did not touch your paper. I bought it when I went to the store."

"Huh?"

"The paper, remember you got all prissy with me this morning about it. I thought you were about to start that crap again."

"Naw, I was just thinking, that's all."

"About what?"

"Oh, nothing." She stares at me for a few minutes more before she resumes reading. I rest my head on my elbows and would have fallen asleep if the phone hadn't rung.

"Hello."

"Yo, I'm about to run through. I hope you made something to eat 'cause I'm starving like Marvin."

"Yeah, we got some grub. My cousin hooked us up. It should be ready soon."

"Good." He hangs up before I can ask him if he wants me to pick up some dessert. Kentee loves cheesecake and I decide to run out and pick up one as a surprise for him. I even have some canned strawberries that can go on top.

"Hey, I'm gonna run down to the bakery and pick up a cheese-cake."

"I got one already, strawberry."

"Say what? Damn, are you reading my mind or something?"

"Girl, stop trippin'. I can't do no shit like that."

"Well, it sure as hell feels like it." She gets up and starts stirring her pots. I say it's a joke, but the more I think about it, the more believable it is. There isn't any other explanation for this. I begin thinking of our last night together before I left New Orleans. We had been invited over to Lasonji's house for a cookout and we were playing jacks on the front porch after stuffing our bellies to near eruption. If she can read my mind, she will remember and start talking about that day too. I got sick that night and threw up all over her porch and her momma made me clean it up.

"So was that him?"

Every time I looked at it, I wanted to throw up again and the smell was enough to gag a maggot. My Aunt Alice wanted to read the vomit, but Momma wouldn't let her. I just cleaned it up as fast as I could and Momma made us leave. We moved two days later.

"Hey, are you listening to me?"

"Sorry, I didn't hear you. What did you say?"

"I asked if that was your friend."

"Yeah. He's on the way."

"Umph."

"What's that supposed to mean?"

"Nothing. It just slipped out."

"You said it for a reason. Why do you do that?"

"Do what?"

"Start saying something, then say you didn't say anything or it just slipped out. It's driving me nuts."

"What sign are you?"

"Huh? What are you talking about?"

"Your zodiac sign. Which one are you?"

"I don't pay attention to that nonsense."

"When is your birthday, I forgot." She has forgotten all about stirring her pots and is giving me such an intense gaze it is creeping me out.

"June second."

"I knew it." She goes back to stirring as if we hadn't been in the middle of a conversation.

"You're a Gemini. That explains it."

I'm getting agitated. "Explains what?"

"Tarcia, let's not fight. Can't we just have a nice, quiet dinner?"

*She's right. I don't want to be all mad when Kentee gets here. I just want him to make a good impression so she can get off my back about him. We can continue our discussion later.*

"Okay. I'll go set the table." I push through the swinging doors to the dining room and the table is already set. *How did she know I wanted to eat in here? I normally eat in the kitchen.*

"Oh, by the way, some chick by the name of Meeka left you a message on the phone."

Shocked, I let go of the doors and they hit me in the face. Memory whooshes over me. I wonder what she said. Did Lasonji listen to the message? That would explain her cocky attitude. Damn, I don't have time to listen to that shit. He's almost here.

"Oh, yeah, what did she say?"

"I didn't listen. When I found out it wasn't for me I hung up. I was expecting a call from Aunt Joyce."

"I'll listen to it later. Thanks for setting the table."

"I thought it would be more romantic."

"Yeah, it is romantic with the candles and everything. How did you find the time?" Kentee's at the door before she can answer but I'm sure she wouldn't have said anything worth hearing anyway. She's good at evading questions.

# *Kentee*

I'm worn the fuck out and should have taken my black ass home, but my stomach won out over both my heads. I hope Tarcia doesn't give me any lip about being late because I will surely eat, drink, and run instead of laying down the pipe on her as I'd planned. Tarcia is a nice-enough girl, but she's too clingy. She strangles a motherfucker with her constant whining and that shit gets old quick. If it wasn't for her banging pussy, I would never see that heifer again.

Leah didn't do anything to help my mood either. She looked beautiful when I dropped off the kids. Her skin was glowing and she had her hair fixed up all pretty. *How in the hell did she have time to get her hair done when she was supposed to be so busy working?* I tried to push up on her and she reacted like I'd been gargling garbage.

"Kentee, move."

"What?"

"You're all up in my space."

"Your space? There was a time when your space was my space."

"Yeah, but those times are over." She pushed me back farther and if I hadn't shut the door, I would be out on the stoop looking like Yogi Bear.

"That's what I want to talk to you about."

"Oh no, I'm not about to get into that discussion with you tonight. I've got to get the children ready for school in the morning. As it is, I'm already an hour behind schedule thanks to you. You have no idea how difficult it is to juggle all this alone. One little thing can upset the whole schedule."

"See, that's why I left you. You never have time for me."

"You selfish prick. You just don't get it. When we became parents, we had to make sacrifices, but you never got it. We've got three children depending on us to raise and protect them. It's always been about you and damn everyone else."

"Leah, that's not what I meant. Damn, why you trying to twist my words and shit."

"I ain't twisting shit. Just think about what you said. Well, what about me? Did you ever stop to think about how I was feeling and what I was going through?"

"Yeah, but—"

"But hell. You didn't think about anyone else but your damn self, especially when you left us to fend for ourselves. So don't you weave your lips to say some dumb shit like that to me ever again."

"God, you sure are sexy when you're mad." I stepped toward her again to give her a kiss.

"Kentee, I think you need to leave now before we each say something that we'll regret."

"My only regret is that I let you go."

"Good night, Kentee."

"Leah, please."

"No, Kentee, it's late and I have things to do." Her chin was fixed and stubborn and I didn't want to make her any madder, so I left. The door closed before I can start begging. The sound of the lock catching was like a knife in my heart.

"Damn, that's not the way it's supposed to go down." Slapping the steering wheel, I get mad at myself for rushing her. I knew I would not win her back in a day, but my patience is wearing real thin. I drive to Tarcia's house in a total daze, barely paying attention to traffic signals or the speed I am going.

*She would not be acting all high and mighty if she didn't have ole dude all up in her face all the time. Shit, the first thing I'm going to do when I get her back is take my children out of that center. She is also gonna have to quit that job. She's gotten too damn independent for my taste.*

Even as I knock on Tarcia's door, my mind is still back at Leah's house.

"Hey, baby!" Tarcia rushes me, wrapping her arms around my neck and her legs around my waist. She damn near knocks me down as she plants a big kiss on my lips. I struggle to remain standing as she curls her legs around my knees.

I unwrap her from my body as gently as I can so she won't start pouting.

"Uh, can you at least let me in the house before you attack me?"

"Oh, I'm sorry, baby. I'm just so happy to see you. I've missed you."

"I see." She grabs my hand, dragging me into the house. Slamming the door, she is on me again, forcing her tongue in my mouth and grinding her hips against me. Against my will, my body starts to respond to her ardent kisses as my arms wrap around her waist, bringing her closer.

"Ahem...dinner is ready."

I had forgotten all about Tarcia's cousin as I peel my lips away, and obviously Tarcia had too. I open my eyes to this incredible vision of loveliness leaning against the wall. Her beauty was understated but very visible despite her tomboyish outfit. Pushing Tarcia away, perhaps too forcefully, I run my hands down the crease in my pants and straighten my shit. I give her my most engaging smile, but she doesn't return it. Pouting at the snub, Tarcia folds her arms in front of her chest.

"Lasonji, this is Kentee." She looks me up and down with the most concentrated stare I'd ever encountered. It feels like she is stripping me of my clothes and my manhood. My dick shrivels against her cold gaze.

"Hi, nice to meet ya."

"Dinner is ready." She leaves the room without saying another word. Bewildered, I look at Tarcia. She twirls her finger alongside her head indicating her cousin is a nut. *Nut or not, the babe is fine.*

We sit down to eat and Lasonji passes out the plates. I want to start a conversation, but I'm so hungry I can't help but to dig right in. Lasonji stops me before I get the next spoonful in my mouth.

"We say grace around here." Chastised, I put down my spoon, bowing my head. Normally, I do thank God for providing a hot meal but this had been such a crazy day, I'd forgotten. I hold the food in my mouth, unwilling to swallow until grace is completed. The burn starts slowly as the insides of my cheeks heat up. As it increases, my eyes start to water. I look around to see if anyone else is having problems, but they are engrossed in prayer and they aren't paying me any attention. I have to get rid of the food in my mouth, either by swallowing or spitting it out. The prayer drones on as the flames slide down my throat into my stomach like lava from a volcano. I've had Cajun food before, but never as spicy as this dish. I will Lasonji to pray quickly so I can have a sip of water.

Oblivious to my pain, Lasonji rambles on, thanking God for the morning sun, the twinkling stars, and the air we breathe. If I knew her better, I'd swear she was punishing me. I suffer in silence until she finally says, "Amen."

I grab my water glass and empty it with one long swallow. Tarcia refills it and I drain that glass too. I hesitate before I take my next mouthful. I'm torn because it tastes so good, but damn, it's hot as hell. Neither Tarcia nor Lasonji appear to be bothered by the spiciness. Unable to stop, I alternate between food and water until my plate is empty.

"Girl, you put your foot in this," Tarcia says.

"Thanks."

"Uh, it's very good, spicy but good," I add.

"Spicy? I thought I went light on the spices."

"Kentee hasn't had authentic Cajun food before."

"How you know what I've had before?"

"Oh, excuse me." I laugh to take the sting out of my words, but I don't want her speaking for me.

"So, Lasonji, how do you like Atlanta?"

"It's okay. This isn't my first visit. In fact, I might just decide to stay here permanently."

"What? You never mentioned that before," Tarcia says.

"You never asked me. I'm tired of fighting the weather in the Big Easy, plus I can make more money living here. New Orleans will still be my home, but I might just take up roots in Georgia, too. We'll see."

"That's cool. If you need a guide, I'll be happy to show you around." Tarcia kicks me under the table.

"Ow, what was that for?"

"Oh, I'm sorry I didn't know your leg was right there. I was just flexing my feet." Lasonji smirks at us, but doesn't comment.

"What did you put in this? It tastes familiar, but I can't put my finger on it."

"Kentee, it's a family recipe, so I can't tell outsiders. I guess you will just have to marry my cousin to get the recipe." A sliver of ice slides down my throat, choking me. My throat muscles constrict, trying to expel the blockage as I struggle for air. I can't move my tongue or produce enough spit to swallow. Frantic, I massage my neck while banging the table trying to get some attention to my distress. I try in vain to work the ice down without throwing up all over the table. Tarcia watches, but it is Lasonji who jumps up and starts pounding me on the back, lifting my hands in the air. When I can breathe normally again I thank her.

"Whew, that was a close one."

"Yeah, you were turning blue black."

"Thanks for your help."

"Would you like some more water?"

"Naw, I'm done for now. Thanks, dinner was great." Tarcia is pouting again because she didn't move quick enough to help me.

"Would you like some cheesecake?"

"Naw, I'm done." I get up to clear the dishes but Lasonji takes them from me.

"I've got the dishes; you two go on and watch TV or whatever."

"Nonsense, you cooked this great meal, the least I can do is help with the dishes. Right, Tarcia?"

"I wouldn't know since you've never offered to help me with the dishes. I'm going to read my book."

"Why you playing my cousin like that?" Lasonji says to me.

"Huh, I ain't playing her. I just want to help you. Is that a crime?"

"Humph. Look, I don't need to start no trouble up in here. Go be with your girl before she blows a gasket or something."

"She'll be okay, just let me help you."

"I said no, okay? Please, I am asking you nicely. Go handle your business."

"Alright. Later." I find Tarcia stretched out on the bed with her back to the door. I can tell by the rigid posture of her body she's pissed at me. That is another one of Tarcia's problems. She's jealous of everyone with whom I come in contact. I sit on the bed next to her, but she doesn't even acknowledge my presence.

"Hey, can a brotha get a drink up in here?"

"You know where it is...be helpful and get it yourself."

*Bitch.* I pour a stiff drink and down it with no chaser. Pouring some more into my glass, I go in the kitchen for some Coke to add to my drink. All the dishes are clean and there's no sign of Lasonji. I hadn't been gone but five hot seconds and she's finished, food put away and everything. *How in the hell did she get done so fast?* I should have paid more attention to this detail at the time but I was thinking of a way to get some ass and go home.

My original plan was to eat and run, but I know if I leave on this sour note Tarcia will blow up my phone for the rest of the night. Tarcia's a good-enough person; she's just insecure to the point of distraction.

"Do you mind if I turn on the television?"

"Suit yourself." I reach over her and grab the remote from her nightstand. Taking off my shoes, I prop myself up on her pillows and switch on the set. I flip through the channels, but nothing catches my attention.

"Ain't nothing on." I peep at Tarcia, but she's still ignoring me. *I didn't come over here for this shit. I could have stayed at my momma's house and been ignored.*

"Got any DVDs?"

"You know where they are." My patience is wearing thin. Putting my shoes on and getting the hell on wouldn't be a thing to me, but instead I flip through the movies. Tarcia loves books and movies so I know I will find something to occupy me until it's time to roll out.

Surprised to see the porno movies on top of the DVD player, I open one of the cases.

"Did you leave these out for me?"

"No, I had to do something while you were MIA."

"Ouch. It hasn't been that long."

"Maybe not for you, but for me it's been a minute." I don't mind her watching porn. In fact, I encouraged it as long as I was watching it with her. I guess I'd been falling down on my job. Seeing the movies makes me think about how selfish I'd been over the last couple of weeks. I expected her to remain faithful, but I hadn't been giving her any reason to be. I was about to put in a disc, but I see she already has one in the player. Curious, I hit play and go back to the bed.

Two beautiful women and one man are going at it. Instantly, my dick gets hard. In my mind, I replace the women on the television with Tarcia and her cousin. The man in the DVD is me. Unconsciously, my hand slips down to my nuts and I gently tug at them. My nuts swell and my shorts stifle their growth. I cup my hands over my dick so Tarcia can't see my erection. Enthralled, I watch homeboy suck one mocha breast and one cinnamon one simultaneously. He is on his knees on the bed and they are standing. He is in player's paradise and I would gladly change places with him.

He tells the mocha lady to spread her legs and she does. Lying on his back with his head hanging off the bed, he motions her forward and she squats over his face. The cinnamon lady straddles his waist and begins to suck his dick. My dick swells as I watch her breasts jiggle around, swatting his balls. I can't take it anymore. I'm about to turn it off when Tarcia strokes my leg.

"I didn't think you were paying attention."

"Hush, unless you want me to stop."

"I ain't saying anything else." She unzips my pants and reaches inside my briefs, taking out my dick. My eyes remain fixed and focused on the television as she blows on my dick. A drop of pre-cum rises to the tip and she greedily laps it up. I smother a moan.

"You gonna have to be quiet. My cousin is in the next room and you know how thin the walls are."

"Yeah, okay." I know perfectly well her cousin is in the next room. I was praying for some fluke in nature to occur and for her to come in and join the party. I struggle to get my pants off.

Tarcia could suck a mint out my mouth and through my dick. That's how talented she is. She knows how to please a man with her mouth and her pussy. If someone can just get past her other quirky habits, she's a good catch.

On the television, everyone has moved onto the bed. Cinnamon is eatin' out Mocha and the brother is nailing Cinnamon. His eyes are rolling around in his head and he has a smile plastered on his face. I turn down the sound because it's distracting me. I want to see them getting it on, but I also want to concentrate on what I have my hands on. I also don't want to blow my load before I have a chance to nail Tarcia just as good.

"Take off your clothes." My voice is low and husky. She doesn't waste a second getting out of her outfit and pulling back the covers.

"Where were we?"

"It's been so long, Kentee."

"I know, baby. Tell me what you want."

"I need to feel you right here." She puts her finger in her vagina, pulls it out, and holds it up for me to lick. I come close, but she pops the finger in her mouth. My tongue follows her finger and she plays with it as she plays with my dick. Another moan slips out, but this time I think it's her. Then again, it could have been both of us.

I push her back on the bed and bury my face between her legs. She gasps and wraps her arms around my head, locking it in place. I couldn't move if I wanted to and believe me, I don't want to 'cause she tastes so sweet. She is bucking off the bed trying to get closer and I'm holding her steady so I can at least breathe as I slurp up her juices. She shouts as she comes and I know her cousin has to hear it loud and clear.

"Damn, baby!" I chuckle, raising my head to look in her eyes. She pulls me forward and licks her juices off my face.

"You ain't done yet. Put it in."

I immediately plunge my dick in her quivering pussy; her muscles draw me all the way in to the hilt.

"Aw damn, baby, hold up, not so fast. I don't want to come yet." If anything, this makes Tarcia pull me in deeper. Her nails rake my back and if her pussy wasn't so damn good I would stop her from marking my back. Girlfriend flips the script on me and I'm no longer interested in the tape. I have all I need underneath me. Instead of me nailing her, she gets me to blow before my time. I collapse on top of her, too whipped to crawl over to the other side of the bed.

"Damn, baby, that was sweet."

"That's what you get for making me wait so long."

"Give me ten minutes and I'll be ready to go again."

I roll over on my side and promptly go to sleep.

I had no intentions of staying the night, only wanted to catch a few winks, but daylight awakens me as well as the need to pee.

Tarcia rolls over and snuggles against my back with her hands firmly around my waist. Spooning, we both start to drift back to sleep. I forget all about the need to pee. Tarcia's pussy was so good, I can't remember why I was staying away, but that is my dick talking, not my mind.

"Kentee," Tarcia whispers.

"Huh?"

"Where did you go yesterday?"

"Huh?" *Where the hell did that come from?*

"I just want to know what you did yesterday with the kids."

"Since when are you interested in my kids?"

"I've always been interested in anything you do."

"Hush now and go to sleep."

"Do you still love me?"

"Yeah, I still love you. Now go back to sleep."

"Okay. But I have one more thing to say. Promise me you won't stay away so long next time."

"I promise." I can feel her cheesy smile against my back. When I say I love her, I mean it. I do love her, but I'm not in love with her. I'll agree to anything just to get a few more minutes of shut-eye. Hopefully I won't regret this promise in the days to come.

## *Tarcia*

I pretend to go to sleep as I hold my Kentee in my arms but I'm too excited to sleep. His promises allay my fears that we are breaking up. I release a pent-up sigh I'd been holding in my heart for months. "I got my man back," I mouth silently.

Kentee's divorce is final and I know it will be a matter of days before he proposes again. I'm so anxious for us to get on with the rest of our lives. I don't care if we just jump a broom in the backyard; I want to be Mrs. Simmons. His absence over the last few weeks scared me so much. He had me thinking that since he was a free man, he didn't want to be bothered with me. His promise put those fears to rest.

Millions of images run through my mind. Hell, I might even invite his children to the wedding. *Naw, girl, stop trippin', 'cause if they come to the wedding, that bitch Leah will come and I definitely don't want to see her ass on what will be the happiest day of my life. Maybe his niece and nephew can be in it instead.*

Kentee mumbles in his sleep and even though I strain to hear him, I can't make out his words. I drift off to sleep with those thoughts still on my mind.

*Today is my wedding day and I can't sleep. Instead, I am up washing and folding clothes. Kentee and I are going on our honeymoon and I want the house to be perfect for our return. I've already scoured the down-stairs, cleaning the bathroom, kitchen, and living room. Now all I have to do is put up the clothes and maybe grab a few hours of sleep. It wouldn't be good for the bride to have bags under her eyes.*

*Grabbing the basket of laundry, I head up the stairs, humming a tune that dies on my lips as my feet stop moving. The wooden snake that Lasonji sent me from Mardi Gras last year is sitting up instead of lying on the floor like it normally does. Kentee hates the snake and I was going to move it into the guest bedroom, but I haven't gotten around to it yet.*

*I shake my head, trying to clear that vision from my mind since there is no way the wooden snake could sit up on its own. I have to be trippin'. When I look back into the bedroom, the snake is as it should've been. Damn, I really do need a nap. I continue up the steps and as my foot hits the last step the snake's head swings around, looking right at me. Its eyes glow first green and transform to red. With lightning speed the snake starts toward me. Throwing the basket at the snake, I start running back down the stairs screaming at the top of my lungs. Fear like I've never known causes my heart to beat like it's trying to escape my chest. Hot tears burn my cheeks and blind me as I continue to run, but the more I run the closer the snake gets. Finally I reach the bottom of the steps with the snake right at my heels. I can feel its hot breath on the tendon of my ankle. I push against the front door as hard as I can, trying to get it open. However, I should have pulled instead of pushed. Too scared to look back, I push hard enough to break down the door. A loud crash jolts me awake.*

Kentee is on the floor. "What the hell is wrong with you?" He jumps, up grabbing his clothes.

"Oh, Kentee, I am so sorry. I was having a bad dream."

"Dream my ass, you damn near punched a hole in my back."

"I was trying to get away from the snake."

"Snake, what snake?"

"It was coming to get me." I'm shaking uncontrollably, and my tears are blinding me.

"Tarcia, you ain't making no sense. I'm outta here."

"No, Kentee, please don't leave me." Kentee pauses for a moment to stare at me, but after a few seconds he continues to get dressed.

"I got to go anyway. I got to be at work soon."

"Please, Kentee, don't go. I'm scared."

"Shit, you scared me too. I'll holla at you later." He's out the door before I can throw on clothes to follow. I hear the front door slam and the house is quiet except for my deep sobs of anguish. I feel like my heart is being ripped out for the second time. Needless to say, sleep is out of the question.

I pad into the kitchen, the wooden floor cool against my bare feet. I put the coffee pot on and cut a slice of cheesecake to have with my coffee. Since I live on the ground floor the management didn't require me to carpet the apartment. It is ten dollars cheaper a month to have the hardwood floors and I prefer it that way most of the time. I have large scatter rugs throughout the apartment to spruce up the place.

Lasonji comes into the room just as the coffee pot begins to whistle. Silently, she gets out her own mug and pours water into both cups. I cut her a slice of cake and we eat.

"Do you want to talk about it?"

"No. Not really." Tears are still rolling down my face. My hands are still a bit shaky, making it difficult to hold my coffee cup.

"Did he hit you?"

"No, it was nothing like that."

"Oh, I heard the crash. Scared the shit out of me."

"Yeah, me too."

"One minute ya'll were mating like rabbits and the next..."

"Oh, wow, we tried to be quiet."

"Girl, I understand. Sometimes you just have to holla." She starts laughing and I join her. Part of me is embarrassed, but the other part of me remembers each exquisite moment.

"I might've lost him for good this time."

"I know you said you don't want to talk about it, but maybe it will make you feel better getting it out." I ponder on how much or how little I want to tell her.

"I had a bad dream and pushed Kentee out of the bed."

"Well, I'm sure...oh shit..." She burst out laughing so hard the table rattles.

"Lasonji, it ain't funny."

"Girl, you should see your face." She continues to laugh.

"Well, it was a little funny. Kentee's eyes were wild. He was look-ing around the room trying to decide who he was going to hit."

"I'll bet. Did he break anything?"

"I thought he broke his back." We give in to the laughter and it makes me feel better. The shaking stops. Now we both have tears running down our faces.

"What the hell did you dream about?"

"It was our wedding day. I was taking the wash upstairs."

"You don't have an upstairs."

"It was a dream, silly."

"Oh, my bad."

"The snake was sitting up looking around the room."

"Snake, what snake?" Lasonji becomes very serious.

"You know. The one you sent me a few years ago."

"You still have that thing?"

"Sure I do. It was a gift, remember?"

She shakes her head. "Go on."

"I thought I was seeing things because when I looked back at it, it was lying on the floor just like it's supposed to." I wait for her to interrupt again, but when she doesn't I continue. I am getting the same creepy feeling I had in the dream.

"So I went on up the stairs. When my foot hit the last step, the snake turned on me and started chasing me. I thought I was pushing open the front door, but instead I pushed Kentee off the bed." I laugh self-consciously. Speaking about it out loud makes it sound stupid.

"Your door opens in, not out."

"Huh?"

"Your front door. It opens in, you can't push it out."

"Damn, girl, it was a dream. Don't make it all technical."

"Did it leave its skin?"

"What?"

"The skin. Think, Tarcia, did it leave its skin!"

"You are scaring me."

"And you're scaring me. Answer the damn question."

"How the hell should I know? I was running."

"I gave you that snake for protection."

"You did what?" I jump up out of my seat, pissed. I pace the floor staring at Lasonji in disbelief. "I told you I didn't want that kind of shit in my house."

"Hey, to you it was just a gift and if I had my way you would have never known it was anything more." I rush from the room to get the damn snake with Lasonji quick at my back.

"No." Grabbing my arm, she spins me around to face her. I struggle to get my arm back. She's hurting me and I start to hit her, but she blocks the slap.

"Did it leave its skin? This is important, so think about it." I slide down the wall and sit on the floor. Lasonji sinks to the floor as well.

"I don't know, it happened too fast."

"Where was it?"

"In my bedroom."

"Come on." She pulls me to my feet and leads the way into my bedroom. The snake is gone.

"Where is it?" I whisper as the shakes return.

"Where was it the last time you saw it when you were awake?"

"Right there, next to the dresser in between the chair and the floor lamp."

"You sure you didn't kick it under the bed?"

"No, I would have felt it."

"What about Kentee? Would he have taken it?"

"No, he hates it."

"Figures."

"What's that supposed to mean?" She doesn't answer me. She drops to the floor and looks under the bed. I back up toward the door, scared of what she might find.

"Turn on the light." We had been using the light from the hallway to illuminate the room. I hesitate as fear grips me.

"Now, Tarcia. We've got to see if the skin is still here." Shutting my eyes, I flip the switch. She continues looking under the bed and when that proves to be futile, she crawls around the floor. By this time, I have backed out into the hallway. She reaches the door and closes it partially. When it opens, she holds the skin between two fingers offering it up for my inspection.

"What does this mean?"

"The snake is gone. It has chased out the evil spirits."

"That's good, ain't it?"

"I would feel better if it would've taken its skin with it." She carries the skin out, holding it away from her as if she is afraid to let it touch her.

"Lasonji, you are scaring the shit out of me. What does this mean?" She spins around.

"It means it ain't over. Finding a snake skin means a jinx is present."

"Then throw the shit away."

"I wish I could. It ain't that simple."

"It's a toy snake, for crying out loud, not a real one." She just looks at me and shakes her head. Her face is somber and unreadable.

"So what do we do?"

"I don't know. I've got to do some research."

"Research? You send some shit to my house and when it gets fucked up you don't know how to handle it?"

"Yelling at me is not going to change a damn thing. I did it to protect you. Hell, did you ever stop to think what would have happened if you didn't have it?" She shut my mouth up real quick. She places the offending skin on the table. I want to protest, but I'm not thinking all that clearly.

"How the hell does a toy snake shed its skin?"

"Be right back."

"I'm right behind you. Ain't no way in hell I am staying in here with that thing by myself."

# *Jasmine*

"Sammie, it's time that you meet your father's side of the family."

"Uh...do you think that's a good idea?"

"Of course it is. Daddy has two brothers and three sisters. It's only right that you get to meet them before it's too late. They are all up in age now."

"I don't know, Jazz. I know me and your mom are cool, but what will the rest of the family say to an outside child?"

"Well, you can be sure that they will say anything that comes to their minds. If they say something out the way, just ignore it, it comes with age. They don't have to be politically correct. Besides, it doesn't matter what they think about something that happened years ago. The point is you deserve to meet your family and I want them to meet my sister."

"Have you talked this over with your mother?"

"Yeah, in fact, this is her idea. Sammie, you don't have anyone left but us. Trust me on this. They will love you just like we do."

"If you say so, but I have to tell you I have a bad feeling about it."

"That's your fear of the unknown. Just think about how different things would be if you didn't step to me that night we met at the club. We would have sailed through life without ever getting to know each other."

"If I remember correctly, we stepped to each other."

"Same difference. You just got to take a chance and step out there, embracing life. Don't worry about a thing. Momma is planning the whole thing. All we have to do is show up next Saturday."

"Next Saturday?"

"Yes, next Saturday. This gives you over a week to prepare. I knew if I told you too far in advance you would chicken out."

"You ain't even lying. I still got time."

"No, you don't. Mom went through a lot of trouble to get this together. The aunts and uncles don't get out much these days. They are anxious to meet you."

"I'll bet they are."

"Girl, stop, I'm serious. I talked to Aunt Mavis last week and she was excited. I've been the only grandchild in the entire family. None of Daddy's brothers or sisters ever had children. They need someone else to dote on."

"Alright, then, let me go figure out what I'm gonna wear."

"Sammie, don't get all stressed out. Just wear something casual. It's going to be in our backyard, so it won't be formal at all."

"Okay, I'll holla at you later."

"C-ya, sis."

# Sammie

It is hard for me to get excited about meeting my father's family, especially since I don't even know him. I have only seen pictures of him and they are twenty years old. I'm not like Jasmine. She is confident, witty, poised, and outgoing. She's everything that I'm not and I don't need any strangers to remind me of that.

While I appreciate the gesture of welcoming me into the family, the thought of being on display and under scrutiny makes my knees weak. *I wonder if she will let me bring my boyfriend, Buddy. He won't let anyone hurt me, and I'll feel more comfortable with him around.* I immediately call Jasmine back.

"Jazz, can Buddy come to the cookout?"

"Yes, of course, sis. And why don't you invite Leah and Craig too?"

"That would be wonderful. I can't help but to feel as nervous as a cat in a living room full of rocking chairs."

"Interesting analogy, that's funny."

"Girl, I haven't been able to think of anything else since you told me. What if they don't like me, Jazz? It will break my heart."

"See, Sammie, you are looking at this the wrong way. You are not there on display. It's your right to be there. So what, your mother was not married to our father at the time of your birth.

If it wasn't for me, he would have been and the shoe would be on the other foot. You've been deprived of your roots all your life. It's time, girl, that you knew from whence you came."

"You make it seem so logical and easy. I just don't want them to compare me to you."

"They won't because we are two different people. Even though we look alike, we are different and the differences are what make us so close. If we were clones we'd probably hate each other."

"Wow, I never thought of it that way."

"Then please start thinking of it that way because whatever happens, you're my sister for life."

"Thanks, sis, I needed to hear that. Let me go so I can see if Buddy can make it. Oh, promise me you won't leave me alone too long. I don't want to get all nervous and start dropping shit."

"Stop worrying, I'll be right there."

"Alright, let me call Buddy to see if he is gonna be able to come." But instead of calling Buddy, I sit down to collect my thoughts. I don't want to sound needy. I know enough about relationships to know that some men get turned off by that. So far in this relationship, I've been able to pretend to be confident, poised, and self-reliant. He doesn't need to know what an emotional wreck I am inside. I'd shared some of my past with him, especially as it related to my mother, but he still doesn't know my deepest dark secrets and I plan to keep it that way. Buddy is the best thing that has happened in my life and I don't want to jeopardize it.

I go in the kitchen waging a mental battle to decide between having a drink versus a cup of coffee. My rationale for choosing a drink over coffee is that I am already hyped. I need to calm down and nothing calms you down quicker than a glass of gin and juice.

Two drinks and one hour later, I call Buddy. He doesn't answer so I leave a message. I am finishing my third drink when he returns my call, and I am so laid back, I can't remember why I was upset in the first place.

"Hey, baby."

"Oh, you sound tired."

"I am. We've had three live feeds today and I still have to host the party tonight at Visions. If I could get out of this one, I'd go right home and go to sleep."

"Poor baby. If you were here, I would take care of ya and make the stress go away."

"I know you would, but baby girl, I'm too pooped to handle you tonight. I would be no good to you."

"I bet I could change that."

He chuckles. "I have no doubt about that. So what's up? I got to get moving to the club."

"Oh, yeah...I did call you, didn't I? Well, Jazz's mother is throwing a cookout next Saturday to introduce me to my father's side of the family. I wanted to know if you would come with me."

"What time? We are running hot and heavy this month because it's our anniversary and every jock has to work something all over the city."

"It's going to be early since my dad's brothers and sisters are up in age. The youngest is seventy-four, I believe. I'm sure it won't last long. You don't have to stay for the whole thing, but I could use some support."

"How early?"

"Noon."

"That's good. I could swing through before I go on location at four."

"Thanks, baby."

"Shoot, I need to see you as much as you need to see me."

"That's what I love about you."

"Love you too. Gotta go, but I will holla at you in the morning. Sweet dreams, boo."

"I'll be dreaming of you."

"Damn, you sure paint a picture for a brotha that makes it hard to think about work."

"I'm sorry, I didn't mean to make it hard for you to work, but I intended to make it hard for something else. 'Night." I hang up to his laughter. *So what was so difficult about that? He's nothing but a big old puddy tat and I'm his bowl of milk. I got drunk for nothing.* I stumble into my bedroom and fall out on the bed with my clothes still on. My last thought before passing out is of my ex-husband, Jessie, which is like living through an episode of "Nightmare on My Street."

Jessie was abusive, both mentally and physically. He beat me down so bad I almost killed myself trying to get away.

# Leah

As usual, Kentee was late returning the children and my schedule has been shot to hell. Regardless of how many times I explain to him how important my schedule is, he continues to act as if it doesn't matter. That, coupled with his repeated attempts to push up on me, has me wondering if having him in their lives is worth it.

"Kayla, I want you to take a bath in Mommy's bathroom. Do you have all your homework done?"

"Yes."

"Are you sure?"

"I'll double-check after I finish my bath."

"Good. Malik."

"I can run my own bath water. I'm a big boy now."

"That you are. Please don't play in the tub. We are running behind schedule."

"I don't play in the tub. That's Kayla." I laugh because he isn't telling a lie. If I gave Kayla a few minutes, then walked into my bathroom, I'll bet water would be all over the floor. I would let Malik use my room since he is so quick, but I'm hesitant because my tub is so much deeper than theirs. I would only allow him to use my tub if I were in there with him, but he is at the age where he doesn't want me to see his private parts, which is a good thing.

With only Mya to attend to, I lead her to her room and help her take off her clothes. As I help her into her robe, she sits on her bed in an apparent daze. *I wish I could look into her brain to see what she is thinking.* The ringing phone distracts me from my musing. I have to rush across the hall to get it since I do not keep a phone in Mya's room. The ringing could send her into a fit since she cannot process loud noises. I grab the phone on the third ring.

"Hold on for a second. Kayla, no playing. You've got to get ready for bed, okay?"

"Okay."

"I'm back." I glance at the caller ID to see whom I'm speaking with and am pleased to see it's Sammie.

"Hey, girlfriend."

"Hey yourself, stranger. What you been into?"

"Same old thang, girl, same old thang. I'm just trying to make it day by day."

"I hear ya."

"Look, I won't hold you because I can hear you trying to get the kids settled for the night. I just wanted to know if you and Craig want to go to a cookout with me next weekend."

"I'll have to check with Craig, but it sounds good to me."

"Cool, let me know. Jazz's mother is throwing the cookout to give me a chance to meet my dad's side of the family."

"Wow, that's real sweet and unselfish of her."

"I know and I appreciate it, but I can't help being apprehensive about it."

"That's understandable. Look, I left Mya unattended, so I'll call you back after I talk to Craig, okay?"

"Sure. Talk to you later."

"'Bye." I am not out of the room good before the phone rings again. This time it is Craig.

"Hey, boo."

"Just checking to make sure the kids got back on time."

"They're back, but not on time. I'm bathing them now, so I will call you back, okay?"

"Sure."

Mya is sitting in the corner when I go back into her room. Malik has put on his PJs and is already in bed. Smiling at his efficiency, I run Mya's bath.

"Did you have a nice time with your daddy?" I sign to her. She just looks at me, so I don't press her. She has her moments when she wants to talk, so I assume this isn't one of them. We finish the bath and she allows me to dress her. After I kiss her good night, she lies on her pallet and closes her eyes, but I know she isn't sleeping. That is another thing about Mya—she doesn't sleep with her eyes closed. When she's truly asleep, her eyes are open. Sometimes it scares me but that's just another trait of her autism.

The sad part about this disease is that no two patients have the same symptoms making early diagnosis difficult and oftentimes leading to misdiagnosis. Craig was the first person to detect Mya's hearing deficiency, which led to her first surgery. We found out that Mya had water in her ear canal. This was drained and tubes were placed in her ears. As a result, she isn't allowed to play in the pool like her brother and sister.

From there, also with Craig's help, Mya started taking sign language classes and when that appeared to be working, the whole family took classes so we could communicate with her when she is in a talkative mood. Kentee even agreed to take the classes, a real shocker for me. So things have improved tremendously over the past two years. We still have a long way to go with her behavior and her social skills.

Autism affects one out of 166 children a year and the numbers are growing. Fortunately for Mya, we met Craig, who helped me push her past barriers that we couldn't overcome alone. Pausing to kiss Malik, I turn on the nightlight and turn off the overhead.

"Good night."

Kayla is still in my tub when I return to my room, but stops splashing as soon as I step into the bathroom.

"Sorry, Mommy." She proceeds to bathe while I mop up the water on the floor. She finishes quickly and scurries to her room. After she gets her pajamas on, she pulls out her book bag. As I suspected, there is unfinished homework.

"Kayla, this is the last time that you are going to pull this stunt on me. It's not funny and it's not cute. The next time you try this, you won't be able to go with your father. Do you understand me?"

"I'm sorry. I won't do it again."

"Okay, now hurry up. Do you need any help?"

"No. It won't take me long."

I leave her to her homework and take a quick shower. It's already past ten o'clock and I still want to call Craig back before it gets too late. We both have to get up early in the morning.

Kayla is done by the time I finish my shower and is sitting on my bed looking at television.

"Oh, no, sweetie, it's past your bedtime."

"I was waiting to give you a kiss." She kisses me and skips off to her room. Strangely, they didn't say anything about what happened with their father over the weekend. Normally, Kayla would not be able to shut up, but she didn't utter a word. I start to go in her room and ask her, but have second thoughts. Nine times out of ten something happens that would piss me off and I wouldn't be able to sleep tonight if I knew, so it is better to just leave this alone for now. It will more than likely come up in the next few days. It always does. Kayla could not keep a secret if she carried it in a bucket. Somehow it always spills out.

Alone at last, I call Craig back, but because of the lateness of the hour our conversation is short.

"Do you want to go to a cookout with me next week? Sammie and Jasmine are having one."

"Isn't that a Kentee weekend?"

"Well, yeah, but I thought if you didn't mind, we could spend some time over there."

"I was trying to surprise you with a short trip, but if you have your heart set on going to the cookout, then we can do it later."

"Do I look like I got 'fool' written on my forehead? I'd rather get away with you."

"Won't Sammie be upset with you?"

"She'll get over it. I didn't confirm it with her. I told her I had to check with you. The only reason I even thought about going is because she is going to meet her dad's family for the first time."

"Wow, now I feel bad taking you away at such a critical time for her."

"She won't be alone. Jazz will be there, and of course Buddy will be there too. Sammie will understand. She knows that we don't spend nearly enough 'quantity' time together."

"What we don't have in quantity, we make up for in quality."

"I know that's right. Well, I'll see you tomorrow, baby."

"Alright, I enjoyed you this weekend."

"I enjoyed you too. Good night." We don't talk about love too much or where our relationship is going. We've both been there before and carry our own sets of luggage. It would be great if we could step things up a notch but until that happens I'm content with the way things are between us. The next thing I know, the alarm clock is ringing, marking the beginning of another work week.

# Tarcia

Lasonji is in her room poring over some books and I am pacing in the hallway. Part of me is glad that she has those reference books, the other part is pissed that she brought them into my house after I had asked her not to. Her face is grim. She has just about torn a whole box of Kleenex to shreds as she flips pages. If that isn't enough to make me nervous, the damn tapping of her feet on the hardwood floor certainly makes up for it.

"It says here that the absence of the snake means the evil has gone."

"That's a good thing." I start to relax.

"However, the shedding of skin means that the jinx is still present. We have to flush out that evil and dispose of the skin, so it cannot harm us. We also have to make certain the snake didn't shed twice."

"Twice, why would it do that?"

"If the jinx is for you, then it would leave a skin for each of your personalities."

"Each of my what?"

"You're a Gemini. It stands to reason, there are two of you."

"Girl, how many times have I told you I don't believe in that crap?"

"Whether you believe or not is irrelevant at this point, wouldn't you say? And despite your denial, there are two of you. I've met them both—one I call Tarcia and the other I named Marcia."

"Oh, now you're trying to say that I'm a nut."

"No, I'm not saying that. What I am saying is that you have two distinct personalities in the same body. Lots of folks have two personalities but their distinction is muddled."

"So who am I now?"

"Girl, I don't mean that someone is taking over your body like in *The Exorcist*. Both of your personalities are still you." Exasperated, she gives me her undivided attention.

"Then make me understand."

"The Tarcia side of you is reasonable. I can talk to you and even if you don't agree with what I am saying, you will hear me out. Marcia is close-minded and will not entertain any such thoughts. Understand?"

"Yeah, but I thought everyone is like that."

"They are up to a point. Marcia goes beyond that point. She is unreasonable to her own detriment. Everything cannot be logically explained. Marcia doesn't believe that. If she can't explain it, it does not exist."

"Oh, I get it."

"Are you willing to admit something strange is afoot?" I hesitate for just a moment before nodding my head.

"Good, that means I am speaking to Tarcia." She opens the books again as I continue to pace. She has me rethinking my entire life since I left New Orleans. My mother was a Gemini too. Her birthday was two days after mine.

"Did my mother have two personalities too?"

"I can't really recall. Back then, children did not speak unless spoken to, but if I were to guess, I would say no."

"Why not?"

"She wouldn't have run away. Her dominant side would have forced her to stay and figure out how to co-exist in the mystical world. That is why it's so important that I figure out what all this means. If there's only one skin, I need to know why. The other one could very well be hiding in the house, or it could've ridden the evil out of here and shed someplace else."

"Truth is, there's no way to know for sure which personality dominated her."

"So true. Give me a few minutes to understand what I'm reading."

She has a point since I cannot think of any logical explanation for the intensity of my dreams or the whereabouts of the snake.

"Oh, okay. Sorry." I am too scared to go to my room or any other room in the house without Lasonji, so I just sit on the floor in the hallway. This way I could keep an eye open for any trouble headed my way, if it is visible, that is. However, fatigue wins out over fear and before I know it, I am sleeping, my head resting on my knees.

# Jasmine

"Ain't this a bitch? I know this hoodrat is not going to stand me up." I anxiously tap my foot on the floor. I hate waiting more than anything else in the world, and I warned that buster to be on time. Glancing at my watch for the umpteenth time, I loudly suck my teeth.

"Shoot. And to think I was planning on breaking the brother off tonight, but he just lost those privileges. That's why I don't fool with these thugged-out motherfuckers. Always perpetrating, talking yang and don't mean shit they say. All game."

I reach over to check my cell just in case Mike left a text message. Flipping the phone shut, I jump when it starts ringing. Arranging my hair out of my face, I bark into the phone. My hands firmly planted on my hips, I wait for Mike to explain himself.

"Damn, girl, you need to take one of those anger management classes they are giving out at the local high school," Sammie says, laughing.

"Bite me," I reply. I glance at my watch again accepting the fact that there's no way Mike and I will get dinner prior to the start of the play.

"Uh, look, I ain't trying to argue with you. I just wanted to tell you to have a good time," Sammie says, sounding like she's preparing to hang up.

"Well, I might not be going."

"Say what? What happened?"

"Mike happened. He hasn't shown up yet. We already missed our dinner reservations and now it looks like we are going to miss the opening if he doesn't get his black ass here in the next few minutes."

"What time is the play?" Sammie asks.

"Eight, and it's already past seven. My gut told me not to go out with this man, but I wanted to see the play so badly, not to mention he had front row seats!"

"Yeah, I feel ya, but you don't want to walk into a Tyler Perry show late because he will call your ass out in a heartbeat."

"Don't I know it, and I ain't in the mood to have someone clowning me. I am so mad I could spit. Mike hasn't called or anything. He better be dead or dying!"

"He must not know who he is dealing with. Obviously, he ain't read the 'How to Treat a Diva' book." Sammie hates it when her sister is upset.

"Obviously, but what really chaps my ass is that for the last three months he bugged the shit out of me to take me out and when I agree to go, he pulls this shit."

"Niggras ain't right."

"I wish I would have held on to the tickets but he insisted on holding them. He said it was his insurance that I would keep the date with him."

"Well, I can't blame the brother there because if you had held on to the tickets you would have rolled out on his ass with a quickness."

"You damn right, and thought nothing about it."

"Well, never fear, good ole Buddy to the rescue. The radio station was giving out tickets at the station this morning and the lady who won them didn't pick them up, so Buddy said I could have them if I wanted them. He's on the way over to drop them off."

"Are you shitting me? He's bringing you two tickets?"

"Nope, I'm not shitting you and yes it's two tickets since he knows me well enough to know that I wouldn't go by myself. Come by and scoop me up, so we won't be all late and shit."

"Thanks, Sammie. Remind me to kiss that man of yours."

"Uh, you know you my sista and I love you, but there will be none of that kissing-on-my-man shit unless I do it."

"I promise to keep my tongue in my mouth."

"That's not all that will be in your mouth if you even point your lips in his direction."

"Okay, I get the point. I'll be there in about fifteen minutes. Be ready. We're gonna have to haul ass to get there on time."

"I'll be waiting by the door."

"Cool. I don't want to be late and become the butt of a joke at the hottest play in the country. Tyler tapes his plays! Hell, with my luck, that tape will be the one he puts on sale." I hang up and dash around the house grabbing last-minute essentials.

I am still pissed off at Mike for standing me up, but now my anger is placed on slow boil until I hear from the rat bastard again. There will be hell to pay if I don't get to see the play at all. I turn the radio up loud and let the top down on my convertible as I race to get to Sammie's house.

Thinking of Sammie brings an instant smile to my face. She is really blossoming under the love and affection of Buddy Love. He showers her with attention and makes sure she always has something to do. In fact, we have switched roles over the last two years since she has been hanging with Buddy.

I discovered Sammie was my sister shortly after my thirtieth birthday. We both had the same father, but our mothers kept the information from us until we literally ran into each other at a club. We looked so much alike we had to get to know each other to see if we were related.

In retrospect, it really was kind of strange how we met. We had been traveling in the same circles for years and never once ran into each other. If Sammie hadn't gotten into that fight at the club, I might have missed her again.

She had just finished kicking some girl's ass and was about to be thrown out of the club when our eyes locked and I just knew she was my sister. Finding Sammie was like a small miracle to me. I was so lonely and she came into my life exactly when I needed her.

I had just gotten divorced from my husband and my self-esteem was severely battered. Sammie's love helped me through the hard times. We shared our horror stories and I learned that my life had not been nearly as bad as it could have been. Sammie taught me to be thankful, even for the bullshit, because it helped get me through.

Sammie's life was really hard up to that point. At least I had loving and supportive parents. Sammie's mother hated her and she never even knew who her real father was until she met me. Her mother had lied to her for years, making her believe that her husband was Sammie's father. It wasn't until after he died that she learned the truth. That's why it is so important to me that next week's cookout comes off without a hitch.

I was so deep in thought that the car appeared to have driven itself the fifteen miles that separated my place from Sammie's. Without even realizing it, I've arrived. I see her boyfriend Buddy going into her apartment, so I allow them a few minutes of privacy before I interrupt them.

Buddy is a good guy and even though I experience moments

of jealousy because she is in a relationship and I'm not, he is the best man for my sister. Buddy and I met over four years ago. He was the radio personality at a club and tried to push up on me, but I was only interested in him as a friend. He had access to all the places I wanted to be seen in and he didn't mind one bit sharing those places with me.

Through him, I became a regular party animal with VIP access to the hottest clubs in ATL. I think that's why it took me so long to meet Sammie—I was hanging with the celebrities while she was getting down with the regular folks. I introduced Buddy to my sister and they have been hanging tough for the last two years. I don't mind because he is showing her the love that she's been missing all her life.

Sammie is the one in the know now. She knows about all the parties and I'm not mad at her. Sammie gets in free and I go along to keep her company. Talk about a win-win situation. I get to spend time with my sista and be in all the right places at the right times. So why aren't I happy?

I jump out of the car, rushing to the door. The trip down memory lane is going to cost us some valuable time, so Sammie needs to hurry up and say her good-byes.

Buddy opens the door before I can knock.

"What's up, baby girl?" He smiles real big, opening up his arms for a hug. I allow him to give me a brotherly hug and then push away just in case Sammie is watching. So far I've managed not to display any overt jealousy and I intend to keep it that way.

"Is Sammie ready?"

"Yeah, she's just waiting on you. You two have a good time and if you feel like it, swing by Visions for the after-party. I'll leave passes for you at the door."

"Thanks, Buddy, we'll see."

"Hey, sis, we better shake a leg if we don't want to be late. Buddy bought us some chicken, so we won't have our stomachs growling throughout the play!"

"Oh, Buddy, you are a real sweetheart." He really is a special kind of guy. I wonder why he never appealed to me in that way.

Almost immediately I try to erase that thought out of my head. Nothing good would come out of this type of thinking. I had my chance at Buddy and I didn't want it, end of story.

"We got to rock and roll, girl." I wave at Buddy and go back to the car to give them a few minutes to say good-bye.

I see their mouths move over a few words and their arms entangle as they share a heated kiss. The kiss irritates me. I am being a bitch as I allow a green-eyed monster to control my thoughts. I might have felt differently if I'd not gotten stood up. Being stood up and watching a couple who is obviously in love is not the recipe for a good cake.

Sammie gets in the car wearing a shit-eating grin. She looks so happy I can't help but smile too. I feel ashamed of my jealousy. Sammie deserves to be happy and I am just going to have to find my own happiness.

"Let's do this!" I throw the car in reverse while giving Sammie the once-over.

"Dag, sis, you are rocking that dress!" Sammie has lost some weight and she is looking good. She has on a sleek dress, black on one side and white on the other, that slims her look even further. Her hair is braided down her back with long silver earrings dangling from her ears. She still has a slight bulge in her stomach but it's hardly noticeable when she stands up.

"You ain't looking too bad your damn self! Have you heard from that trifling nigga yet?" Sammie lights a cigarette and rolls down the window to let out the smoke.

"Light one up for me too, please."

"Do what? Don't tell me you're smoking again?"

"I just want one, okay?" I don't dare take my eyes off the road, but I can feel Sammie's gaze burning my skin. I quit smoking two years ago and have been bugging the shit out of Sammie to do the same ever since my mother was diagnosed with cancer.

"I don't know if I want to contribute to your backsliding."

"Light the damn cigarette, girl. I don't need no lecture from you about it." The closer I get to the Fox the madder I get. This is not the way I planned this night. I was supposed to be just coming out of Houston's with a fine-ass man; he would be driving and I would be profiling. I should've been in the front seat of his cream-colored Benz with the leather interior, chilling to the sounds of Lena James as the wind blows through my hair, sipping Hennessy and laughing my ass off.

"Jazz, I ain't the one that stood you up."

"Ouch."

"Damn, that didn't come out right."

"No, it didn't, but your point is well taken. Sorry, girl, I'm just mad at myself for even giving the nigga a chance."

Sammie hands me my cigarette and I inhale deeply. I immediately start coughing. I toss it right out the window.

"That'll teach your ass." I start to bitch, but she was right. I gave up the habit for a reason and my lungs aren't going to allow me to have a pity party at their expense.

"Yeah, I give up. I ain't trying that shit no mo." We arrive ten minutes later and it takes us another fifteen minutes to find a parking spot.

"Are you okay now?" Sammie asks.

"Yeah, thanks, girl. I was just tripping."

"You ain't even lied." Before I could start to fuss at her good, my cellie rings. I look at the caller ID before I answer. Attitude is back in full force and effect.

"What?"

"Damn, baby, why you snapping on me like this?" Mike asks.

"Uh, excuse you?" I unhook my seatbelt and nod to Sammie to do the same. We need to get inside. I open the door and the warning bell starts chiming, reminding me that the keys are still in the ignition. I snatch them out and slam the door shut. Sammie's door echoes mine.

"Where you at?" Mike demands as if he is entitled to an answer.

"None of your damn business." We start walking. I walk fast and Sammie is struggling to keep up with me. I cannot believe he has the nerve to call acting like everything is okay.

"Look, baby, I know you're mad, but I couldn't help it. I got sent on a run and I just got back. I was out of range so I couldn't call you."

"Whatever."

"It's true. I'll make it up to you even if we have to travel to South or North Carolina to see the show." He is practically begging. Part of me wants to believe him, but that is the part of me that got stood up.

"Like I said, whatever."

"You still haven't told me where you are?"

"Regardless of your half-assed excuse, it's still none of your damn business. I gotta go." I wasn't about to tell him that I am going to the play.

"Oh, alright, then, I guess I'll go home and go to bed. It's been a long day."

"'Bye." I snap the phone shut.

"What was his excuse?" Sammie asks.

"His lying ass said he had to make a run outta town and he was out of range to call me. Claims he's gonna make it up, even if he has to take me out of town to do it."

"You believe him?"

"Hell to the fucking no! He blew his chance. I wouldn't go out with his ass again if I was wearing gasoline drawers and he had the only water hose in the state."

"Aw, damn, Jazz, not the gasoline drawers."

"Yep. He's probably screwing some skeezer as we speak. I say good riddance to bad rubbish."

"So why didn't you cuss his ass out?"

"What good would it have done to continue fussing with him? Would it change anything right now?"

"Well, I guess you got a point. I think you let him off too easy."

"I didn't say it was over. I'll make his ass sweat for a minute before I tell him to kiss my entire black ass."

"Damn right."

"If the nigga is going to treat me like this and I ain't even slept with him, imagine how his ass would act if I give him some."

"You definitely got a point."

"So I lead his ass on for another couple of months and then when he least expects it, I will pull the damn rug out from under his ass. I might even make another date with him and stand his ass up just so he knows what it feels like."

"Turnabout is fair play."

"Let's talk about it after the play." She pulls out the tickets from her tiny purse and hands them to a lady dressed in black with a mini flashlight. She skims the tickets and we're directed to floor seats about ten rows from the front.

"Sammie, these seats are great!"

"Girl, I am surprised too. Buddy didn't tell me where we were sitting. I assumed since these were complimentary tickets they would be farther away, especially on the first day of the show."

We settle in our seats, neither of us feeling the long lines at the refreshment counter. We decide to wait until intermission to get our drink on.

Promptly at eight, the lights dim and the play begins. Buddy is hosting the show. This man is full of surprises.

I lean over and whisper to Sammie. "How come you didn't tell me Buddy is the MC?"

"I didn't know either."

"Hey everybody," Buddy addresses the crowd from the stage. "How the hell is ya'll doing? Welcome to the show. Before we get started, I wanna say a special shout to my lady, you know who you are. I love you, baby girl."

I glance over at Sammie as her mouth forms a perfectly shaped O. I would be lying if I said I'm not envious. Sammie is my sister. I was the one who introduced her to Buddy in the first place, so I have no right to be jealous of her. I reach across the armrest and grab her hand, smiling though my despair. The lights go out as we hear Madea announce she is in jail.

This is not my first Tyler Perry play, but it is Sammie's. She's laughing so hard I think she is going to pee on herself. Our eyes are glued to the stage as one scene flows into the next until intermission is upon us. By now, we both are a little thirsty and I need to go to the bathroom.

"Why didn't you tell me this guy is so funny?" Sammie asks.

"I tried to get your hot ass to slow down long enough to watch one of his DVDs, but you always wanted to go out. I got his entire collection at home."

"They ain't bootlegged, are they?" We laugh again. Tyler makes it known how he feels about bootleg copies of his plays. And now that he has started doing movies as well, that is another threat that he has to watch out for. I give Tyler all his props because he went from being homeless to a millionaire. But the thing I love most about Tyler is that he didn't forget about where he came from. He gave back to the community choosing to live right here in Atlanta with the people who made him.

Buddy comes over to ask Sammie if she wants to take some pictures as we head to the lobby.

"I'll meet you back here, okay?" Hurrying off to the bathroom, I see a long line is already forming and I want to be able to still get a drink before we take our seats again.

I luck up at the bathroom by getting there before the real crowds come in. I think people must have gotten their drinks first and they are going to pay the price.

In the lobby, I order two Hennessy and Cokes for Sammie and me. I push my way against the flow to get back to where Sammie is taking pictures. Buddy must have pulled some strings because he got Madea to come out and take pictures with them.

"Come on, Jazz, get in the picture," they call to me.

I hear a commotion brewing behind me. This ghetto woman apparently wants her picture taken with Madea, but her date isn't trying to hear it. I chuckle to myself thinking everybody can't be like my sis. I turn around to see who is causing such a ruckus, but the smile dies when I see Mike with his arm draped around this light-skinned heifer.

Mike is so busy trying to hush his date, I am able to walk up on him before he notices me. He looks like a deer caught in headlights. If it hadn't been such a painful surprise, it might have been funny.

Madea, hearing the commotion, starts to perform right here in the lobby.

"Looky here, looky here. I done told ya'll you can't take black folks everywhere. Some of ya'll don't know how to behave out in public. It's a shame, a crying shame. What he needs to do is hit her upside the damn head. I'll bet she'll shut up then. Umph. Now, sister, dear, if you wanting to get this here picture, ya'll betta hurry up 'cause I gots to get back in my cell before they find out I'm missing."

I want to wait to see if Mike will acknowledge me or just ignore me. Quandary is written all over his face. The look disgusts me and I twirl around, giving him my ass to kiss. I cross the rope to the photo area and join my sister taking pictures.

"Was Madea talking about me?" Mike's date ignorantly asks.

I want to say, *"Hell, yeah, she is talking about your loud ass,"* but instead I allow my eyes to burn a hole in Mike. I'll bet he will never forget the fury they hold. And if he does, I will always have a picture or two to remind him. That high-yella bitch isn't even worth his efforts to lie to me and since his woman of choice is showing out, I decide to show him I don't need his sorry ass either.

After a few more pictures, Madea excuses herself, then kisses us both on the cheek. I look to see if Mike is still watching, but he is gone. Handing Sammie her drink, we go back to finish watching the play. She is babbling on and on about how down to earth Tyler is, but she doesn't notice the pain that I'm in.

The rest of the play passes in a blur. The only thing that I can see clearly is Mike with this stupid-ass look on his face. I can't understand why Mike would treat me in such a backhanded fashion. It is true I haven't given him none, but he claims he respects me for it. Rat *bastard!*

# *Jasmine*

"Do you want to go get something to eat?" Sammie asks.

"Naw, I'm kind of tired. I think I just want to drop you off and go home."

"Are you alright? I can ride with Buddy if you're too tired to take me home."

"No, if you want me to take you, I can. It's just that I don't feel like hanging out."

"This doesn't sound like the sista I know. What's wrong, Jazz? Didn't you enjoy the play?" She's right. I'm envious of her relationship and it isn't making any sense. I know I should share with Sammie about seeing Mike at the play, but my mouth cannot form the words. I'm not used to being treated in this fashion and I am ashamed to admit that I've gotten played!

"I'm alright, girl. To be honest, the green-eyed monster got a hold of me for a minute, but I am okay now."

"Green-eyed monster? Jazz, what are you talking about?"

"You and Buddy. You two have come a long way, and I guess I got to feeling sorry for myself since I don't have anyone special in my life."

"But, Jazz, that is your choice. You can have any man you want."

"I know, but I can't really explain it better than I have. It's not just the man thing; it's everything. I need to find something that will give my life purpose."

"Purpose?"

"Yeah, a reason to get up in the morning."

"Sounds like a job to me," Sammie said, laughing.

"That's exactly what I'm talking about."

"You, work? Girl, don't you know how good it is not to have to do that shit? I'd cut off my left arm if I didn't have to put up with this corporate bullshit every damn day. You are living in a stress-free world of your own making, girl. You better appreciate that shit."

"That's the point, Sammie, I don't appreciate it. I'm bored out of my mind. At least a job would give me something to bitch about and if I don't like it, shit, I can quit."

"Yeah, I see your point. It's easier to take bullshit when you know that you don't have to. What kind of work would you want to do?"

"Promise me you won't laugh, but I really would like to work with children."

"Are you for real?"

"Yeah, you know I love kids and since I can't have any of my own I figure the next best thing would be to work with them. I've even considered adoption."

"Damn, how come I didn't know you felt this deeply about this?"

"I just finally admitted it to myself. I'm not going to make any decisions yet. I think I am going to go on a vacation to sort out how I'm really feeling."

"Oh, vacation, sounds like fun. Want some company?"

"Naw, girl, I think I need to be by myself for a minute. You know the old saying, if you can't figure out where you've been, how are you gonna know where you want to go?"

"I hear ya. That's the kind of journey I need to take myself."

"Enough with this depressing shit. We can talk about it some other time. Go find your man and ya'll have some fun for me too. I'll wait here for your call to make sure you have a ride."

"Alright, sis. I love you."

"Yeah, I love you too. Thanks for the play. I had a blast."

"Me too. I'll holla when I find him."

For a few moments neither of us moves. I want Sammie to hurry up because the longer she waits, the more likely it will be that Buddy would have left. Although her house is not far from mine, I am aching to be alone. Besides, I know that if I say anything else, it won't come out right. Sammie releases her seatbelt, gives me a kiss, and waves good-bye.

My cell phone rings as soon as Sammie shuts the door. I pluck it off the side of my purse and glance at the caller ID. I am not surprised to see Mike's name flash across the screen. I send the call to voice mail. I don't feel like dealing with his shit right now. I have enough on my mind without adding his bullshit in the mix.

Sammie calls to tell me that she found Buddy. Relieved, I drive home as if the bats of hell are chasing me. All I want to do is take a hot bath, pour myself a cool glass of wine, and curl up with a good book. With a heavy sigh, I get my ass out of the car. Dumping my purse and shoes on the sofa, I pad into the bathroom in my stocking feet. Pausing, I light a few candles as I turn on the water and add some bath salts.

In the kitchen, I grab a glass for my wine and bring it and the entire bottle to the bathroom with me. I only stop long enough to fill up the ice bucket to keep the wine cold. Removing my clothes, I allow cleansing tears to fall with each discarded item. I'm not crying over Mike. He's minor in the scheme of things.

I'm not even crying because of how lonely I feel. It runs much deeper than that. I am crying for all the years I wasted away without a purpose. I never stopped to think about which direction I wanted my life to take. I was content to live in the moment, any moment, and I'm crying for the one thing that I could never get back—time.

I slowly lower myself into the water. My tension releases into the air and my body relaxes. As I take my first sip of the wine, the phone rings. Instinctively, I rise to answer, but then change my mind. Whoever it is can wait. I ease back onto the cold vinyl pillow stuck to the back of the tub and grab my book. Moisture drips from my forehead and I use the back of my arm to wipe it away. The phone rings four times before the answering machine picks up. It is Mike. I can hear his begging ass urging me to pick up the phone, but I'm not feeling it.

While I soak in the tub, a plan forms in my mind. Everyone has something to motivate them. For the last five years, since my divorce, my only motivation has been having fun. But I finally realize that there is more to life than just having fun. Everything in life has a purpose, including pain, especially if you use that pain to motivate change. For too long, I've been complacent, settling for fast men and bling bling. It's time I move though my pain.

Learning to trust again has been my biggest problem. My ex-husband hurt me so badly when he cheated on me that I vowed to never give my heart to any man again. Maybe I wouldn't have felt so bad if he'd cheated with another woman instead of a man. It is time for me to let go of the past and embrace the future.

After the cookout next week, I will go on vacation before I make some drastic decision about my future. I'm not sure I want a job, but I am going to look into it before I leap. I am also going to explore adopting a child. I've been toying with the idea for a long time, but never really believed I could do it until I said it today. The thought makes me feel stronger somehow.

Energized, I jump out of the tub trailing water behind me. The idea of a vacation is looking better and better. While I'm away, I will concentrate on where I want my life to go from this point.

Logging on the internet, I search Yahoo Travel for the perfect vacation. I feel alive for the first time in years.

# Jasmine

Cookout day is finally here. Mom and I have been very busy planning and arranging everything. The flowers have been delivered, the waiters are due at ten, and everyone else is expected at twelve. The food is being supplied by Justin's restaurant and should arrive by eleven. They promised it will still be hot. Yep, everything is running smoothly. I turned the ringer off on my phone last night because Sammie was blowing it up. She is nervous and I can understand it, but enough is enough. I mean, how many times can I keep telling her that everything is going to be okay?

I was about to turn the ringer back on, but someone is knocking on the door. I expect to see Sammie when I peek through the peephole, but am surprised to find Mike grinning at me.

*I'll say one thing. That nigga has some fucking balls just dropping by my house all uninvited.* Balls or not, it is not enough for me to open the door. I'm not upset anymore about him being with another woman, because, after all, he is not my man. I am upset that he didn't think enough of me to cancel our date.

Mike knocks several more times before he slips a note under the door. I wait until I hear his car peel away before I retrieve the note.

Dear Jazz,

First let me say that I am very sorry about last week. I found myself in a difficult situation and instead of being a man, I chose the coward's way out and lied to you. I'm sorry for this, I really am. When I close my eyes, all I can see is your face and remember the pain I caused you. I don't like the way it makes me feel inside one bit.

I think of you as my sunny day and now the only thing I see in my forecast is rain. The only person I can blame for this is me. I know you must hate me by now, but I tried to call you and you wouldn't pick up the phone. I hope in time you will allow me to make it up to you.

When I said that I wanted to take you away to see the play, I meant it and the offer still stands. Please let me make this up to you. Please. The lady you saw me with last week was an old girlfriend. I'd purchased the tickets for us when they first went on sale months ago. I assumed she wouldn't be going because we were no longer seeing each other, especially since she moved out of town. I wouldn't have extended the invitation to you to go to the play if I had any idea that she would be showing up. She was on my doorstep when I got home. She flew in specifically for the play. I did what was easiest for me. I took her and lied to you. I know now that both options were unacceptable.

I understand that I destroyed my best chance at happiness that I've ever had, but I hope one day you will forgive me. That woman means nothing to me and I don't mean anything to her. She left the very next day and I promise you, she slept on the sofa.

I know you probably don't believe me, but I had to tell you my side of the story, the truth this time. I'm not begging for a second chance because I think I deserve it. I'm begging because I need it.

I know I'm not worthy, but if you give me half a chance, I will make it up to you. I will give you a few days to think about it and I'll call you. Please pick up the phone. Terribly sorry, Mike.

I read the letter four times, and each time I can't decide how I feel. I don't know whether I believe him or not. It is a beautiful letter. That is, if it is true. I fold up the note and place it on the coffee table. I make a snap decision that I pray will not come back and bite me in the butt. Irregardless of the circumstances, Mike still lied to me and I was not about to enter into a relationship with a liar. Been there, done that, end of story. As I turn on the ringer on my phone, I decide to get dressed. I have to get downstairs to help out just in case someone arrives early. I don't want Mom overdoing it. When I finish dressing, I call Sammie.

"Hey sis, do you want me to swing by and pick you up?"

"Obviously, you haven't listened to your messages. I've been calling you all night. I was about to do a drive-by to make sure your ass was okay."

"I'm sorry, girl. I was taking some me time. So do you wanna ride or what?"

"Yeah, I'd really appreciate it. I don't want to walk in the lion's den alone. Plus I had this awful dream last night and I wanted to talk to you before the cookout."

"What was it about?"

"Well, we were at the cookout and everything was going good and we were actually having fun until Buddy walked in."

"Buddy? That should have made you feel better."

"I know, right? But as he got closer to me he started to change. Instead of his regular gait, he was pimp-walking, giving folks the finger as he passed. By the time he got to me, it wasn't Buddy. It was Jessie. I started screaming at him and everyone was looking at me like I was crazy."

"Girl, we have to do something about your active imagination. It's on overdrive."

"But, Jazz, it was so real. I could even smell his cheap-ass cologne. I woke up shaking and sweating."

"I think it's a mind game with you. Every time things start going well for you, you bring Jessie in to bring you down and get you depressed. It's almost like a security blanket with you, to keep you from being totally happy."

"Do you think so? Because if this is something I am conjuring up in my mind, I will put a stop to it right now. I'm sick of seeing his tired ass either in my dreams or in person."

"I know that's right. Look, if you want to go with me you'd better get dressed. I need to get back here to help Mom."

"I've been dressed for the last hour. I have changed my clothes at least twelve times and finally I just said fuck it. I don't know who is going to clean up the mess I made trying to decide what to wear."

"Unless you got money for a maid, you will, 'cause I ain't about to help you clean up your damn room."

"Dag, sis, I would help *you*."

"You're only saying that because you know I have a maid. I'll be through in half an hour. Don't change clothes again, hear? I'm sure what you were wearing the first time was fine."

"Yeah, I know. That's what I finally decided to wear. I'll see you when you get here."

"Fool, stop trippin'. It ain't that serious."

I'm not about to tell Sammie that the aunts and uncles can be a handful if they are allowed to pass the bottle around. As it is, they are likely to say anything out their mouths. But I feel confident that since the cookout is so early none of them would have had a chance to get their drink on. Plus, they promised Momma to act right.

Taking one last look around my apartment, I grab a few of my CDs to stir things up. I know that they like old school, so I had Sammie ask Buddy to make us a few more CDs, and she will be bringing them. I will make sure the DJ keeps things mixed up. The phone rings before I can actually pull the door closed. Debating whether to answer or not, curiosity gets the better of me and I grab the phone. It's my mother.

"Oh, hey, Mom, I was just leaving to go pick up Sammie."

"There's been a change in plans. I need you to pick up your Aunt Mavis."

"Ah, damn, why did she wait until the last minute to tell me?"

"You know how your aunt is."

"Why doesn't she ride with Aunt Rosa? They live around the corner from each other."

"Well, it's Rosa's fault she wants to ride with you. Rosa told her she is too old to be riding in those fast and fancy cars."

"So she had to prove her wrong, right?"

"You guessed it."

"I can see it now. She is going to ask me to put the top down and I'm going to argue with her. She'll pout and I'll wind up putting it down and spending the next twenty minutes chasing her wig."

"Sounds like you've done this before."

"Yes, I have."

"Baby, I'm sorry. If there was another way to do this, I wouldn't have called you."

"It's not your fault, Mom. I don't mind picking her up, but Sammie has been trippin' for the last forty-eight hours and she is counting on me to come get her."

"Well, can't you get both of them?"

"Yeah, I could've if Aunt Mavis didn't wait so long. There is no way that I can pick them both up and be back in time to help you with the food."

"I know, baby. I'm sorry."

"It's okay, Mom. Plus, it ain't your fault. Sammie will just have to understand."

"Yeah, because Aunt Lenora will nut up for sure if we leave her there alone with Aunt Rosa."

"Yeah, I guess Sammie will understand. I'll call her from the car. I just hope Auntie is ready, 'cause the last time she had taken a laxative and I had to stay out in the car for forty-five minutes waiting for her to finish."

"Why couldn't you stay in the house?"

"You know how Aunt Mavis gets down. See ya later."

I hang up the phone laughing, but I am not looking forward to the next call I have to make. Sammie must have sensed something was up because she hit me right up on my cell.

"Where are you? I have walked a hole in my carpet."

"I got bad news, sis. Mom just called and I have to pick up Aunt Mavis. There's no way I can get you both and still help Mom out, so you are going to have to drive yourself."

"Shit."

"I know, but Aunt Mavis said her arthritis is acting up and she can't drive. If I don't go get her, there is going to be hell to pay because she is the peacemaker between Aunt Lenora and Aunt Rosa. Trust me, you don't want to see them get all riled up."

"They are sisters. What's the beef?"

"They dislike Aunt Rosa because she is the oldest and they think she treats them like children. They will kill each other if Mavis ain't there to stop it."

"Oh, well, I understand. I just wish I wasn't so nervous."

"It's going to be fine. Why don't you come to Mom's now? This way you will already be there when folks start arriving and you won't have to walk in alone."

"Yeah, I think I will do that. But hurry up, okay?"

"Okay. I'll be there as soon as I can. Oh, and help Mom out if things start happening. If I don't keep an eye on her, she will go overboard and be sick for a month."

"Alright, then, I'll see you there."

I could hear the disappointment in Sammie's voice, but there isn't anything I can do about it. It is too bad Leah can't make it because this is sure to be quite a party, but I understand her need to get away with her man. Shoot, that vacation I was thinking about is looking better and better.

# Leah

Craig has arranged a weekend getaway as he said he would and it isn't a minute too soon. The last two weeks have been stressful for us both. For some reason, Craig's temper has been short with me and even the staff is commenting on his curtness. Of course, they don't realize the extent of our relationship, so they feel free to bitch in front of me. Craig is acting differently. He hardly wants to spend time talking over the phone like we normally do. And when I come to get the kids, he seems too busy to walk me to my car let alone have a conversation. Maybe it's just me—I'm still relationship shy after Kentee. Now it seems like our relationship is fizzling, so I automatically jump at any opportunity to revive it.

However, Craig is acting like he has a chip on his shoulder. He doesn't speak during our six-hour drive to Tunica unless he wants me to hand him something. My thoughts are running rampant. I'm feeling scared. *Has he finally had enough of my emotional baggage and is only taking me on this trip for a final rumble in the sheets?*

At the hotel, I feel defeated in spite of all the luxury around me. Craig and I walk in silence to one of the restaurants in the casino. Even the thought of playing the machines does not excite me as much as a smile from Craig would. My thoughts are on the kids and what they are doing instead of on my man. We are not holding hands like we normally do and I don't like it one bit. His behavior is frightening me.

"This restaurant has a seafood buffet. Would you like to try it?"

"That will be fine." I don't feel like having a whole bunch of conversation, so a buffet will be perfect. If he didn't have anything to say during the drive, what are we going to talk about now? We wait on our table in silence and I can feel the tension mounting. He finally touches me as the waitress tells us to follow her and I practically jump out of my skin. He places his hand on the small of my back, urging me forward. His fingers feel cold and clammy. I shudder. He touches me again and I am grateful, but there's no warmth. I don't want to lose him, but I'm not going to beg. Been there, done that.

"Are you cold?"

"No, I'm fine."

The waitress takes our drink orders and we get in line. Many of the people we pass have cups full of change on their tables. One guy has five cups of dollar coins.

"Wow, I wonder how much he won."

"I'd be more interested in knowing how much he lost."

"Ain't that the truth?" We lapse back into silence as we fill our plates. Normally, I don't like buffet food because it's never hot enough, but I am starving and cannot wait to get back to the table and dig in.

From the look of Craig's plate he is pretty hungry as well. It is piled high and if everyone else wasn't taking as much or more food I would be embarrassed.

When we sit down, I find the nerve to question Craig's behavior. I put down my fork, giving him my full attention. "Why are you being so quiet?" I am hungry as hell, but my fear of losing Craig spurs me on. He acts as if he doesn't hear me, so I repeat my question.

"I know I've been a bitch, but are we okay?" My heart beat seems to pause as I wait for his response.

"We're okay, baby. I'm just thinking of ways to make this your most memorable weekend. I want everything to be perfect for you."

"Memorable? Baby, you are scaring me. All week long you've been short and I felt like I was bothering you most of the time when I called you."

"I'm sorry, baby. Trust me, you haven't done anything wrong. I've been stressing, trying to stuff a seven-day vacation into two and a half days."

"Craig, I'm with you. That's as good as it gets for me. I'm not impressed by anything else but being with you." I pick up my fork, giving my food the attention it deserves. I believe his simple explanation and try to finish our meal in peace, despite the nagging worry worm in my gut.

"So do you wanna hit the casino after dinner or do you want to take a drive?" Craig asks.

"I'm down for whatever, baby. We can stay right here in the hotel if you'd like or take a drive. It's on you, especially since you did all the driving to get here."

"Let's take a drive. The casino will be open all night long and you can even come down after I go to bed if you want to."

"Oh, I wouldn't feel good about coming down here again without you. I like to gamble, but I'd rather spend my uninterrupted time with you."

"You keep talking like that and we won't be seeing any of the fine city or the casino." He smiles for the first time in weeks. "I tell you what. We'll take a short drive and hit the casino for an hour or two when we get back. After that, I'm sure we can find something to do in our suite. I believe they even have pay per view. How does that sound?"

"Sounds like a plan to me!" I finish my plate while fighting the temptation to get a piece of cheesecake.

"Get your cheesecake, woman, I know it's killing you." I am full and don't want to have trouble sleeping, but I have a sweet tooth that won't quit and he knows it. He tops his meal off with a cup of coffee while I sinfully eat my cake.

After leaving money on the table for a tip, Craig ushers me out of the restaurant and to the car. He drives as if he knows exactly where he is going and I can't help but wonder how many other ladies he's brought to this same area. Unwilling to dwell in my prior misery, I remain quiet while I enjoy the scenery. I drift off to sleep even though we have been driving for less than fifteen minutes.

"Black folks, feed 'em and they out like a light." Craig's voice rouses me from sleep and I punch him on the shoulder playfully as I wipe the corners of my mouth, praying for no moisture that would indicate that I was drooling as I slept. Looking around, I realize that we are parked in front of one of those wedding chapels you usually see in Las Vegas on the old Elvis movies. I turn to Craig, not sure what to make of this new development.

"Now, don't nut up on me. We've talked about this before. The bottom line is I'm tired of waiting. Are you down for doing this tonight?"

"Stop playing. This ain't even funny."

"Do I look like I'm laughing?"

"You're serious?"

"As a heart attack, baby. Despite what you think, patience is not my long suit."

"I know what your long suit is."

"Hey, kill the jokes right now. Are you ready to do this? Life is not promised to us. One of us could die tomorrow; I don't wanna waste another minute of my life without you as my lover and wife."

"Are you sure?"

"I've never been so sure of anything in my entire life. We can do a big ceremony later on, but tonight I want to make love to you officially as my wife."

"But, Craig, there is so much to work out. The kids, where will we live…don't you think we should talk about this more?"

"If you love me, Leah, there is nothing else to talk about. We will work out those issues together."

"So what are you waiting on?" I was trying to sound seductive despite my nervousness.

"You, just say the word."

"Yes."

Tears flow from our eyes and mingle together when he presses his face forward and gently kisses me on my eyelids. I cannot think of a more moving experience in my entire life. Not even the births of my children moved me as much as this very moment. My heart feels like it's about to burst. I can't get out of my seat-belt fast enough to run around to his side. Throwing my arms around his neck, I hold on so tight, I just don't want to let go. Our kiss is passionate and long.

He breaks the kiss. "We have to hurry, baby, they will be closing soon." He doesn't have to tell me twice. I practically drag him into the building. I can't believe we are going to actually do this. I keep expecting to wake up at any moment, even as we are filling out the paperwork. But it isn't a dream and less than fifteen minutes later, I am Mrs. Craig Simmons-Richmond.

What surprises me most is the size of the diamond he places on my finger. Obviously, Craig has been planning this for some time. The diamond is quite large, set in yellow gold and surrounded by four smaller diamonds. I want to ask Craig how many karats it is but I think better of it. I don't want him to think I'm either ungrateful or just plain old tacky.

"How long have you been planning this, Mr. Richmond?"

"Been thinking about it for some time, Mrs. Richmond, but I honestly didn't plan on popping the question this weekend. I wanted to wait until we had more time to be together, but you lit a fire in me that would not go out until I made you mine. Plus, that ring was burning a hole in my pocket for weeks. Come on, I promised you some gambling before we consummate our marriage."

Being around people is the last thing I want. I am so excited. I want to call my mother and Sammie to share my good news. I know we will face some big adjustments as far as the children are concerned, but I am confident our love will see us through. The hardest part of any new marriage, when there are children involved, is getting the children to accept and feel comfortable with your mate. Since we are past that hurdle, I am sure they will adjust quickly to our new living arrangements.

For a nanosecond, Kentee crosses my mind, but I quickly block that dark cloud before it douses my internal sunshine. This is Craig's and my night and I claim it with gusto. There will be plenty of time during our ride home to work out the particulars. Until then, I just want to relax and enjoy my new husband. I steal a look at him and his grin is almost as big as mine. Ironically, just a few short hours ago I thought he was going to break up with me and now, we are married. I am so tickled, I start laughing so hard that tears leak from the corners of my eyes.

"Hey, what's so funny?"

"I'm laughing at myself for being so stupid."

"Stupid? I don't get it." I continue to laugh because I feel plain silly for ever doubting this wonderful man sitting beside me.

"The whole way up here, I was thinking that you were bringing me here for one last romp in the bed before breaking up with me. You've been so distant the last few weeks. I thought you were tired of me and my emotional baggage."

Craig pulls the car over to the side of the road. "Are you serious?"

I nod my head. The pain in his eyes is obvious.

"I'm so sorry, sweetheart. I never meant for you to feel anything less than love from me. I'll admit I was preoccupied with trying to make this a fantastic getaway. I didn't mean to cause you pain."

"It's okay now, baby."

"No. It's not. Promise me that if you ever feel insecure, or if I appear to be acting an ass for no reason, call me on it. Can you do that for me, baby?" He lifts my hand from my lap and gently kisses my palm. "Can you?"

"Yes, I can."

"Good. In order for us to survive, we have to communicate. So stop that holding-in stuff, especially if it causes you pain. If we don't confront things head on, they will only fester."

People are slowing down their cars, peering into the windows. It was only a matter of time before a state trooper pulls up to see if we're stranded or in need of assistance.

"Uh, baby, do you think we can move so as not to get killed on the first day of the rest of our lives?"

"Yeah, uh…my bad." We both laugh as the tension in the car breaks.

"Wow, for a minute, you sounded just like Malik."

"I know, right? He is starting to rub off on me." Craig reaches out and grabs my hand, placing it in his lap. I try to caress his dick, but he shakes his head.

"No, baby, you can't do that unless you want to wind up in a ditch. I'm hot enough as it is."

"Later?"

"Oh yeah, you can count on that."

# Kentee

"Hey, Ma, how are you doing?"

"Oh shit!"

"Huh? What kind of greeting is that for your only son?"

"The only kind you deserve since the only time I hear from you is when you have Bebe's kids with you. The answer is no. You will not drop those kids off with me today."

"Aw, Ma, they're your grandkids, for Christ's sake."

"And they are your kids, so deal with them."

"I am dealing with them. But I'm tapped out of ideas about how to entertain them."

"You've had them less than twenty-four hours and you're burnt out? Here's a novel idea. Stop trying to entertain them and be a father."

"I don't know how to do that."

"You should have thought of that when you were making 'em."

"Could you just watch them for a little while? I have an errand to run and I can't take them with me."

"Then I suggest you wait and make your little run after you drop those rug-rats back home 'cause they aren't coming here."

"Why must you keep calling my children names? You act like you don't even love them. Is that it? You don't love your own grandchildren?"

"So you say they're my grandkids. I can remember when you and Leah first split up you told me that they weren't yours, and now you want me to claim them. Make up your damn mind. Are they yours or not?"

"Uh—"

"Speak up, cat got your tongue?"

She has me there. I'd told so many lies I forgot whom I'd told what to. I never doubted the paternity of my children, but I didn't want Leah to come in and turn my family against me after the split. So I did what came naturally, I lied to protect my own ass.

"Fine, Ma, but when my kids grow up and don't know who you are, don't act surprised."

"That mind shit might work on some of those hoochies you play with in the street, but it damn sure ain't going to work on me." She hangs up the phone before I can say anything else.

"Shit!" *Now what am I going to do?* I can't drop off the kids at my girlfriend's house because I promised Leah I wouldn't. I have every intention of keeping that promise, especially since my current girlfriend doesn't know I have children and I plan to keep it that way.

Wait. I promised I wouldn't take the kids to my girlfriend's house. I didn't say anything about my friend's house. Tarcia isn't my girl anymore. She is just a friend with benefits. And since she already knows about the kids, I won't have to lie to her. Slapping my hands together, I gather the kids, jump in the car and head over to Tarcia's house before she can get out in the street with her freaky friends.

"Daddy, we're hungry," Kayla whines.

"What? Your momma didn't feed you?"

"She said we didn't have time to eat because you were on the way."

"Damn." Slamming my hand down on the steering wheel, I fight the urge to yell at Kayla. The noise startles Mya and she begins to whimper. Realizing things are going downhill fast, I know I have to act quickly before things spiral out of control.

The yellow arches light up the sky like a beacon calling me in. Fast, cheap, and good. Everybody loves McDonald's, even adults. Pulling into the drive-thru, I quickly place our orders. I decide against going inside 'cause I don't want Mya to act a fool. She has come a long way with her eating habits, but she still does not tolerate strangers looking at her.

While I wait for them to finish eating, I scheme on what I am going to say to Tarcia to convince her to watch the kids. I know she isn't going to be happy about seeing them, but I am hopeful she will keep a civil tongue in her mouth, especially after the way she acted the last time I saw her. She damn near punched a hole in my back and scared the shit out of me. I am counting on the fact that she still holds a torch for me. Her scheming ass will probably use this favor to get me back in her bed. *That's a small price to pay for what I'm about to do.*

Tarcia answers the door on the second ring, looking like a deer caught in headlights. For a minute, I am scared that she is going to slam the door, but then her entire face lights up. I can tell she is happy to see me until she realizes I'm not alone.

Her expression becomes an icy façade as she crosses her arms over her chest. She is flashing hot and cold at me as if she is waging an inner battle.

"Hey, baby." As I step in closer to grab a kiss, she turns her head so it lands on her cheek instead of her lips. Undaunted by her attitude, I continue working our way into her apartment. For a minute, she holds her ground and blocks my way, but ultimately she steps aside.

"What are you doing here?"

"I missed you. And, and...the children missed you."

"No, we didn't," Kayla says. I silence her with a look and she lowers her eyes.

"We were in the neighborhood and thought we would stop by. Go sit down, kids." Tarcia, with a scowl on her face, still has her arms folded. She isn't making this as easy as I thought it was going to be.

"So, how have you been? Can we sit down?" She doesn't answer, but I act as if I'm not expecting her to and sit down anyway. The children sit right next to me, forcing Tarcia to sit on the love-seat. Kayla is sulking; Mya is gazing out the window. Malik turns the channel on the television, clearly ignoring us all.

Tarcia snags a cigarette from the pack on the cocktail table. Normally, I would chastise her for smoking in front of my kids, but since I am about to beg for a favor, I don't want to piss her off. Her eyes are burning so brightly, she could light her cigarette from within. Instead, she uses the lighter that is also on the table, blowing smoke in my direction. I can tell she is hot with me, but she's going to have to get over it and quickly. I have shit to do and time is ticking.

"Say, where is your cousin? Is she still staying here with you?"

"You would know that if you came around more often, now wouldn't you?"

"Ouch, go for the jugular now, why don't you."

"I'm just calling them like I see them. Last time I talked to you, a few weeks ago, you were on your way over here and I haven't heard from you since."

"I've been out of town on a big project. It was at the last minute."

"Oh, cut the shit, Kentee. You said you were on your way. What did they do? Call you right before you turned in my parking lot?"

"Almost. I had to go home and pack and I knew you wouldn't believe me, so I just didn't call. I'm sorry, baby." I can feel Kayla's eyes burning a hole in my face. I am beginning to think that coming here wasn't such a good idea, but I am committed. I have to get across town to pick up a package within the next half hour or I will be in some serious hot water with some very difficult people.

"Tarcia, can you do me a favor?"

"No."

"I haven't even asked it yet."

"You don't have to. I know your sorry ass. You want to leave your kids here while you go God knows where and with whom."

I glance at my kids to see if they heard her call me a "sorry ass," but mercifully their eyes are glued to the set, except for Mya. It is bad enough their mother called me a "sorry ass;" I don't need for them to hear Tarcia calling me that too. If I don't correct that soon, before I know it they will be calling me "sorry ass" instead of Daddy.

"I ain't going with anyone. I gotta pick up a package for Lil' John and they can't go."

"You should have thought of that before you picked them up from their mother."

"I didn't know it at the time. He called after I got them and their momma had already left the house. She won't answer the phone and now I am stuck."

"Sounds like a personal problem to me."

"Come on, Tarcia, don't be like that. You know I still owe Lil' John for bailing me out of jail."

"Again, this sounds like a personal problem. Take 'em to your new girl's house."

"Ah, babe, you know you are my only girl."

"I am? You could've fooled me. I ain't seen or heard from your ass for close to a month and you say I'm your only girl? What, do I have *idiot* written on my forehead?"

"How many times do I have to tell you, I've been working?"

"So whatcha been doing with your dick? I know you're dipping it somewhere because it damn sure ain't been in my pussy."

"Damn, girl, watch your mouth. There are children in the room." I look around to see if they are listening to our conversation, but if they are, they're hiding it well. "Whether you like them or not, they are still children."

"Humph."

"Come on, Tarcia, if you let them stay here for a little while, I'll bring you back a little something-something."

This gets her attention. She is the greediest bitch I've ever known.

"Like what?"

"What do you want?"

"Break me off some of what you're going to get. And don't tell me you ain't gonna take none 'cause I know you."

"Girl, are you trying to get me hurt or killed?"

"No. I just want a piece of what you're gonna take anyway. Do we have a deal?"

I take a few precious minutes to think about it, but the reality is I don't have much of a choice at this point. I was planning on skimming at least an ounce off the top. Lil' John always gives me a bonus for timely deliveries, so I can afford to break her off a small piece.

"Okay."

"Don't be gone all day either. I don't have anything for them to eat, and me and my cousin are going out later and I'm not taking them with me."

"So your cousin is still here?"

"Why you so interested in my cousin?"

"I'm not, I was just asking. I can't win. You jump on my ass when I don't know and you jump on me when I ask questions."

"Just hurry up and get back."

"I'm coming right back."

Lasonji comes in from the guest bedroom looking lovely as ever in her no-nonsense way. I smile and greet her. "Hey, how you doing?"

"Fine. Tarcia, can I speak with you for a moment in the kitchen?" She turns without waiting for a response and they leave the room.

Lasonji's reception was even icier than Tarcia's. Without realizing it, I check her out, but Tarcia's evil eye busts me, and her annoyance is etched on her face. She follows Lasonji into the kitchen while her eyes dare me to watch Lasonji's ass. I try to hear what is so important that she has to interrupt our conversation, but they keep their voices down.

They are evidently fighting about something, but as long as it doesn't interfere with my little run, I'm not going to sweat it. That's Tarcia's cousin and she has to deal with her shit, not me.

"Kayla, I want you to mind Ms. Tarcia while Daddy makes a run. Don't give her no trouble and when I get back, we'll go and get some ice cream, okay?" Kayla nods her head, but she is fighting back tears. I know they don't want to stay here any more than I want to leave them but my back is against the wall. They absolutely cannot go with me where I am going and I have to go.

"And watch out for your brother and sister, okay?"

"Yes, sir."

"Yo, Tarcia, I gotta run. I'll be back soon." Without waiting for her to come back into the room, I jet. I don't know what it is about that cousin but she gives me the creeps. Every time she has looked at me, it's like she's looking into my head and I don't like it. Perhaps she knew that I was using her cousin and she didn't approve.

"Oh well, two tears in a bucket, fuck it." I hop in the car and peel out of the lot before Tarcia can change her mind and fuck up all my plans. I do have one other stop to make before I come back, but Tarcia doesn't need to know about that.

# Tarcia

"I can't believe that you allowed that man back in your house after what happened the last time he was here."

"We didn't find anything, so what's the beef?"

"Did you ask him about it?"

"Uh…"

"So you just let him in, no questions asked, and you allow him to leave his kids here. You don't know anything about them kids."

"I've been with them before. They know me."

"I didn't say anything about them knowing you. I said you didn't know them. For all you know, they could be conduits to the dark side."

"Oh, come on, Lasonji, they're children, for Christ's sake."

"Haven't you ever heard of the devil's spawn?"

"Oh, there you go with that shit. I'm not going there with you again. You worked me up so bad the last time, it was a week before I could sleep through the night."

"Well, I'm glad that you have started sleeping again because I haven't. That skin is still out there whether you want to believe it or not, and the fact that it appeared when your man was here means they are connected."

"Give me a break."

"I'll give you a break. But I want to show you something before I go." She turns and walks out of the kitchen and into the dining room. Without asking my help, she pushes the dining room table to the far corner of the room. How she pushed that table without moving the scatter rug is a mystery to me. It is heavy as shit and took three men to carry it in, but she shoved it aside as if it were weightless. I expect to see scrape marks on the hardwood floor, but surprisingly it appears to have been freshly polished. It's unlikely because the room hasn't been used since the night of the dinner. I am distracted from the clean floor by a strange marking that is on the wood.

The drawing looks familiar and unfamiliar at the same time, if that is possible. My heart pounds and I can feel the blood rushing through my veins. I look at Lasonji, hoping that she will clarify this for me, but she just stares at me. She does not look at the drawing and that worries me more than anything. Perplexed, I get closer to it. Heat emanates from the floor, rising to meet the cool air from the air conditioner. The room feels more like a jungle than a dining room.

"What the hell is that?"

"Answer your own questions. Who was sitting there?"

"Me...Kentee...what does it mean?" Despite my fear, I get down on my knees and try to wipe it up, but it won't come off. It is engraved into the floor but that doesn't make sense.

"This wasn't here when I moved in." I start to hyperventilate. Falling back onto my butt, I propel myself away from the drawing. As sweat pours from my face, the room begins to sway before my eyes. "Cover it up, please!"

Lasonji just stands there staring at me.

"Did you do this?" I ask Lasonji. I don't want the children running into the dining room to see what is going on, but at the same time I want an explanation from her.

"You know the answer to that, so stop trippin'. I'm going out. If you don't take your spiritual well-being seriously, then that's on you. I'm going to protect mine."

"You're going to leave me here with that?"

"It's been here since the dinner."

"And you didn't tell me?"

"You didn't want to hear it, remember?"

"But I didn't know."

"Well, you do now. Listen, I won't feel safe until the matter of the snake is resolved. Plus, it's time I start looking for my own place anyway."

I immediately start to panic, but not because of the engraving. For a minute, I forget all about it. I cannot afford to have Lasonji move right now. The money she is giving me is keeping my head above water while I search for a job. My unemployment benefits don't start until next week, but it won't be enough to cover the bills. I need Lasonji to stick around until I have a steady paycheck coming in.

"Girl, I'm sorry. I guess I wasn't thinking. I thought since we didn't find the other skin, everything was okay. I mean, damn, you haven't said anything about it for over a week. Tell you what, Kentee's only going to be gone for a few hours. I'll keep the kids in the living room and you can have the rest of the house to yourself."

"No, I need to get out to clear my head. I can't think with all this energy up in this house. Just keep them out of my room and hit me on my cell when they have left." She slams the door on her way out.

"Let the doorknob hit you where the good Lord split you, bitch."

I throw the rug over the drawing, using my feet to straighten it out as best I can. When it is completely covered, I can no longer feel the heat. I try to push the table back into place, but every time it gets near the rug, the rug bunches up and exposes the picture. After several tries, I give up.

"How the hell was she able to move the table without disturbing the rug?"

# Sammie

I arrive at Jazz's mother's house just as a florist truck is unloading large bouquets of lilies. They are beautiful, in all different hues of pink, yellow and white. Looking around the circular driveway, I see that mine is the only other car present, so I heave a sigh of relief. Unless some limousine service dropped off the rest of the family, I am the first guest to arrive.

Jazz is the only grown woman I know who lives at home with her mother by choice and is happy about it. She says they keep each other company and they are more like friends than mother and daughter. From what I can see, they are. I envy their relationship. My own childhood was troubled and my mother and I never got along until right before she passed away.

*If only our relationship could have been like Jazz and Andrea's, maybe I would have turned out differently.* But there is no sense crying about that now. What's done is done and I have to believe that God doesn't make any mistakes. My life is what it is.

I follow the delivery guys around to the back of the house and go in through the back door to help Andrea.

"Hello?" The kitchen is empty, but the air is filled with the smell of fresh lemons. The table is piled high with paper plates, cups, plastic silverware, and red, pink, and yellow napkins.

"Hello," I call again. I move from the kitchen into the living room. I don't want to startle Andrea, so I make sure to walk heavily instead of tiptoeing around like I normally do when I am uncomfortable with my surroundings. Although I have been to the house on numerous occasions, I never will forget my first visit to this mini-mansion. I could not help but feel bitter because of their obvious opulence compared to the humble home I was raised in. I finally understood that money would not have made our house into a home. Love, given freely, makes all the difference in the world between a cardboard box and a penthouse suite.

Andrea rushes into the room, rousing me from my memories.

"Oh, Sammie, I didn't hear you come in." Andrea holds out her arms to me and I walk into them, squeezing her tightly in return. She smells like she has just gotten out of the shower and I inhale her scent deeply. Despite our rocky start, I fell in love with Andrea and consider her to be my second mother.

"Sorry about the mix-up, but your father's folks can be downright demanding at times."

"It's okay, Ma. I needed to do this by myself anyway." I break free of her embrace. "Can I help you with anything?"

"No dear, the caterers will be here any minute. Why don't you put your purse in Jazz's room and relax a bit before folks start coming."

"Nope, I told Jazz I would keep you from overdoing it and I intend to do just that. I will stow my purse, but I'll be right back."

The house is more like two apartments joined by a main staircase. Jazz's room, as Andrea called it, is off to the left, consisting of two bedrooms, a sitting room, bathroom, two walk-in closets that are larger than my bedroom, and a small kitchen area. She has a balcony off her bedroom with steps leading down to the backyard providing her a private entrance if she chooses to use it.

Unlike my room, hers is bright and airy and void of clothes and abandoned shoes. She even has an entire wall devoted to her collection of purses. Every time I see that wall, I can't help but to laugh because before I met Jazz, I had two purses to my name. Now, I'm not happy unless I get at least two a week. Jazz is definitely rubbing off on me. Not wanting to dilly-dally any longer, I rush back downstairs.

The kitchen is a hub of activity as I walk around looking for Andrea. The caterers, along with three servers, had arrived and taken over the kitchen. I want to help, but there are so many folks milling around. I'm the only one who doesn't have any purpose for being there. I wander back outside as the grill is being set up. All the workers are dressed in white pants and long white jackets. Most of the men are wearing hats and the ladies have their hair tied back in tight buns. When I return to the kitchen I find Andrea slicing some cakes. Without asking, I grab a knife and get to work.

"I was looking all over for you."

"Oh, I'm sorry, dear. I got hung up on the phone talking to Uncle Marvin. He got his invites mixed up and thought he was coming to a poker party instead of a cookout."

"Now that's funny. Is he still coming?" I secretly hoped that he would cancel since that would be one less person staring and judging me.

"He'll be here. He isn't one to turn down a free meal. Just don't pay any attention to him if he starts sipping from a bottle in his pocket. I asked him to leave it at home, but he doesn't rightly pay me any attention."

*Great, that makes me feel better.*

Right, just what I need, a drunken uncle I've never met to liven up the party. Thinking of booze, I could use a drink myself. I finish cutting up the last of the cakes while Andrea answers the phone. I go into the dining room and pour myself a double shot from one of the crystal decanters on the buffet table. I really don't care what it is; I just need to knock the edge off my uneasiness.

"Where are you going to put the cakes?"

"We'll leave them inside because of the heat. We can put them back in the dining room until we are ready to have them served." With the cakes all wrapped, I look around for something else to do.

"What now?"

"Now we fix us a drink and relax before the troops come marching in."

"Amen to that." Jazz was worried about her mother for nothing. She has enough sense to sit back and let the hired help do the job they are being paid for.

"Did Jasmine tell you about your aunts and uncles?"

"Not too much. She said she didn't want to scare me away."

"They can be a handful, but most old people are. They feel like their age gives them the right to say anything that comes to mind."

"Well, I can understand that. After all, age does have its privileges."

"Yeah, but sometimes they go too far. So don't let them get all up in your personal space. None of them have been married or had any children, but to hear them tell it, they got all the answers."

"None of them married? Wow, that's strange for a whole family not to marry."

"Yeah, except your father."

I had almost forgotten why we are gathering in the first place. I spent so much of my life thinking my stepfather was my daddy;

it is hard to believe my birth father is someone else and even harder since I never got to meet him. "So tell me about his brothers and sisters. How many are there?"

"There are six of them; your daddy would have made seven. Rosa is the oldest. She is eighty-two; Leonara is seventy-nine, Rufus is seventy-eight. Marvin and Mavis are twins at seventy-six and Maceo, the Romeo of the bunch, is seventy-four."

"How old would my dad have been?"

"He would have been sixty-eight."

"Wow, that's a big break in between kids. There is no way I would wait seven years to have another child."

"Yeah, your daddy was a shocker. His mom and dad, rest their souls, thought they were through until he snuck in there."

"I'll bet."

"And his brothers resented him, especially Maceo, since he was enjoying his status as the baby until your father came along."

"This is all so new to me. I'm not familiar with the feeling of having brothers and sisters. It has always been just me."

"I understand. I was an only child as well. I met your father when I was sixteen and we became childhood sweethearts. We lost contact for a while when he enlisted in the army, but we got together again soon after basic training. He and your stepdaddy were real close, so when they got assigned to their first tour of duty, your father sent for me and your stepdaddy sent for your mother."

"Wow, I didn't know that. Jazz told me ya'll were close, but not that close."

"Yeah, we had a double ceremony and lived next door to each other for years. Whenever one was transferred, the other followed at the first opportunity. We traveled that way for years. Your mother and I kept each other company while the men were away."

*I wonder when the cheating started and better yet, how they were able to carry it out living so close to each other.*

Jazz's arrival stops any further conversation and not a minute too soon. I could feel the tension rising as we strolled down memory lane. I feel the need to apologize for the pain my mother inflicted, so I am relieved to have escaped the moment.

"What are ya'll doing in here? The guests are starting to arrive."

"We were having cocktails and catching up. I don't get to spend as much time with Sammie as you do." Andrea rises from the couch to greet Mavis.

"Mavis, you look…uh…you look…" She turns to Jazz for help, but she is busy trying not to bust out laughing.

"I look scared, damn it," Mavis says defensively. "That's how I look. This here chile done scared the shit out of me with all that fancy driving of hers."

Unable to hold back her laughter, Jazz's shoulders begin to quiver and Andrea's stoic face dissolves into gales of laughter. I try to hold back my laughter, but I can't help myself.

Mavis whips around at the sound of my laughter and stumbles back, clutching her heart. "Sweet Jesus, I didn't see you back there." I immediately stop laughing outwardly, but I am still cracking up inside. Her wig is lopsided with hairs pointing all over the place. Her lipstick is smudged around her lips and her eyes are fixed and dilated. Jasmine got it together enough to make the introductions but Andrea is still laughing.

"Aunt Mavis, this is Sammie."

"I can see that. She looks just like that brother of mine. Matter of fact, she looks a lot like you, 'ceptin' you're not as fat."

It feels so good to hear someone else say that I look like Jazz, I almost missed the comment about my weight.

"Sammie's not fat. She's big boned just like Daddy."

"Big boned, my ass. That chile ain't missed many a meal. Show me to the bathroom, so I can get my wig on straight. I told you not to put that damn top down." Andrea pulls Mavis out of the room. Mavis was only in the house two minutes and I'm ready to leave. There is no way I am going to sit through three hours of this shit, old folks or not. I can hear Andrea fussing as she leads her down the hall.

"Sammie, don't pay her no mind," Jazz says. "She's been bitching since I picked her up. She called me lard-ass all the way here, so please don't get upset or offended by anything she says. She's old and set in her ways."

"Jazz, that's no excuse for being rude. How would she have felt if I said something about that three-dollar wig she's wearing?"

"Three dollars? Dag, Sammie, the taxes on the wig are more than that."

"Then she was robbed, but don't try to change the subject. If this is any indication of what I'm in for, then I'm out. I don't need this shit at all."

"I promise, the other aunts and uncles will be nice. Aunt Leonara will set Mavis straight as soon as she gets here. Have another drink and grab a shrimp while you're at it." She pours me another glass and I swallow it all in one gulp. It burns all the way down to my toes, but I feel better. My stomach is too twisted for food, so I pass on the shrimp.

Andrea returns with Mavis and instinctively I tense up, waiting for some more barbs aimed at me. However, instead of slinging insults, she comes over and gives me a hug.

"Lean down, chile. I can't reach you up there." Unsure of her motives, I lean into her and she gives me a genuine hug with two firm pats on my back.

"You're the spitting image of my brother. It's so nice to finally meet you."

I look at Andrea, wondering what the hell she said to her in the short amount of time they were gone. She smiles at me and nods her head reassuringly. Mavis is so petite; I could have lifted her up if I'd wanted to.

"Ma, Uncle Marvin and Aunt Rosa were pulling up when we got here. I guess they went on to the back. We came here first to freshen up."

"Umph, 'we' my ass," Mavis mumbles.

Listening to this little old lady cussing is funny as hell. She just doesn't look like the type to me. Despite our rocky beginning, now I feel like I am going to like her.

"It's nice to meet you too, Ms. Mavis."

"Hey, I don't want to hear none of that 'Ms.' shit. I'm your auntie and we is all family up in here. Fix me whatchu been drinking, so as I can go deal with that old bat Rosa." I can't move. Mavis switched from hot to cold so fast, it is hard to see where the next punch will come from, but I am thankful it's not directed at me. Andrea calls to the waiters to fix the drinks as we all move to the backyard.

*Okay, Sammie girl, show time.*

# Leah

"Hey, how about stopping at this one?"

"Sam's Town?"

"Yeah, I've been seeing all these billboards that say they have the 'loosest' slot machines in town. Let's give it a try."

"Well, do you wanna play or do you want to play?" I look at Craig, confused, but his meaning becomes clear.

"I wanna play." We head back to our hotel without another word being said. I am feeling excited and nervous at the same time. We are about to make love for the first time as husband and wife.

"Hello, room service, can you send up one of your strawberry cheesecakes and two bottles of your best champagne?"

"Cheesecake and champagne? What are you trying to do to me?"

"I'm trying to make up for driving you all the way to the third-largest gaming district in the world and not letting you play."

"But you said we *were* gonna play." I pretend to pout, just as he is pretending to be making up for anything. My heart swells with love. "I'm going to freshen up."

"Can I come?"

"Someone has to wait for room service."

"Damn, you got me there, but I'll be in as soon as they are gone."

"I'll be waiting." Grabbing my toiletry bag, I playfully run toward the bathroom. I am feeling as giddy as a child. Rather than take a quick shower, I run the bathtub, filling it with bubbles made from shampoo. If I were taking the bath alone I would have used my own bubble bath, but I'm not sure how Craig would feel about taking a bath in Victoria's Secret.

I twist my hair up off my shoulders into a neat French roll and remove all my jewelry except for my beautiful wedding ring. I admire its reflection in the vanity mirror. It is perfect in both size and shape. Craig catches me as I am practicing how I will show off my ring when we get back to Atlanta.

"Ahem, what are you doing, my dear wife?" Caught, I spin around to face him. My heated cheeks are evidence of my embarrassment. Normally I am not influenced by material things, but I cannot tear my eyes away from my ring.

"I can't help it. This ring is beautiful."

"Not as beautiful as you." He is naked and obviously wants some attention. His gaze travels from my feet to my neck, stopping as he stares in my eyes. Breaking from his tempting hold, I step into the tub. Craig produces two flutes and an iced champagne bucket from behind his back.

"Are you just going to stand there pointing at me or are you going to play like you promised?"

"Oh, I'm gonna play, on that you can depend." He pops the cork and our eyes follow its path as it bounces against the ceiling. My eyes follow Craig's every move.

"Am I being selfish?" he asks me.

"Huh?"

"Because tonight I don't want to share you with anyone, not even strangers. I want to be the sole focus of your world, just you and me. So I ask you again, am I being selfish?"

"Well, if you are, I like it."

He steps into the water, never taking his eyes off of me. He offers me my glass as we meet, standing, in the middle of the tub. He nuzzles my neck, resting his chilled glass against my back.

"That's cold, Craig."

"Ah, but I will warm it right up. Turn around." I do as he instructs, sloshing water onto the floor. Pulling my back against his chest, he caresses my neck and shoulders. His lips trail a fiery path over my shoulder blades and down my arms. His hands move in a circular motion over my stomach, inching up to my breasts. I wait to feel his touch, pressing my toes against the tub to get closer. He chuckles, breathing in my essence, his arms holding me tighter.

"You are so beautiful," he says softly. I close my eyes and remain still allowing his touch to linger. His hot breath and warm kisses heat my blood. I moan in ecstasy. This is how I'd pictured an ideal marriage.

"Turn around." I do as he instructs, closing my eyes in anticipation. Icy cold champagne jolts me from my fantasy. The champagne runs down my breast to the tip of my erect nipple. Craig holds his glass beneath it catching each drop. Raising his glass, he smiles in mock salute. I watch as he drains his glass.

He washes my breast with his tongue, gently kneading it. I moan loudly from deep within. My clitoris clenches, beckoning him to come closer. He pours more champagne on my other breast, but this time he gives the glass to me. My eyes meet his as I drain the glass. It is still very cold and delicious.

"Is that better?"

"Much, but if I don't sit down soon, I'm going to fall down."

"Do you think I would let you fall?" I am breathing deeply,

sucking in air each time he blows on my erect nipples. I want him to go on forever, but I also want and need more from him. I need to feel his body pressed against mine. I need him to pierce my soul the way he has my heart. My greedy hands try to pull at him, but he is intent on seducing me in his own way.

"Slow down, boo, we've got all night." He may have all night, but I'm about to bust a nut right here and now.

"Craig, we can take it slow the next time. I need you inside of me now." He pauses, his eyes search mine, then he quickly turns me around and with one short thrust is inside of me. Pushing deep, I can feel him burrow like a coal miner's rig, trying to reach my core, the core of my essence. With my palms flat against the wall, I match his pace pound for pound. He's riding my ass like a jockey riding a wild stallion.

"Girl, you feel so good. I just want to…I want to…damn, girl…I wanted to take my…I'm coming, baby."

I feel him shoot off inside of me as I reach behind and grip his ass, driving him in deeper. I want to hold back, but I can't any longer.

"Lawd," I scream as I come with him, riding the waves of pleasure. We don't sit in the tub. We plop down, causing more water to run over the sides and for some reason, it is funny as hell. We aren't drained, we're whipped. We lay in the water until it's no longer tolerable and our fingertips begin to wrinkle.

"If we don't get out soon, baby, we are going to be sick," he says.

"I know, you go first because I am going to need some help."

"Oh, it's like that?"

"Yeah, you worked me over real good."

"Are you complaining?"

"Not on your life. I'm conserving my strength for round two."

"Is that so?"

"Help me out and I'll show you." I don't have to tell him twice. He carries me straight from the tub to our waiting bed. Pulling the covers up to our chins, we play footsie until we both have feeling in our limbs.

"Ding-ding-ding-ding."

"Huh? What's that?"

"Round two."

"Ahhh."

# Tarcia

With more questions than answers, I walk back into the living room. Just that quick, I had forgotten what had started the fight with Lasonji in the first place. *Kentee is starting shit and his ass ain't even here.*

My glare shifts contemptuously between the door and the residue of Kentee's relationship with that other bitch Leah. I am fuming and I don't know whether to phone his ass and cuss him out or get a belt and beat the shit out of his rug-rats. *What possessed me to say yes in the first fucking place? What possessed him to ask me when he knows damn well how I feel about his children and their mother? All I know is that he better hurry his ass up because I ain't going to be responsible if they start acting the fool and shit.*

It wasn't always like this. There was a time when I tried to be nice to his kids, but that was when I thought we were going to be this big old happy family. When he lost the house because he couldn't afford it and his child support payments, I gave up all pretense of liking them and, to be truly honest, they never liked me anyway.

Not trusting my raw emotions, I decide the best place for me to be, for me and them, is my room. I figure if I ignore them, maybe they will have sense enough to be quiet and leave me alone until their father comes back. At this point, entertaining them is out of the question.

"Ya'll sit here and watch television. Okay?" They don't even bother to look in my direction and I resist the urge to reach out and touch each one of them. I go in my room, leaving my door slightly ajar so I can hear them if they start to get into anything they shouldn't be. If I'm lucky, Kentee will be back before the cartoons go off for the morning. I switch on my own television and pick up the book that I had been reading when Kentee knocked on my door.

*The Tribe* by Gregory Townes sucks me in from the first page and I am having trouble putting the book down. His vivid descriptions of destructive times that are parallel to events happening in today's streets have me flipping from fact to fiction. I become lost in the story, experiencing the same terror as the characters of his book.

I became so absorbed in the book that I apparently drifted off to sleep. A painful spasm jolts me awake and a tightening in my chest is causing my pulse to race. For a moment, I don't know where I am. It feels like someone has placed a large object on my chest and I can't move it enough to allow air into my lungs. My vision is blurry, but I attribute that to my sleep-crusted eyes. My main concerns at this moment are catching my breath, and the fire that is burning in my lungs.

I try to see the clock on my nightstand, but my eyes will not cooperate and the display is not clear. For a brief second, I wonder if I am still dreaming. The pain, however, is convincing me I am not. As I struggle to sit up, my arms feel as if they are encased in cement, but I fight nevertheless. My head pounds as my chin rests on my chest. Finally, my eyes adjust and I notice dancing shadows in the living room through the slightly ajar bedroom door.

*Lasonji must have left the television on.* It's strange that I don't hear the sound, but I'm still not thinking clearly. My chest is killing me as another coughing spell takes over my body.

Thinking a glass of water will soothe my parched throat, I stumble to the door. I have no idea how long I had been sleeping, but it is getting dark outside. The acrid smell of smoke greets me when I push open the bedroom door. The sofa is totally engulfed in flames. Sheer panic propels me to the front door. I don't think of grabbing anything. My only thoughts are of getting out of the house. I stumble and fall just short of the door.

"What the hell?" The room is filled with smoke, so I cannot make anything out clearly. My eyes are burning as tears stream down my face and into my mouth. I use the end of my T-shirt to cover my nose as best I can. Using my hands, I feel around the floor looking for the object that tripped me up. Behind me, the fire is getting hotter and glass is exploding. I have to get out of here; it is too late to save anything.

I touch a hand and that's when I remember the children. Huddled together, they are lying in front of the door. Rising to my feet, I manage to drag Kayla through the doorway into the hall. I don't stop to check to see if she is breathing. I am acting on pure instinct alone. No longer able to stand, I crawl back into the apartment. The heat is so intense, I feel as if my skin is falling off, but I have to get Malik and Mya out of the apartment.

My determination to get them out is paramount. For the first time in my life, I am thinking about someone other than myself. I silently pray that the babies are not already dead. Despite my hatred of their mother, they do not deserve to die. Finally, I reach the twins but I don't have enough strength to pull them out. I am sleepy and my lungs feel as if they are about to explode. The carpet is on fire and the flames are racing toward us.

"God, please," is my last thought as I collapse on top of them.

# *Sammie*

*ear* is not the word I would use to describe how I feel upon entering the backyard for the picnic; *terror* is more accurate. Despite the reassuring glances from Jazz and Andrea, I feel like I'm walking into a lion's den wearing raw meat.

At first, no one notices me, allowing me a glimpse of the family dynamics. For the most part, the siblings are paired up, all talking to be heard. Music is playing softly in the background and waiters are circulating around the yard passing out drinks and snacks. I try to sneak over to a chair under a tree without being spotted but Jazz calls me out.

"Everybody, this is Sammie, please make her feel welcome." If she was standing next to me, I would have punched her in the face. I don't want the spotlight turned on me; I would've felt more comfortable if I could have gradually made my way around introducing myself at my own pace. Now, I have no choice but to suck it up, give the princess wave, and pray for a freak accident to take me away. No such luck—Pandora's box has been opened as they all come over as fast as their legs can carry them to meet me.

"Well, lookie here, lookie here. Ain't you just a chip off the old block?" A tall, slightly balding, cocoa-brown man with twinkling eyes steps over to me, arms flung wide, grinning from ear to ear. Confused, I look around, not sure what to do.

"Don't just stand there; give your Uncle Maceo a hug." Without waiting for me to move, he swoops down on me. His arms practically suffocate me as he rocks me back and forth. I don't even have a chance to raise my arms to hug him back.

"Maceo, give the chile some room. She don't want you sweating all over her."

"Aw, shucks, Rosa, stop hatin'. This here is my niece."

"Boy, she's all our niece. Now step back so I can see her." Maceo releases me, but instead of moving away, he stands beside me. He makes me nervous because he is eyeing me like I'm Sunday dinner, instead of a family member.

"Dag, Rosa, she looks like you used to. About forty or fifty years ago." He mumbles the last part just loud enough for everyone but Rosa to hear. The other sisters start to laugh.

"What are ya'll cackling about?" Rosa demands as she watches her two sisters.

I could tell she is a real firecracker. I definitely don't want to get on her bad side.

"Yeah, you do look like my brother, alright, God rest his soul." Without another word, she turns around and walks away. I didn't realize that I had been holding my breath until she is seated. Her eyes never leave mine as introductions are made to the remaining siblings. I'm not comfortable until everyone is off in their own circles again, leaving me alone.

"That wasn't so bad, now was it?"

"I don't know, Jazz. I'm still in shock. You didn't tell me how strong the family resemblance is. It's like looking into a mirror and seeing the future."

"If we're lucky. I can only hope I look as good as Aunt Rosa when I get her age. She still has all her teeth and she walks five miles a day."

"Wow, that's impressive."

"Mavis and Leonara own a beauty shop in Clarkston and a little boutique next door so they keep quite busy too."

"Do they still do hair?"

"Sometimes, if you are one of their favorite customers and it's a special occasion. They don't keep up with the latest styles, so they leave that to the operators."

"Why don't you go there to get your hair done?"

"Girl, I see enough of them on holidays. If they were doing my hair, they'd be all up in my business."

"I know that's right. Why do women run their mouths when they go to a salon?"

"I don't know, girl. It must have something to do with the fact that women come in there all tore up, no makeup, expecting to leave like glamour queens."

A waiter passes us drinks and I greedily take two. Jazz gives me the eye, but I ignore her. She is used to being on display. I, on the other hand, am not.

"So tell me about the brothers."

"Uncle Rufus is the quiet one, always thinking. He's retired from the railroad. Marvin is retired too but I swear I never knew what he did. I don't think anybody knows for sure. All I remember is that he always had money and wasn't stingy with it. He was the one who bought the beauty shop. Uncle Marvin looks after Aunt Rosa. He's the only one who can stand to be around her for more than an hour or two. Uncle Maceo probably hasn't worked a day in his life. He's the player. He's had more women than Carter has liver pills and still considers himself to be a pimp."

"I can believe that. He keeps staring at me."

"Girl, he's harmless. He got drunk at Christmas one time and told us the only way his dick would stand up by itself is if he is hanging upside down." Caught off-guard by a visual, I spit half my drink on the lawn. Jazz pats me on the back until I can breathe normally again.

"Girl, you damn near killed me with that one."

"Hey, I'm just telling it like he told us. We were sitting around the kitchen table after the other uncles and Aunt Rosa left and out of nowhere, he started talking. To this day, I don't think he remembers saying that to us because he sure be getting his mack on every time a skirt walks past him."

Jazz goes to check on her mother, and I just wander around. Everyone is eating, so I start to feel more at home. I feel stupid for getting all worked up about this party in the first place. I don't know what I was expecting, but it darn sure wasn't the open-armed reception that I received. A genuine smile is on my face as I fix myself a plate and the smile gets bigger when I see Buddy come in the gate. Putting my plate to the side, I rush to greet him.

"Hey, baby!" I give him a big hug and a kiss on the lips.

"How ya doing, beautiful? You okay?"

"I'm fine. I worked myself up into a tizzy for nothing."

"See, I told you."

"Yeah, you did. I thought you weren't going to be able to make it."

"Honey, wild horses could not have kept me away." He kisses my cheek, squeezing my hand.

"You hungry? I was just fixing my plate."

"I'm good. Where is Jazz and Ms. Andrea?"

"In the house, I think." I want to introduce him to my new family, but I'm not sure what to call him. I don't want to say my friend and possibly offend Buddy, but I don't want to call him my fiancé either because he hasn't said those magical words yet, defining our relationship, so I say nothing. What I didn't know was that Buddy had already met the family some years before.

Everyone is having fun, including me. Buddy and I dance to a few records amid the catcalls of Uncle Maceo, and there is a lively game of cards going on at the picnic table. I am happy and feeling secure like I'd never felt in my life. Suddenly, I'm a part of a family.

"Baby, I gotta run." I look at my watch and realize that Buddy has stayed a lot longer than he had planned and would have to seriously hustle to make it to the club on time.

"Wow, look at the time. Thanks for sharing this with me. Will you be coming over after your set?"

"That's my plan unless something comes up at the last minute. I'll call you and let you know either way."

"Okay." I walk him to the gate as he nods to the family. He stops and hugs Jazz and Andrea. We almost make it to the gate when Uncle Maceo lifts his head up off the table.

"Hey, Jazz, ain't that the young fellow that was sniffing your drawers a few years back?" Silence fills the yard. Suddenly there are no buzzing insects, even the music stops. Once again all eyes are on me and I just want the ground to open up and swallow me whole.

"Uncle Maceo, stop trying to start shit with your drunk ass. Buddy is a long-standing friend of the family. I introduced him to Sammie." *Good looking out, sis.* We start to move toward the gate again, feeling relieved.

"Umph. Like mother, like daughter. Marvin, I'm ready to go." Aunt Rosa gets up from the table and beats us out the gate, giving us her ass to kiss.

# Tarcia

When I wake up, I'm on a stretcher in the parking lot with an oxygen mask on my face. The whole building is now in flames and firefighters are running back and forth trying to contain the blaze. I watch everything I'd worked for go up in smoke. I am still in shock, unwilling to believe how quickly my life has changed from sugar to shit.

Around me, I can hear my neighbors crying and demanding answers, but I am too stunned to speak. I can't even remember how I got out. The last thing I remember is looking for somebody, but I can't remember whom. Lifting the mask, I search the crowd for my cousin, but don't see her. While I watch the building crumble before me, I am battered with mixed emotions. I hate that building. It represents all that my life has become since I had gotten involved with Kentee. Now, I don't even have that. What am I going to do now?

When Kentee and I first got together, I thought my whole life was about to change. He moved me out of the projects where I had been living with my mother and brothers and into a beautiful house. He said he was going to take care of me and our baby and that we wouldn't want for anything. And in the beginning, I didn't.

We had a quiet wedding and a small reception, with just my

mother attending. He told me that all of his family lived out of town and could not make it in time for the ceremony. He was attentive, always home on time, and I never had to wonder where he was.

But that quickly changed when he found out that I wasn't pregnant after all. He accused me of trying to trap him, which I vehemently denied. Things began to change after that and not for the better. I try to focus on the chaos around me now, but I cannot get past the pain in my heart caused by Kentee. I wouldn't have been in this damn apartment if it weren't for him. First we lost the house, then I discovered while he was in jail that not only were we not married, but he had another family on the other side of town. If I were smarter, I would have cut my losses then, but I loved him so I stayed. Lying to myself that things would get better, I excused his many absences and his lack of attention. I even babysat his children. *Oh my God, where are the children?*

Jumping up from the stretcher, I start running from cluster to cluster, looking for them. I remember pulling Kayla out of the apartment and going back for the twins. They have to be here somewhere if I made it out.

I look around at the faces of my neighbors and I shiver from the cold looks they are giving me. I am used to those looks and focus on finding the kids and getting my hands on Kentee. Already I am scheming on a way to use this mishap to reclaim my place in his life.

If I were paying attention, I would've seen them huddled with my next-door neighbor while crying to someone on the phone. But at the moment, they are just pawns to be used to get what I really want—Kentee.

I see them just as a short wiry lady with graying hair parts the chaos and starts toward the kids. They start yelling louder, so my confused mind thinks she is trying to harm them.

I feel the penetrating eyes of my neighbors as we all watch our possessions go up in smoke. The firemen are trying to push us farther away from the apartment building, but I am on a mission. Pushing them aside, I fight to get the kids away from the stranger, but to my chagrin, they start yelling and screaming at me as if I were trying to harm them.

However, the kids' obvious love for this woman and their disdain for me starts to work my nerves. I was the one who saved them from the fire. They should be showing me some love, instead of siding with her. She turns her back on me, using her body as a shield for the children as I keep punching her in the back. I catch a glimpse of her face as she tries to usher them into her car. She reminds me of Leah and that pisses me off.

"Get away from my children," I scream, charging the older woman with all the energy I have left.

I hit her high in the chest and we both tumble to the ground. The wind is knocked out of me, but grandma has something for my ass. She starts whaling on me like I stole something and I cower from her blows.

"They...are...my...babies...bitch, now leave us the fuck alone!"

Malik, Mya, and Kayla all gang up on me and I find myself in the fetal position trying to defend my face. Recognizing defeat, I stay in position until the blows stop raining down on my body. Once again, I slip into a fog.

The firemen managed to save the majority of the building, but I've lost everything. Everything that was not burned was damaged by water.

The paramedics are attending to the scratches and welts I sustained both from the fire and the fight. Grandma and the kids are still there watching me, but the fight in me is gone. My reality slaps me in the face. I have nothing but the clothes on my back. No money, no identification, no credit or bank cards...nothing, and nowhere to go. To take things to a different level, I lost my damn book!

Anger is blossoming in my heart and my throat feels raw from the smoke and the yelling. I look at my watch and realize that Kentee has been gone over five hours. What am I supposed to do? I start to cry like I have never cried before. His children are strangely quiet and lower their gaze whenever I look at them, all except Mya. Her eyes appear to mock me and I am fighting the impulse to strike her, but she is protected by her grandmother and I would not mess with her again.

Mya started the fire. I know it in my heart of hearts, even though the firemen said it is too early to tell. But to me, it only makes sense. The fire was concentrated on the sofa when I entered the living room. Fires don't just start in the middle of a room without a little help.

*That little heifer was trying to tell me that she didn't want to be in my house any more than I wanted her there!* Suddenly, her fingers open and she drops the lighter that she has been holding. It is the same lighter that was on the coffee table when the kids got to the apartment. She smiles for the first time since I've known her. That smile chills me to the bone and I start to shake. My last thought before losing consciousness is *Gotcha*.

# *Kentee*

"**D**amn, Tarcia is going to be all up in my shit," I mutter to myself as I wheel around the corner after exiting 285. The need for speed is flowing through my veins much like the coke that I snorted earlier. I know I should have never tried the product, but I had to make sure I was getting some quality shit, so one thing led to another and now I am high as a kite.

I'm in the doghouse and no doubt my children are starving. Passing McDonald's, I resist the temptation to go in and order three Happy Meals because a sense of urgency that I cannot explain is propelling me to pick up my kids. I only wish that urgency had raised its head before I snorted all that coke.

I don't believe in psychic connections, but something is pushing me forward faster than I need to be traveling, especially since I am buzzing. I need time to get my story straight but my foot feels like it is weighted to the gas pedal and it is taking all of my concentration to stay on the road.

My heart is racing but I attribute it to the drugs. Suddenly I realize that I'm very afraid. Something isn't right and it isn't just the fact that I am late picking up my children.

"Get the hell out of the street," I yell to a man who innocently chose this moment to jaywalk. I lay on the horn, which apparently scares him more than my high rate of speed. "Idiot," I yell back at his receding figure. He gives me the finger and I give it right back to him. When I turn back around to look at the road, I barely have time to stop at the traffic light.

"Whew. Talk about luck." I accelerate this time with a little more caution and care. Getting killed would not help in this situation. I don't question where this parental concern is coming from because truth be told, if I was all that concerned, I would never have left them with Tarcia in the first place. Thankfully, I am only a few blocks away so I start rehearsing my lie.

"Baby, I am so sorry that I took so long. I was waiting at the drop to make the pick-up. Ole dude was late." I decide to keep it short and sweet because the longer the lie, the more likely I am to fuck it up. I just want to give my line, break her off a little dope, and get the hell on. If I can stick to the script I can be in and out in ten minutes.

"What the fuck... " My voice trails off as my eyes try to adapt to the chaos in front of me. My brain seemingly disconnects from my body as I watch firefighters sift through the rubble. The building where Tarcia lived is no more. Throwing the car in park, I jump out.

"Where are my babies?" I scream. My heart is slamming against my chest as tears flood my eyes. All the people who are standing around look lost, but I do not see my kids. I begin praying like I have never prayed before.

I rush through the crowds hoping to see a familiar face, or someone who could tell me what happened. Frantic, I grab the arm of a fireman. "Was anyone hurt?"

"Some smoke inhalation, but nothing serious. No one was transported."

"Thanks." I spin around and see Kayla sitting on the curb with her head in her hands. Next to her sit Mya and Malik, both with vacant expressions on their faces. They look like they have just survived a war.

"Thank you, Jesus," I say, looking up to the sky as I rush toward my children without noticing their grandmother. I pull them all to me, but their arms hang limply at their sides as if they don't have the energy to hug me back. I am so relieved to find them safe. I feel as if I am being given a second chance.

"We are okay, Daddy. Grandma saved us." Kayla's words sound like an accusation.

I start to usher my children to my car, wanting to get as far away from this destruction as possible. In my haste, I've completely forgotten about Tarcia. My children are safe; that is the important thing. I would question them later after I'd gotten them something to eat. Needless to say, my buzz was gone.

With the kids in the car, I attempt to go around and get into the driver's seat when I feel this searing pain in the back of my neck. Then Tarcia jumps me and is riding me like I am a horse. She is screaming, but her words are garbled and I can't understand what she is saying. We tumble to the ground and I manage to get her underneath me. She loosens her grip, but the pain in my neck continues.

"What the hell is wrong with you?"

Pushing myself off her prone body, I raise my hand to the back of my neck. My fingers feel wet and when I look at them, they are covered in blood. The pain is intense, but I don't know what the source of it is. Tarcia is huffing and puffing like a slave.

"You and your damn kids," she says in a deep and demented tone that I'd never heard her use. She appears possessed and consumed with anger and I want to get away as fast as possible. I begin backpedaling to the car, as this is not the time nor the place for a physical altercation. My luck, I'd wind up back in jail. I touch my neck again because it feels like the blood is going down my arm. My hand touches an object that cuts my finger.

"What have you done?" I scream at her in disbelief.

Feeling dizzy, I begin sliding down the side of the car. Tarcia stares as if she is enjoying my pain. She has a sly smile on her face as if she has a secret she isn't willing to share. Darkness takes over as I fall to the ground. I can hear my children crying, but I couldn't get up if I tried. I try to focus on their words and when I do, my body freezes. There aren't screaming for their daddy to get up or asking if I am okay; they are calling for their mother. I feel like they are saying, "Fuck Daddy. We want our mommy."

# *Tarcia*

I saw Kentee weaving through the crowd, and I assumed his anguished expression was for me. Boy was I wrong, because all of those worry lines disappeared when he found his children. He gathered them up in his arms, and then he was leaving without even checking to see if I lived or died. Something in me snapped. I wanted to hurt him beyond repair. The next thing I knew, I was hanging on his back with the jagged edge of a beer bottle jutting out of his neck. I wanted to kill him. In hindsight, it was my selfishness that kept me from understanding his actions, but that glimmer of knowledge does not help me one bit now.

I have to wait in jail until he regains consciousness and to see what kind of time I am facing as a result of my assault on Kentee. I really wasn't trying to kill him, I just wanted him to acknowledge me and my pain. I was tired of taking a backseat to his children and that fucking Leah.

I punch and pull at the small pillow that they gave me and try to get comfortable. I am lucky that I don't have to share my cell with anyone. I've heard horror stories about what goes on in the prison system and I'm more than a little afraid. I pray for sleep and an early court time. I am hopeful that Kentee will come to my rescue.

But on the off chance that he does not come through, I have my own backup, and if I have to resort to those measures, Kentee better watch his ass! Irritated beyond belief, I start to act a fool.

"Where is my phone call?" I demand in my most commanding voice. I have to say it three or four times before I get an answer.

"Lady, you need to shut the hell up," the guard says.

"I know my rights. I watch *Law and Order*. I deserve a phone call."

"*Law and Order* is television. This here ain't no make-believe. You are in here for the real deal and you will get a phone call when I say you get a phone call."

"You are violating my rights."

"Dial 1-800-Who-Cares because I surely don't."

"I wanna speak to your supervisor!"

"Lady, you don't want to get on my bad side because all kinds of shit can happen to you in here. You don't want to make me mad."

I shut up real quick. I'm not certain that he can make it bad for me, but I am not about to take that chance. The guard laughs at me and it takes all my self-control not to tell him to bite me. I return my attention to my pillow and again try to punch it into a comfortable position.

"Do you think I can get another pillow?"

"Ha! In your dreams. You seem to think you are on vacation. This is the big house, baby, and the only benefits you get are those I decide you need and a pillow ain't one of them."

Humbled, I decide to keep my comments to myself. My fear is growing. This man doesn't like me and I sense that he is going to make things hard for me. Unfortunately, I don't realize how hard until much later in the night. Somehow, I drift off to sleep. My dreams are troubled; I keep seeing Kentee as he slides down the car, his face contorted in pain. It is difficult for me to watch this scene being replayed over and over in my head, but I am stuck on it. I guess because my future freedom is affected by his reactions.

In my dreams, that bitch Leah shows up to nurse him back to health. That vision alone causes me to wake up in a cold sweat. The last thing I want is to chase him back into her arms. Kentee went back and forth between us like there was a revolving door with prizes being given out at every stop. I drift off again, but the dreams are tormenting me as I fight against my covers, trying to get closer to Kentee to tell him how sorry I am for the attack.

In one dream, I finally get to speak with him and he forgives me for trying to hurt him. This is the dream that disturbs me the most because in the dream we start to get physical. I can almost feel him touching me, kissing me, tasting my steamy pussy.

# Tarcia

Around three-thirty in the morning, I wake up when a pair of hands roughly snatch me from my dreams and yank down my pants. Clarity hits me full force as I realize just how much authority my jailor has over me. He clamps his hand over my mouth and whispers in my ear.

"Don't you say a mother-fucking word 'cause I can arrange for your ass to die in here and no one will be the wiser." He doesn't have to tell me twice. I will take this rape and fight it when I get outside of his reign.

He flips me over and roughly pulls my shirt over my head. I'm not wearing a bra, so my breasts are fully exposed to him. He begins to eat at my breasts and I start to get real scared. He's sucking my nipples. He is trying to eat my damn boobs! He is pinching and biting me like I am on the buffet at Ryan's.

"Why are you doing this?" I whisper, fighting back against the pain he is inflicting.

"Because you're a mean-ass bitch who needs to be taught a lesson."

"I'll be good, just stop."

"I ain't stopping until I am ready to stop and the more lip I get, the longer it will be." He thrusts his dick inside me. I try to make myself enjoy what he is doing to me, but it's hopeless. No matter which way I look at it, I am being raped and he isn't wearing a condom! I try to close my eyes and not think about all the diseases he could be exposing me to, but it does no good. It is what it is and I cannot do shit about it until after I'm out of here.

"Just relax and I might make your stay more comfortable. Hey, I might even give you an extra pillow."

All the anger that I previously held against Kentee is coming back two-fold and I am ready to kick some jailor ass! I allow him to stick his fingers into my pussy before I clamp down on his hand and go for his eyes. I try to snatch them right out of the sockets and his howls ring out in this otherwise quiet wing. My fingers are dripping blood and I don't intend to let go until either he is blind or someone comes along to witness my assault; whichever comes first doesn't matter to me.

With his free hand, he tries to knock me aside but I am determined that I will be the last female he assaults. Hell, I am already in jail. What else could they do to me? So I hold on for dear life until he passes the fuck out.

# *Kentee*

Although the paramedics are already on the scene, they are reluctant to move me until the police arrive. Lucky for me it isn't a life-threatening wound or I could have bled to death waiting on them. The whole time I am waiting, Tarcia is yellin.' The police placed her in handcuffs and she is in the car, but I can still hear her mouthing even as they drive off.

The police insist that I go by ambulance to the hospital 'cause I'm two seconds away from driving myself. I am still feeling light-headed and the pain is intense despite the drugs they give me en route to the hospital. Lucky for me that psycho bitch missed my artery or things would not have gone so well.

"I can't believe that bitch stabbed me!"

I decide not to press charges against her. She knows too much about my business to have her singing to some judge. But unfortunately, the decision is not up to me. DeKalb County decides whether they want to press charges. I don't envy Tarcia being caught up in a system that likes to keep people that look like us locked down, but she brought it on her own damn self. I was just making sure my kids were okay.

Thinking of my kids makes my head and heart hurt. I can still hear them crying for their mother even though it was me who was bleeding. I reach for the phone to call my ex–mother-in-law. The officers told me they allowed her to take the kids home while I was being transported to the hospital. I didn't even know she was there, but I thank God she was. It would have killed me if they sent my children to DFACS because of that dumb bitch.

Paula answers on the first ring. I don't hear any crying in the background, so I assume the kids have settled down and gone to sleep, or worse, their mother came and got them. I know I am in for a serious tongue lashing from her the next time I speak to her.

"Hello," Paula says.

"Uh, Paula, this is Kentee. How are the kids?" It is clear from her tone that she really doesn't want to be talking to me.

"They're fine." She left off the "no thanks to you," but it is in her voice.

"Uh…did they go home with their mother?"

"No, they're here; Leah won't be back until tomorrow." *Where did Leah go? Who is she with? Why didn't she tell me?*

"Oh, okay. Can I speak with Kayla?"

"They're sleeping. They had a rough day."

*They had a rough day. What about me? Hell, I got stabbed! Isn't she even going to ask if I am okay?*

"Alright then, I guess I will talk to them later." She hangs up, leaving me holding the phone. Fear and jealousy eat away at my stomach; fear that Leah won't let me see my kids again and jealousy that she might be away with that guy from the day care center. Kayla talks about him a lot and I get the impression he's spending a lot of time with them outside of the center.

I'm not ready to accept another man in Leah's life. It doesn't matter that I cheated on her, or that I left her for another woman. She still belongs to me and when she gets back from wherever the hell she went, I am going to make sure she knows it. I'm not about to have no other man playing father to my children! Jumping out of the hospital bed, I am impatient to get back home so I can start planning on how I can win Leah back.

*I'll just tell her I made a mistake. I'll tell her she's the only woman in the world for me and that it took being away from her to realize it. I'll tell her it's over with me and Tarcia. I won't mention Tarcia stabbing me unless Kayla has already told her. I'll ask her if I can move in with them. Yeah, that's what I'll do. I'll tell her that I don't like them living there all by themselves. That it isn't safe for her to live alone. If I get her scared enough, she won't hesitate to let me back in. If she won't let me back into the bedroom right away, I can always find a piece on the side until she comes around. Yeah, that sounds like a plan. I got to get out of here. Hey, I will buy her another ring! Diamonds are a surefire way to a girl's heart.*

I walk out of the hospital without waiting to be released. I hop a bus back to my car and my first stop is the pharmacy to fill my prescription for pain medication. They made a big mistake giving me the drugs before I signed the bill. Once home, sleep claims me and I start dreaming as soon as my head hits the pillow. I dream Leah and I are a family again.

# Tarcia

D read grips my stomach and makes me feel like I'm about to vomit. *What have I done?* The guard is lying in the corner of my cell with blood still oozing out of his eye. The blood forms a puddle on the floor and each drop echoes against the walls. I'd acted in self-defense, but looking at the evidence of my hatred scared the shit out of me.

What surprised me the most was that no one came looking for Mister Slick Dick. His radio was beeping and folks were calling, but he didn't respond. I am quite sure my tormentor would never see out of that eye again because his eyeball was hanging down on his cheeks and appeared to be drying up like a prune.

The guards didn't discover his body until lunchtime, some nine hours after he attempted to rape me.

"We've got a man down. Open number sixteen."

They threatened me with a stun gun as they wheeled him out. Can't they see that I'm not a threat to anyone? Haven't I been through enough? I just want to wake up and let this nightmare be over.

"Your court date just got bumped up," says the guard as he slams the door shut. This is scaring the shit out of me. I've never been to jail and don't know what to expect. I am hoping they will let me speak to an attorney, but so far, I've been ignored. Briefly, I worry about Kentee, but he is the least of my problems right now. I am confident that he won't press charges against me, but if he does, he will rue the day. However, this situation with the guard is really bothering me. If the guard hadn't been in my cell trying to fuck me, he would have never lost his eye.

Within the hour, I am transferred into another holding cell. I ignore the catcalls as I walk in my prison-issued uniform, carrying my one pillow, blanket, and shoes, to my cell. They had me remove my clothing because it was stained with blood. I can't decide who I am madder at, Kentee or the damn guard whose name I never knew. My new cell is further along the hallway, but this time I'm not in it alone. I wearily enter the cell, unwilling to turn my back on either the guard or my new cellmate.

*At the rate I am going, I will never leave this place. Why is everyone fucking with me?* My roommate is a straight-up he/she who does not waste any time letting me know how they feel about sharing a space with me.

"What the fuck is this? This ain't no damn hotel!"

"Bitch, you don't pay no rent, so I can put anyone in this cell I desire!" the guard says. He has a point and I have to struggle not to laugh at his witty retort. My cellmate shut his mouth up until we are alone in the cell.

"I got bottom bunk."

"No problem." The silence in the room is weighted as if it has a life of its own. I am curious about what this obvious drag queen did to land behind bars, but I am not about to be the first one to start a conversation. Instead, I hoist myself up on my cot and try to nap. Chauncey, as I learn is his name, has other ideas. He wants to know whom he is sleeping with.

"Why you here?"

I debate on whether or not I should tell him the truth. I want to establish right up front that I'm no damn joke, so I told him.

"I stabbed my cheating-ass boyfriend and I blinded one of the guards that tried to rape me."

"Damn. So you a bad bitch, huh?"

"Let's just say I don't take no shit from nobody. If you step to me, I'm jumping in that ass."

"Well then, I think you and I are going to get along just fine 'cause I don't take no shit either."

"Fine, you stay in your space and I'll stay in mine."

"Cool. And if shit starts to get fucked up, as it tends to get, I've got your back, but will you have mine?" I don't know how to answer that. I am in unfamiliar territory. "Look, honey, this ain't no place to be trying to be the Lone Ranger unless you want to wind up in a corner with a broomstick up your ass."

I shudder at the visual. "I got you, sista."

"I ain't a sista yet. When my ass gets out of here, I will finish the process."

"That's entirely too much information for me. But if I read you right, we like the same thang, so I hope not to be here long enough to fight you over a damn dick."

"*Touché*. But the men I am after ain't gonna be interested in you. They know what they want before they even get here. I ain't trying to change nobody. I just want to get my nut on!"

"Shit, you should have been with me about nine hours ago. If you had been, maybe that guard would be able to see how to tie his shoes. I fixed his ass; I dug his eyeballs out the sockets and left his ass to rot. If there's one thing that I can't stand, it's a rapist."

"Gurl, you ain't even lied. Wish I would have been there. He wouldn't have to rape me; I would've given him my shit spit-shined and polished. Shoot, girl, I ain't had no dick in a minute. I might have raped his ass." Despite the severity of my situation, that is funny and I cannot contain the laughter. I am beginning to like my cellmate.

"Shit, why'd he have to pick on me? I've already got one case; I sure don't need two."

"You ain't lying, chile. These guards don't take too kindly to you hurting one of their own, even if they are wrong."

"But he started the shit; I didn't want his attention or his nasty dick."

"Wait till your ass has been here as long as I have. You will be begging for a dick! Me, I ain't turning none of it down."

"How long have you been here? If that's too personal, you don't have to answer."

"Naw, it's all good. I've been inside for ten years on a twenty-year sentence. I'm up for parole so they transferred me here to await my hearing. I am trying to keep my ass on the low-low and get the fuck up out of here."

"Damn. Ten years is a long time," I reply, feeling sorry for him.

"Tell me about it. This ain't no place for punks or pushovers. You'll have to butch up if you are going to make it. If you don't, some ho will have your ass bent over a table fucking you with anything she can get her hands on."

"Wow. You see that shit on TV, but I never believed it really happens."

"Damn, gurl, you got a lot to learn. In here it's all about respect. Don't look folks in the eye. Keep to yourself and if someone steps to you, handle your business, 'cause if you punk out, then your life here will be hell."

Fear grips me again. I was never much of a fighter growing up. I'd surprised myself with my ruthless attack on the guard and my foolish impulsiveness with Kentee. I never meant to stab him. I just wanted to scare him.

"Where are you from?" I am curious about Chauncey's accent, which is familiar and foreign at the same time.

"Born and raised in New Orleans."

"I should have guessed. I was born in New Orleans too, but I've lived here most of my life."

"So what are you in for?"

"I already told you. I stabbed my boyfriend in the neck with a broken bottle."

"Damn, you must have caught him acting like a puppy."

"Worse. I was watching his children from a previous relationship and they set my house on fire. I lost everything and he acted like I didn't matter."

"Ouch. You got anger management issues."

"That son-of-a-bitch has put me through hell. I wanted him dead!"

"I hear your pain, but those puppies ain't worth this hell hole." Sadly, I realize he is right. I gave up my freedom for a few seconds of satisfaction.

"If I have to stay here longer than a day, he is going to pay dearly."

"And just how are you going to accomplish that, my Tasmanian devil?"

"I don't know yet, but if I don't get out soon, I will have plenty of time to think about it. Someone, either his stupid-ass ex-wife or that trifling nigga, is going to pay."

"Oh, I smell a loud bark coming out. Don't tell me the puppy is married too?"

"He was when we first got together, but he left her for me," I proudly announce.

"Lawd, talk about drama!"

I realize my new cellmate is correct. I have been floating around in a pot of shit for the last few years. Ever since I laid eyes on Kentee my life hasn't been the same.

"Yeah, it's been a trip."

"You could put a curse on him."

"A curse? Oh, Lawd, not you too. I had to hear that shit from my cousin and I frankly just don't believe in that shit."

"It ain't up to you to believe. If it's done right, the proof will be in the pudding."

"What exactly are you talking about?" I hate to admit it, but he has my curiosity going.

"Rootwork."

"I don't know any rootwork." My hopes are dashed before I can get excited about the prospect of revenge.

"Maybe not, but I do." Chauncey sits looking at his nails as if he isn't involved in this conversation. I, on the other hand, am very interested in finding out how he can help me.

"Look, you've been through a lot so you need time to think about this before you agree because once this shit is started, there ain't no backing out. The effects of some of these spells are irreversible."

"Why are you so willing to help me? What's in it for you?" I am suspicious of his motives. I've only known him for a short time and already he is pledging allegiance to me.

"It ain't nuthin' to me. I'm in here until they let me out. What else is there to do?"

It sounds reasonable enough to me, but I'm not thinking in my right mind. I had forbade my cousin to use black magic in my house and I know she loves me, but I am willing to trust a total stranger to do the same thing. Go figure.

"So how do we get started?" Now I am eager.

"Don't you want to think about it for a while?"

"No. I've done enough thinking. It's about action now. Plus, I don't know how long I'm going to be with you. They've bumped my trial up to this evening."

"Dag, they got you on a fast track. That ain't necessarily a good thing."

"That's what I'm afraid of."

"Okay. I need some information from you. I need your full name and address, your date of birth, and the exact nature of the problem you've had with the person you want to put a spell on. I will also need his name, address, and date of birth. Make sure you write a statement as to what you want this spell to do for you, and I will start working on the rest."

"Wow, that's it?"

"For now. Oh and I need a lock of his hair or some other personal item."

"Will a sample of his blood work? Some of it got on my bra when I stabbed him."

"That's perfect. Here's some paper." I take the pencil and paper and begin writing down the things Chauncey asked for. I was surprised that he is allowed to have these items in his cell but something tells me to expect the unexpected with Chauncey.

"Shit, what do I put down for an address? Remember my apartment burned down. That's what got me here in the first place."

"It's still your residence. It's where all your stuff is, burnt to a crisp or not."

"I don't know his address either. We haven't lived together for several months. He claims he is living at his mother's house, but I doubt that."

"That's not as important since you have his blood. Blood is the most powerful talisman in black magic."

"Talisman? I thought a talisman was an object, like an amulet or good luck charm."

"It can be. It all depends on what type of magic you're practicing." He is chuckling as if he said something funny and I begin to feel uneasy even talking to him.

My mind is whirling a mile a minute. If I can use black magic on Kentee, I have to decide what it is that I want. Do I want him to be my love slave, or do I want to destroy every relationship he has after me?

"I want a little bit of both. I want him to be impotent around any female except me. I want to ruin him financially and I want women to be repulsed by him."

"Do you want me to make him have an urge for men? Ummm... that could be fun."

"Naw, I ain't trying to waste a good dick. Sorry."

"Well, if I were you, I would rethink this 'financial ruin' business 'cause a broke nigga ain't no good to ya!"

"Yeah, you have a point. I don't want to be taking care of his grown ass."

"I know that's right. That is the first thing that will foil a relationship, if the finances are fucked."

"Thanks, good looking out. When can we begin?"

"Well, we don't want to start the love spell until you get out of here because he will be trying to break in this mother-fucker and both of ya'll asses will be stuck. But we can start the others right away. I just have to get a few key items."

"Wow, this is the best news I've heard since I've been in this bitch."

"Well, you be sure what you ask for is what you want because once we've started, there is no turning back."

# Leah

"I is married now!" I say out loud, admiring my ring as we travel back to Atlanta. But questions flood my brain and although I'm not ready to ask them, I feel I need to before we get home.

"Craig, how are we going to do this marriage thing?"

"I don't understand, boo. What do you mean?"

"Where will we live? How do we handle business?"

"We will work it out, baby. Let's just wait to get back to ATL before we start discussing the nitty gritty, but the logical choice of where we live is my house. We can talk about it later."

Instinctively, my backbone stiffens. I don't want to be in another situation where I have no say-so in my house, nor do I want to put myself and my kids in a position where we can get kicked out at will.

"Leah, I know what you are thinking. I am going to put the house in both of our names regardless of what it costs. I will not put you back in the same situation you were in before. And we ain't going to be doing that dumb shit anyway. You are my wife for life."

Immediately, I feel at ease. Craig understands my painful past and is smart enough to know that I don't want to repeat that behavior. That alone speaks volumes to me about my new choice in a husband. We stop at Waffle House to have breakfast. We choose to sit next to each other and even though it is a tight fit, I am glad to be sitting next to my husband instead of just being across from him. Living in his home is the best choice, although I am worried about all his beautiful things.

When we are back on the road again my mind gets to clicking. Unable to put aside my fears, I continue to have doubts. Not about our marriage, but about the people who will be affected by it.

"What about your ex? Do you think she is going to bring us drama?"

"To be honest, I don't know. But you are my wife and I ain't going to tolerate no bullshit from her or your ex-husband. He is going to have to step off. I know he will have to see his children, but I will not allow him in our relationship."

"Hell, I won't allow him in our relationship either. He chose the path that he wanted to take, so he can kiss my natural black ass as I twirl around in circles."

"Oh, no he can't. That's my natural black ass now."

"Craig, you know what I mean." I punch him gently on the shoulder. Secretly I am happy at his playful possessiveness.

"Oh, married less than twenty-four hours and already you are abusing me. What in the world have I gotten myself into?"

"You can pull this car over and I'll show you."

The car swerves to the right as Craig pretends to pull onto the shoulder, but he rights the car and keeps on driving.

"I'll wait because you know what they say about anticipation."

"Yeah, making you wait ain't a bad idea."

We fall into a comfortable silence and I pull my book out of my carry-on bag. I am a read-a-holic and if I have the time, a book is stuck in my face. I am reading *Pretty Evil* by Lexi Davis. This is her first novel and her approach to her story is different and fresh. She has mixed the supernatural with a little comedy and I am enjoying it.

"So how do you think your family will react?" I guess Craig is having a little trouble letting the details go too.

"Mom may be a little pissed because she wasn't invited but she'll get over it. I know the kids will be cool since they are already in love with you."

"We'll make it up to them with a huge reception. How does that sound?"

"Sounds like I thought of it myself."

"And don't forget we have to have a honeymoon."

"I thought we just did!"

"No, baby, not like this. We have to take it to another level. Prior to meeting you, I promised myself that I would never marry again. You and your children changed my heart completely, so I want the world to know about it."

"That's the sweetest thing anyone has ever said to me. Did I tell you how much I loved you today?"

"'Loved,' as in past tense? Are you over me already before the honeymoon?"

"No, silly, you know what I mean." I lightly punch him on the arm again.

"I'm just saying, woman, you are going to be with me for the rest of our lives and you better get used to it."

"I love the way that sounds and when we get somewhere that I can show you, I'm gonna prove it to you!"

"Is that a threat?"

"No, my dear husband, it's a promise. I don't make threats."

Craig's mouth opens and quickly shuts without any words coming out. *Hah*, I thought to myself. *I shut his ass up.* We aren't far from home and already I am planning on ways to seduce him.

"Do you wanna stop by and pick up the kids before we go home or will tomorrow be soon enough?"

"Tomorrow will be soon enough. It seems that I have something to prove to you that does not need witnesses." Craig chuckles deep in his throat and rubs his hand up and down my leg, igniting a fire that I am prepared to put out as soon as we get to a private place.

I root through my bag searching for my cell phone to make sure that everything is okay. I turned it off on Friday because I didn't want anything to disturb my weekend with Craig. After a frantic search, I find it. I have seventeen messages, which is not a good sign since hardly anyone calls me on my cell. I chastise myself for being so selfish in turning it off in the first place. I'm on pins and needles as I listen to the messages.

"Hey, Mommy, are you and Mr. Craig having fun? I'm having fun with Grandma." I smile.

"Hey, Mommy, Daddy is going to pick us up and we are going to spend the night with him. I love you." Again the message is from Kayla. I smile again. I'm not upset that they were spending the night with their father because I had laid down the rules for Kentee. I feel confident that he would not jeopardize his visitation on anything foolish.

Message three says, "Hey, Mommy, I love you. I hope you are having a good time."

Message four. "Mommy, the house is on fire." Kayla's voice is shrill and hurts my ears. I almost drop the phone because the message is so unexpected. I don't know if she meant her grandmother's house or Kentee's. Frantically, I pushed the buttons to hear the next message.

"Mommy, where are you? I'm scared." She didn't say if anyone was hurt or anything. Craig notices my worried look and pulls the car over.

"Baby, what's wrong? You look like you have seen a ghost." I wave at him to keep driving and he pulls back into traffic with his attention divided between me and the road. I heard him, but I cannot answer him. I have to hear the next few messages. My breathing is labored. Craig drives until we reach the exit, stopping at a gas station.

Message six. "Baby, it's Mom. Call me as soon as you get this message." My stomach turns over but at least I know she is safe.

Message seven. "Oh dear, Leah, I didn't know that Kayla was calling you. Don't panic. Everyone is fine, but we do need to speak with you as soon as possible. Don't worry, sweetheart. Things are under control, but you need to know… " The message stops as if her phone died.

Message eight. "Leah, it's Kentee. I need to speak with you. Call me back please."

Message nine. "Leah, please…call me…I have to know…" I am sure Kentee hung up just to piss me off.

Message ten. "Dammit, Leah, answer the fucking phone!" Kentee screamed.

"We have to go to my mother's house now. Something has happened and I can't make it out." *I am trying to hold all my emotions in check, but something is very wrong. The rest of the messages are hang-ups.*

# Leah

The drive back to Peachtree City takes forever. I cannot relax or lose myself in sleep as I did when we first started our trip because my mind is in turmoil. Craig's holding my hand tightly and is my pillar of strength. Every now and then he looks over at me and gives me an encouraging smile. My heart is swelling with love for him as I attempt to smile back while fighting tears of anguish. Through it all, he is managing not to break the law. I know that he is just as worried as I am, but he does not let it show.

"How much farther?"

"Sweetie, we have only traveled about ten miles since the last time you asked me. I know this is tough, but we will get there."

"I know I am being a pest, but my mind is racing a mile a minute."

"Obviously if it were a life-or-death situation, or if Mya was hurt, your mother would have called us back. I trust her enough to know that whatever the situation is, she has it under control."

"You think so?"

"I know so. Why don't you pull out one of those smutty novels that you are always reading and try to relax? We will be there before you know it."

Easier said than done, but I attempt to do as he suggests. It is easier to read than to think of all the what-ifs that are floating around in my mind. I search through my carry-on bag to find my worn copy of *Pretty Evil*. If this book can't keep my mind off my troubles, nothing will.

Craig drives until we almost run out of gas, but I hardly notice. I don't realize that I have to go to the bathroom until we pull into a gas station and I see the icon of a lady on the wall. I jump out of the car without even bothering to grab my purse. I can hear Craig laughing behind me.

I dash into the gas station and bum-rush the door praying the whole time that it will be empty. It takes all I have to run upright and not bend over while trying to hold my water. It isn't until I am perched over the toilet seat that I realize that we are almost home. Craig only had to fill up one time on our way to the casino, so I assume we will be home within the hour.

My stomach is starting to get queasy again and I fight the wave of nausea that is threatening to overcome me. I wash my hands and walk through the store as calmly as I can when I exit.

"Everything come out okay?" Craig asks after I return to the car.

"Smarty pants."

"I have to go too, but, I refused to walk in their carrying your purse." I look down at the floor and remember that I had left it in the car. I smile as Craig goes into the gas station. He comes back with my favorite junk foods: Twizzlers, Sour Patches and Doritos.

"God bless you." I grab the bag of junk and rip open the bag of Twizzlers, pulling out a few before handing him the bag. I have turned him into a junk-food junkie as well. I resist the urge to ask how much farther and pick up my book. Craig rests his free hand on my thigh.

"Are you all right? Do you want me to drive?"

"I'm fine, baby. Finish your book. We will be home in no time."

"Home, I like the sound of that." I shake away my dread at what could be waiting for us there.

# Jasmine

It is only ten in the morning and already I have run out of things to do. Fighting depression, I decide to go to the gym. Things didn't turn out quite like I expected at the cookout. While I had been trying to cheer up Sammie, I was suffering through the worst male drought I've ever experienced.

While Sammie took Aunt Rosa's comment as a barb aimed at her, I took it as a direct hit against me. She was implying I cannot keep a man and I am beginning to believe her. Ever since my divorce, I've had a series of one-night stands, but no one has held my interest longer than a month. Even though Aunt Rosa hasn't had a man since the turn of the century, her words still had bite. Everybody has a man but me. Even Momma is getting back into the groove of things. Sammie was driving me crazy with her pity parties, so last night I turned off the phone. She was flip-flopping around on whether or not Buddy is her ideal mate. I had my own issues to deal with, so I took the night off for myself. I had only switched the phone back on for a second when it started ringing.

"Hey, girl, whatcha up to?" Sammie asks.

"I'm on my way to the gym."

"Girl, you stay in that gym. It ain't like you got to work on your body with the way you be slinging that ass!"

"Well, in order to keep slinging this ass, I got to put in a little work. Besides, working out is not the only reason why I go to the gym. It's like forty percent working out and sixty percent shopping."

"Shopping? You've lost me."

"I go to the gym when I am horny and looking for a quick fix."

"Oh Lawd, I have heard everything now."

"Girl, I can't believe you didn't know this. I mean, that's the very best place to scope out your next lover."

"Enlighten me, because I ain't never heard no shit like that."

"As a rule, you want a man who can do at least one-hundred-fifty push-ups without passing out or quitting. 'Cause a man who can do that will be just a man who will be underneath you and expect you to do the work."

"Dayum, I never thought of that!"

"He also needs to be able to bench press at least two-hundred-and-fifty pounds 'cause you want to make sure he can lift you onto the dick and hold you there while you take a ride. While he is on the bench, check out the package. If he got anything, you'll see the imprint while he's lying flat on his back."

"Oh, stop, you're killing me. Where did you come up with this shit?"

"Girl, men have been doing this for years. I just figured it out."

"What else should I look for?"

"I make sure that they can squat down and stay in that position for a while. That shows me he has staying power and can go the distance. Add looks to that and you've got the perfect male for a little afternoon fun."

"But what if he is gay? I heard a lot of those muscle-builders are really gay."

"I ain't looking for a muscle-builder I just want a man who can perform for me when the time is right. Besides, I've thought of that too. This is Atlanta after all."

"Oh, no you didn't just point Atlanta out on the gaydar chart."

"I'm not saying that Atlanta is the gay capital of the world but just in case it is, I have a way to protect myself. I find a way to make him drop off something to eat at my hairdresser's before I sleep with him."

"Your hairdresser?"

"Yeah, child, he can spot a gay man at twenty thousand feet." Sammie drops the phone and I can hear her laughing hysterically. After a few seconds she gets back on the line.

"Where do I go to sign up?"

"Shut up, you've got a man."

"Yeah, Buddy is cool, but sometimes he ain't feeling me." Sammie sighs.

"Girl, that nigga loves your dirty drawers! Stop trippin'."

"Yeah, you're right, but he ain't in tune with my sexual desires. I get tired of telling him what I want all the time."

"So you saying the nigga can't lay down the pipe?"

"Naw, it's not that. It's my body language…sometimes he can't read it."

"Shit, now you've got me confused."

"Okay, it's like this. If we're lying in the bed watching the boob tube and I want my nipples sucked, I usually lie on my back and raise my hands over my head, giving him full access to the tits, right?"

"Uh…yeah, I can picture that."

"But he doesn't get it. He will rub them instead and that pisses me off."

"Then tell him. He ain't a psychic."

"That's not all. If I throw my legs over his, I want him to play with my pussy, but then he starts sucking my tits instead of doing both at the same time."

I am getting annoyed with my sister. She's acting like a child instead of a grown-ass woman.

"Look, Sammie, not everyone is used to a sexually aggressive woman. If Buddy is not doing the things you want him to do, then you're going to have to teach him to read your signs. These 'signs,' as you call them, are unique to you and unless you want him fumbling around in the dark, you better turn on the light."

"But Jazz, I am tired of being in control of our sex life. I want him to take control," Sammie whines.

"Control…you are not making sense. Listen to yourself. How can he take control when you're asking him to read your mind?"

Sammie is quiet for a minute and I am beginning to think that I have hurt her feelings. This is the first time that I have truly lost patience with her. I decide to try another tactic.

"Sammie, in the past you've had two kinds of men: those who used and abused you for sex and those who allowed you to do the same to them. Every man doesn't have to slap you around to show you how forceful he is. I'm asking you to try something different with Buddy. Show him what you want him to do and when he does it, tell him that it feels good or say something like, 'Oh yeah, baby, just like that,' and I guarantee you, he will remember it the next time."

For a minute, I thought she'd hung up on me.

"Sammie?"

"I'm here…just thinking about what you've said. You make a lot of sense and I don't know why I didn't see it for myself. Do you really think it will work?"

"Oh yeah, it'll work. Trust me."

"Can a girl have a back-up plan just in case it don't?"

"You're a hot mess."

"No, you're the one! Go ahead and go shopping. Call me later and let me know how you make out and I mean that just the way it sounds."

"Will do. Oh, by the way, could you do me a favor?"

"Sure, sis."

"Stop sweating the small stuff. There's enough shit in the world to worry about."

"Okay, I'll try. Thanks."

I hang up the phone. Again, I thank God for allowing me to meet my sister. Preaching to her is actually teaching myself. Now if I would only take some of my own advice, I would be alright. In my past, I never had any girlfriends, but I am starting to like this kinship feeling.

I finish applying my makeup and grab my gym bag on the way out the door, humming one of my favorite songs, *Not Gon' Cry*.

# Sammie

Nothing has been right since the picnic. I'm self-conscious around Buddy and spend a lot of time second-guessing myself. Jasmine was right about my relationship with Buddy. I was trippin' big time. I treat Buddy differently from any other man that I've ever been with and I was about to throw away a good man just 'cause he isn't a mind reader. Lawd, I can't thank you enough for bringing my sister and her wisdom into my life. With a new attitude under my belt, I call Buddy.

"Hey, baby," I say oozing sweetness.

"Hey, yourself. Whassup?"

"Do you have a gig tonight or can I steal you away?" There is a moment of silence and my old insecurities begin to nag at me. The phone starts to slip from my moist palm and I have to quickly switch hands so as not to drop it entirely. An odd ache begins in the center of my chest and spreads into my arms, making them feel heavier. I instantly regret suggesting that he make a choice between work and me because I don't know what I would do if I came up the loser. My mind seeks a snappy comeback just in case he laughs at my proposal.

"Just say the word, baby, and I'm there. I'm supposed to cover Visions tonight, but I think I can get Ryan to cover for me."

"Baby, I ain't tryin' to take money out your pocket, but I really want to see you tonight. In fact, I don't need the whole night. Meet me at the food court at Lenox Mall around six and I will fill you in."

"I'm there, beautiful. See you then," Buddy says, hanging up the phone.

Amazed, I stare at the phone. *That wasn't as bad as I thought it would be.* It is after four so I have a lot of preparations to make. First stop, Victoria's Secret, and I also need to stop by Starship for some adult toys before I meet Buddy in the food court. My plan is to take him into the security corridor and fuck his brains out. I know one of the guards and I'm sure I can persuade him to stand lookout for our late-afternoon tryst.

I jump off the couch and race to the car with my mind spinning a mile a minute. Pleasing Buddy is my primary objective for the evening. I want to really rock his world and shake off all the negative energy I allowed to come into our relationship in the first place. For the first time in my life I have someone who loves me for me and not for what I can get for them. I don't have to do anything but be myself. It is foreign to me and will take some getting used to, but I am willing to try.

I shop like I have on gasoline drawers burning straight up my ass. Running from shop to shop, I am trying to put together the perfect outfit. Since we started dating, I have dropped about fifty pounds and I am amazed at how good I'm looking. I am not the hot sex machine Jasmine is but I can hold my own. Confidence has never been my strong suit, but I feel something I've never felt before—sexy.

Satisfied with my outfit, I admire myself in the mirror. Holding up a finger in the air, I wet it and place it on my ass. I hear it sizzle in my head.

"That's what I'm talkin' 'bout." I've chosen a short purple dress that clings to my newfound curves and dips dangerously low in the front and suggestively in the back. Jazz taught me that less is more, something I'd never known before. She has revamped my whole closet and all my former hoochie outfits are in the trash. They were so ghetto, I could not even donate them to charity.

Lately, my attire is more elegant. I buy a pair of purple sandals and I pick out a necklace and earring set to complement my ensemble.

Next I go to Victoria's Secret to pick out my underwear. In the past, I couldn't wear their bras. They have panties to fit a rhino, but bras made only for a peacock with more padding than cup and that stupid underwire. Whoever came up with underwire bras should, in my opinion, either be shot or made to wear them for forty-eight hours. Nine times out of ten the woman wearing them are flat-chested and trying to hoist up their non-existent boobs. Blessed as I am, I only need something to help my boobs fight the laws of gravity.

Next up, I go to the adult novelty shop outside Lenox Mall and I must admit I go a little crazy. I buy everything from a pleasure feather to a piggy parfait, which is designed to enhance toe sucking, edible body paints, and underwear. I also buy a rockin' rabbit and last but not least, a card game for lovers. Of course, all these items will have to wait until we have more time, but I want to be prepared if he wants to come back to the house after our tryst. This will be the perfect time to introduce my new toys into our relationship. I cannot wait to get started.

Bags stuffed full of goodies, I mingle with the other shoppers trying to get back to the food court. I don't know how Buddy will react to my sexual aggression, but I am eager to find out. Anticipation has pasted a smile on my face I feel won't come off, when suddenly I bump full throttle into Jessie. He has a way of sucking the wind from beneath my wings and setting them ablaze.

"Jasmine, is that you?"

"No."

"Stop lying, heifer."

"If I were Jazz, you would be lying flat on your ass for calling her a heifer. Did you forget the last ass whuppin' she gave you?" I try to step around his trifling ass but he grabs me by the bag. I look at his hand as if it is dipped in shit. My eyes tell him exactly how I feel at being touched by him.

After a few moments he releases his hold. "Uh, my bad, no disrespect intended. I didn't recognize you. You're looking good, girl. Whatcha been doing?"

"Thank you and none of your business. Now if you'll excuse me, I need to be going."

"Not so fast, girl. Can't I holla at you for a minute? Shit, you look just like you did when we first got married."

I am speechless for a few seconds. Jessie does not do compliments and he damn sure doesn't do them with me. He is more likely to call me a nasty bitch than to tell me I look good. I can only stare at him with my mouth half open, waiting for the insult that is bound to follow. He is actually smiling at me.

"Why you looking at me like that?" I ask suspiciously.

"I'm sorry. I got caught up in the past." His words cut through me like a knife. I don't know whose past he is referring to, but the one I am thinking about was not pretty. I am thinking of the times that he beat my ass and made me sell my body to finance his drug habit. Unwanted tears come to my eyes, but they do the job of hardening my heart. I can't afford to get lost in sentiment.

"Look, you can skip down memory lane by your damn self. I

prefer never to think of those times ever again." Once again I attempt to step around him and he blocks me with his body. Stunned, I drop my bag, spilling the contents on the floor. Silently, I look around for help, but there isn't anyone willing to get involved. Piece by piece, Jessie returns my items to the bags.

"I see some shit ain't changed. How much you charging these days? How 'bout you hook a brother up for old time's sake?" Jessie is openly fondling himself despite being in the middle of the mall.

"Fuck you, Jessie."

"Now?"

"Nigga, please, did you forget what you put my ass through? Am I the only one who remembers the ass whippings and the men and women you made me sleep with?" I am screaming at him, unmindful of our surroundings and not caring who hears me. My past is my past and Jessie is not a part of my future. But Buddy doesn't know my past and now I realize that he is in the crowd listening. The look on his face is one of shock and disgust. His mouth is hanging open like a big O.

"If you don't move, I promise you I will start screaming."

"Hell, you already screaming and it ain't doing no good. All you are doing is embarrassing yourself." Jessie is right about that and for a moment I try to compose myself, but then something inside of me snaps. I am through being his damn punching bag and I'll be damned if I will allow him to disrespect me ever again.

"Can't you get it through your thick skull, I don't want your ass?"

"Now hold on, heifer. Just because you done lost a little weight that don't mean you can talk to me any kinda way. I will slap the black off your ass."

"Jessie, I've come a long way from the child you married and abused."

"I didn't abuse you, bitch. You enjoyed every minute of it." My head jerks as if he actually slapped me. I am so mad I had forgotten to swallow and my saliva is dripping from the sides of my mouth.

"Enjoyed it? Are you still smoking crack? You did everything you could to destroy me, Jessie, but it's over. Now get the fuck out of my way!"

"Listen here, bitch, it ain't over till I say it's over." He moves in closer to me. I've forgotten about the crowd gathering around us and my desire to keep a low profile and get the hell away from him. I am operating on pure hatred for all the humiliation I'd suffered at the hands of this man. I am done taking his shit. Using all the strength I can muster, I ram my knee into his groin, fake a move to the left, and spin to the right, running full speed out of the mall. Jessie folds to his knees, groaning in pain.

"It's *Ms. Bitch* to you! How's that for a memory, you rat bastard?" I yell behind me as I hit the exit doors. I am running from my past and my future at the same time. I cannot get the look on Buddy's face out of my mind. Tears flow freely down my cheeks as gut-wrenching sobs escape my chest. Painful memories scar my mind as I run down memory lane too scared to look back. The most logical choice is to flee, but my heart wants to stay and face Buddy to possibly salvage our relationship. *What the hell am I going to say to him anyway?* "*Hey, I used to be a whore, but I'm not anymore.*" That doesn't sound right even to me and I lived through the shit. I slam the car door shut and peel out of the parking lot as if the very devil himself was riding my coattail. I don't slow down until I am five blocks away. I keep checking my mirror to make sure Jessie is not following me.

"Shit, you did it again, Jessie. Why are you so intent on fucking up my life?" I bang my hands on the steering wheel so hard my hands are throbbing. I just can't believe it. Every time I allow myself to think that part of my life is buried, someone drives a backhoe through it. Every other woman that I know who has the misfortune of having an ex-husband has been able to go on with their lives happily ever after. But I luck up and get a man who refuses to let go. It would be different if Jessie actually wanted me, but he moved on and married again. He just doesn't want anyone else to have me.

The look on Buddy's face spoke volumes. He has been through his share of bad relationships and he isn't about to go through no drama with me. He doesn't have to. He is fine, successful, and a mini-celebrity in his own right. The last thing he needs in his career is for it to get out that he is sleeping with a whore.

I didn't make a decision to ease back into my former life, if it can actually be called a decision at all. However I am now cruising the streets of the West End, looking for a way to end the pain—if not for a lifetime, then at least for the moment. Surprisingly, I score in a big way without too much drama. I would have thought it would've been harder to make the large-size purchase without actually knowing someone. But I do it and my confused mind takes it as a sign from God that it is okay to step over the line just this one time. I don't believe for one moment this will be a permanent fix. I just want one for the right here and now and I am going to take it.

# Leah

"You ready?"

"I was born ready."

"I am not talking about that. I mean facing my mother."

"Yeah, I have only your best interest at heart so I ain't never scared."

I laugh and this helps to ease the tension in the car but doesn't remove the fear in my heart. I couldn't understand why my mother wasn't answering her phone despite my numerous attempts to reach her.

"I'm right here, baby. Don't forget it. You are not alone."

"Thanks, honey. I needed to hear that." Despite his assurances, I still don't make any moves.

"Sweetheart, we have to get out of the car so we can find out what's wrong."

"I'm scared."

"I know you are. I'm scared too, but it is what it is and we will deal with it."

"You go and tell me if it's safe to come in."

"I know you're kidding. If things were that bad, your mother would have told you or at least called you back until she reached you."

"What if someone is hurt?"

"Hush, let's not speculate." Together we exit the car and I lean on him as we approach the door. My legs just won't cooperate and if it weren't for him pulling and supporting me, I don't think I could have made it.

"Relax, baby. Your mom's car is here, so that means she's at home. If things were real bad, like one of the kids getting sick, she wouldn't be here."

"I guess you have a point." I try to raise my hand to ring the doorbell, but my hand keeps hesitating. Craig pushes it while brushing a light kiss on my forehead. I smile at him and he pats my arm for reassurance. It doesn't take long for Momma to answer the door.

My relief at seeing her standing in the doorway is incredible. I feel like a weight has been lifted. Now if I can just find out what happened, Craig and I can share our good news. I stand before Momma waiting for her to tell me the news. She smiles, holding her arms wide for me to enter. I grab her, afraid to let go.

"Baby, you're home." I don't respond immediately. It is enough just to smell and hold her.

"You two look like you had fun." As she steps back to look at us, I cannot help but to beam. I am excited and nervous about her reaction.

"Momma, we got the messages. Is everything okay?" She turns around and we follow her into the house. She sits down on the sofa and Craig and I sit on the matching loveseat. The living room is spotless as usual. Something is wrong; I can tell by the way Momma keeps avoiding my eyes.

"Where are the children?"

"Oh, they're still taking a nap."

"Momma, you're scaring me. Please tell me what happened."

"It's nothing now, but I was real worried at the time. That's why I called you. The kids went with Kentee on Saturday. I wasn't going to let them go, but Kayla said you read him the riot act of no funny business."

I smile because she almost quotes me verbatim. Kayla can't hold water in a bucket.

"It's okay, Momma, I did talk to Kentee and he knows the rules."

"Well…he didn't follow them."

"What did he do?" I jump up and start pacing. Craig tries to grab me, but I am heated. I am going to kill that motherfucker if he had my babies around some of his whores.

"Leah, sit back down. It's all water under the bridge now." Reluctantly, I sit. I grab Craig's hand. When my emotions are back in check, Momma continues.

"He dropped the children off at his friend Tarcia's house and apparently there was a fire. The kids weren't hurt, but they were just scared, is all. Kayla called me and I went and picked them up."

"That no-good, sorry, son-of-a-bitch! He promised me that he wouldn't drop my kids anywhere, even at his sister's house. Do you know who that trick Tarcia is? She's the heifer he left me for, the one who I almost got into a fight with at work! Shit, we just had this conversation two days ago, Ma. I can't believe that he would pull this crap. Wait till I get my hands on him."

I am beyond mad. I am ready to fight and if he rolls up here right at this moment I don't know what I'll do to him.

"That's it. I'm through talking with him. I've had it up to here with his lies." I am pacing again. I just want to hit him really hard.

"There's more."

"Huh?"

"Kentee got there before I had to clock that heifer and he tried to take the kids with him. He didn't even know I was there. Tarcia got mad and attacked him and now she's in jail."

"Attacked him? She ain't no bigger than a minute." I'm not feeling sorry for Kentee. I am just trying to get a mental picture of her fighting him.

"She stabbed him in the neck with something. They took him to the hospital, but he's out. He called to speak with the children, but I told him they were asleep."

"Serves his ass right!"

"Leah, I know you're upset, but I raised you better than that."

"I'm sorry, Momma. You're right, no one deserves that." Craig pulls me down beside him and places his arm around my shoulders.

"No wonder he was blowing up my phone. He probably wanted to get to me before I got to you. Well, at least everyone is okay. I was so worried."

"Yeah, they're fine. Kayla took her daddy being hurt pretty hard. The other thing is there is a good chance that Mya started the fire."

"Oh, my God. Why would you say that? She's never played with matches before."

"She was holding a lighter when they carried her out of the house. I asked her what she was doing with it, but she wouldn't answer me. Maybe you or Craig can get her to open up."

"Do the police want to question her?"

"I left my phone number, but so far no one has called. I guess it all depends on what that girl says. She was the only one other than me who saw the lighter hit the ground."

"Craig, what are we going to do if they come after my baby?"

"Baby, there is no sense worrying about that now. Whatever happens or doesn't happen, we will deal with it."

"I don't think we will be hearing from the police. I kicked the lighter under the car and when no one was looking I scooped it up and put it in my purse. If Tarcia mentions it, I will deny it."

"Momma!"

"What? You would've done the same thing if you were here."

"You ain't even lied," I say. Momma smiles at us and I could feel the stress roll off me.

"I'm sorry your trip had to end with such difficult news."

Sensing there is no better time than the present to share our good news, I sneak a peek at Craig and he nods his agreement.

"Ma…" Kayla comes tearing down the hall, flinging herself into my knees. "Mommy, you're home; did you and Mr. Craig have fun? Did Grandma tell you about the fire? Did you know my daddy got hurt by the bad lady? What did you bring us?"

"Hold on, baby, we can only answer one question at a time." Laughing, I pick her up and give her a big hug. She squirms in my arms, trying to get to Craig. Reluctantly, I release her and she flips over to his lap.

"What did you bring me?" Kayla whispers in Craig's ear.

"Don't I get a kiss first?" She kisses him on his cheek and wraps her arms around his neck, hugging him tightly. Malik, with Mya in tow, also comes into the room. Leaving his sister, Malik throws himself at me and Craig. I must admit that as much as I needed the break from the duties of being a mother, I missed my children. Freeing myself, I kneel in front of Mya. I wait until she makes eye contact before I sign hello to her.

Malik is talking a mile a minute, but I tune him out so I can give Mya my full attention.

"Are you okay?" I sign. I am really worried about Mya because she is not able to express herself like her brother and sister. There is no telling what she is holding inside regarding the fire.

"Yes," she answers. Raising my arms for a hug, I am grateful she accepts my affection. With Mya, I've learned to only offer hugs if she is in an accepting mood. Had she turned away or simply stood there, I would have just made a hugging motion, letting her know that I love her. Stepping back, I wait to see if she is going to acknowledge Craig.

The room falls silent as we all watch Mya. She doesn't hesitate to climb up next to Craig on the sofa and place her head in his lap. This single gesture is proof enough that Craig and I did the right thing.

"Momma, kids, we have an announcement." Craig pulls Mya upright so she can follow the conversation. Momma keeps looking from Craig to me, a question in her eyes. Suddenly I'm afraid to tell them, but once again Craig gives me a nod of encouragement.

"We got married." Momma gasps, and her hand covers her heart for a brief second as tears flow down her face. I think she is upset, but her huge smile tells us she is happy for us.

"Thank you, Jesus." She rushes toward me and gives me a big kiss. Of course, this is the reaction that I'd hoped for, but I still feel guilty about not involving them.

"You're okay with this?"

"Yes, I prayed for this. Although I would love to have been there, I will take my blessings any way they come."

"Momma, we didn't plan it this way, we just couldn't wait." Momma hugs Craig as she wipes away her tears. Malik is grinning but Kayla has this disturbed look on her face.

"What's the matter, Kayla?" Craig asks.

"Does that mean that Daddy ain't my daddy no more?"

# Sammie

The message light on my phone is a solid red indicating that not only do I have a message, but my mailbox is full. I vaguely remember hearing the phone last night, but I wasn't ready to speak to anyone so I ignored it. I was on a mission to ease the pain and I worked it until there was nothing left to do but pass out.

Morning, however, brings yesterday's pain back two-fold. On one hand, my guilt at backsliding is gnawing a hole in my heart and the fear of facing the consequences is driving me to seek additional relief. That mentality drives me out of my house at ten in the morning to the bank. I can't use the ATM this time because there is a daily dollar limit for withdrawals and that limit won't be enough for what I need to do.

I plan to medicate myself enough to deal with Buddy and to finally put the Jessie issue to rest. Logic has nothing to do with my withdrawal from the bank. Although I had just gotten paid the day before, my money is already earmarked to pay my rent, car payment, and insurance. After paying these bills, I will be lucky enough to have lunch money, but I don't think about this as I write a check out to cash.

"Ms. Davis, I see you are closing your checking account. Is there anything that the bank can do to keep your business?"

"Uh…no. I'm consolidating my accounts and will be putting this money into my credit union account."

"Very well, I just need you to sign this acknowledgment."

"Acknowledgment, what does that mean?"

"By signing the acknowledgment, you agree to hold the bank harmless in the event checks are posted to your account after you close it and for any uncollected fees. You are obligated to immediately reimburse the bank for any associated fees you may incur as a result of that return."

"Oh, okay." I grab the pen and quickly sign my name. I push the form back to her because one or two things will have happened by the time they find out what I've done. I will either be dead or wishing I was.

"I just have to get this signed by my supervisor and I'll be right back." My skin starts to itch and I fight so hard against scratching, tears form in my eyes. Scratching is a true indicator of an addict and I don't want to portray that image. It feels like she's gone forever when in reality it is less than two minutes. But to add to my anxiety, my cell phone is blowing up. I can't risk answering it even if I'm so inclined. She ignores it just like I do.

"Thanks for observing the no-cell-phone policy," she says, sliding my cash toward me with a plastic smile pasted on her face. "Is there anything else that I can do for you today?"

"No, I'm straight." Relieved, I hurry from the bank praying she will not discover my deception until I am free and clear. It doesn't matter if she finds out after I leave the bank because I plan on disappearing. Guilt is written on my face, but it is not enough to make me turn back. I don't even think about the fact that I allowed them to photograph me and they have my signature on the check, not to mention the acknowledgment. I am being controlled at this point by a stronger desire.

Cruising the streets once again on the West End, I look for the easy score. Logic tells me not to use the same runner, but the new guards aren't as trusting as the one I found last night. They want my credentials and I don't have any. Sure, I could have brought smaller amounts just to keep coming back. But I have enough sense to know that the more times I visit the area, the higher my profile will be in the community. And despite my destructive behavior, I don't want to get caught and tossed in jail, labeled a druggie. I just want to get my stuff, medicate and hibernate.

So I am forced to wait until my contact hits the streets. In the meantime, I hide out in bars. By the time I find him, I am drunk as a skunk and willing to agree to anything to put the all-encompassing pain to rest. By this time, my cell battery has died.

"There you are. I've been looking for you all over."

"Bitch, please, for what? I ain't your baby daddy and I don't owe you no fucking money." Clearly, he doesn't remember me from the night before. This should raise a flag, but my drunk ass ain't focusing on the negative, only the positive. He doesn't deny being a source for my drug of choice and I am not going to let him out of my sight until he provides it.

"Can't we do this off the street?" I'm paranoid and anxious to cop my drugs and leave. But it appears like I am being guided by a force greater than me and I am in no condition to fight it. So when this total stranger decides to get into my car I don't object. In retrospect, this is yet another mistake on my part.

"I've got three thousand dollars and I need to make a purchase right now. Can you handle it?

"I can handle it, but how do I know that you aren't the po-po?"

"I bought some shit from you last night and you didn't have a problem."

He thinks about it for a minute before he responds. "Your first purchase was small potatoes; now you want some meat. How do I know that you ain't posing for the po-po just to get my ass hung up in some shit?"

"You don't and I can't do anything about that. I need an escape and if you can't provide it, I will go somewhere else. It's just that plain and simple. I'm prepared to give you all the money right now." I was taking a big risk telling him how much money I had. If he couldn't provide the weight, there wasn't anything stopping him from hitting me over the head and taking it from me. Lucky for me, money talks; bullshit walks.

He doesn't say anything else and I fight the urge to choke the shit out of him.

"So what do I need to do to make this happen?"

"I got to be a part of it."

"What the hell does that mean? I got to share with you? Oh, hell no."

"Do you want it or not?" Shit, I am beyond wanting it, I need it. But something in my drug dealer's demeanor is different tonight. He isn't a take-it-or-leave-it dealer; he is being driven by his own demons and they join mine. Instead of this being a score for me, it is a score for us and my demented mind sees nothing wrong with that.

"Then let's do this shit." I wait in my car for over an hour while my mark scores. He wants to hit that shit immediately in my car, but I quickly snatch my shit to do it on my home turf. For some reason, I'm not afraid to take this unnamed dealer into my home. To pacify him until we reach my house, I ply him with booze. We are singing old-school tunes when we leave my car, yelling, "Always and Forever"...off tune, loud as hell, as we enter my condo. Stupid me didn't notice Buddy parked outside or think about how it must look to him, me stumbling into my apartment with a strange man.

We're an unlikely pair, but sex is the furthest thing from our minds when we enter my apartment. He wants to get high; I want to forget all the events that led me to this point.

"Hey, what's your name?"

"Why?"

"We are about to get high together so I would prefer to have a name instead of hey you."

"Oh…okay. It's Raymond, but you can call me Ray."

"Thanks. I'm Sammie, in case you didn't know." I go to get my drug shit, but he stops me with a broad sweep of his hand. Inside his coat pocket, he holds everything we need. I realize that my rudimentary attempts the night before wasted product and was nowhere near as effective as the shit Ray has brought to the table. But I wasn't sure I was ready to actually smoke crack. I am scared and excited just thinking about it.

"Wait, what is all this shit?"

"You want to smoke it, right?"

"Uh…I haven't done that before. I just snort it."

"Baby girl, then you have been wasting your money. Let me just cook you up a little and you tell me which way is better." I don't want to say yes because I suddenly remember how sick Jessie acted when he was high on crack, but I'm not capable of rational thought at this time so I allow him to cook my shit. He cooks my rent, car, insurance, gas, and personal utilities with the flick of a lighter and my dumb ass allows it. Nagging welts appear on my arms and I scratch them until they bleed, but this is my only resistance. At the time, I thought it was funny, until it

252 TINA BROOKS MCKINNEY

was all gone. What should have lasted for a few days is gone in a matter of hours. I doze off.

When I wake up, I am alone. The reality of what I've done pushes me over the edge. All of a sudden, it is dark and I can't move even though I have to go to the bathroom. I feel helpless as I pee on myself. I wait to feel the warmth of release, but it is absent. I can hear people around me, but I cannot respond to them. I want to tell them that I peed but my mouth isn't working. I am in a coma.

My thoughts drift to Buddy. My anguish turns to anger as I now decide this is his fault. He witnessed another man push up on me, call me names, and he did nothing to stop him. He didn't act like a man in love at all. "Why didn't he try to help me? He should have been kicking ass and taking names later." I am working myself up to a good mad now, for all the good it is doing me. I couldn't raise my arms to strike even if he brought his sorry ass to the hospital to visit me. This thought depresses me even more than being in a coma. I love that man and it feels like I am in yet another loser relationship despite how well it had been going. That's when I decide to die. I will my heart to stop beating. I don't want to face yet another day alone.

"Lord, I'm tired. Can I just come home?" The loud bleeps of my heart monitor drown out my thoughts and signal the answer to my prayers. I am going home and despite all the dirt I accumulated, God is going to forgive me. Drugs drove me to the brink of a coma, but despair, depression, and the destruction I created keep me there blocking out the light of hope and my future. And as quiet as it's kept, I'm glad. I've been fighting all my life for love and acceptance and I am finally sick and tired. The monitor that is measuring my existence finally earns its keep when it flatlines.

Strangely, I see all this happening, but I am not compelled to jump back into my weary body until I see my sister, Jasmine. Funny that I had forgotten all about her. I did not consider the pain that I would cause her when I decided to check out of life. I don't feel worthy of her love, but that love brought me the will to stay.

# *Jasmine*

Sammie is in a coma and there is a good possibility that she will never come out of it. There is an equal possibility that if she does survive, she might never be the same. I feel so insignificantly small in the scheme of things, but I'm not ready to lose my sister. This is the second time in my life that someone I love is fighting to live and I hate every minute of it. With Dad, I told him it was okay to go to sleep because he'd lived a full life. He would've been bedridden if he had lived and I knew that he wouldn't want to continue living that way. Although I wasn't ready for him to leave, I had to trust God that my father would be in a better place. I am not so willing to accept anything less than full recovery for the sister whom I've just found. "Hell to the no. It can't be over yet."

"Wake up, damn it." I slap Sammie's face with all the fury my hand contains. This isn't about her anymore; it is about the people whom Sammie is leaving behind. I wait until we are alone to show her I'm not playing this shit with her. She can be melodramatic when she wants to be and frankly, I don't have the time or patience for it. She needs to get her shit together—quick, fast, and in a hurry.

"I said, wake the fuck up, damn it. I ain't playing with you,

Sammie." She jerks the first time and withdraws from my fingers, but does not open her eyes or otherwise acknowledge that she felt the slap. I slap her again and this time she doesn't even cringe. Defeated, I crumble onto the bed crying and praying that she'd be given another chance despite her dumb-ass playing. I cry until I have no more tears and then I fall asleep. In my dreams, Sammie is alive and well, but when I open my eyes and focus on the machines I realize it was just a dream.

The doctors had to partially shave Sammie's hair and she has small electrodes on her head to measure her brain's activity. She is heavily sedated and is hooked up to a respirator. Fear of the unknown pushes me away from Sammie's bed. I don't want to look at her body anymore. I go out to the main waiting room, but that holds its own pain.

Buddy and Leah are waiting for me to come out. He is first to stand, rushing me, causing me to stumble back. I'm not ready to be touched, so I hold up my arms to keep him away. His eyes scour my face and I can feel their intensity as he struggles to keep the tears from falling. Leah pulls up short next to Buddy. Her hands are clenched and kneading a Kleenex that has long since wiped its last nose. I look around to see if others are maintaining the vigil with us, but with the exception of Leah and Buddy, the waiting room is empty.

"Any word from Tyson?"

"Not in the last hour. He should be here any moment." I drop to the nearest vacant chair. This would be the first time I would meet my sister's son, but I didn't want it to be under these circumstances.

"Any change?"

Unable to reply, I merely shake my head.

"I want to see her. No, I need to see her." Buddy doesn't wait for permission. He leaves the room with hitching shoulders as he struggles to keep from crying. I always knew in my heart that Buddy loved Sammie but it was never more evident than at this precise moment. His pain is written all over his face.

"So we still don't know any more, do we?" I ask Leah.

"Buddy shed a little light on the subject, but I think that's just the tip of the iceberg."

"What did he say?"

"He said he was supposed to meet Sammie at the mall, but she ran into Jessie first and they got into it. Looks like Sammie got pissed off at the world and shut down. She hasn't been answering any of Buddy's phone calls and she hasn't been to work either."

"Why didn't she call me?"

"Good question. I was thinking about that on my ride over here and the only reason I can come up with is she didn't want to speak with anyone. You would've answered your phone and probably cussed her out. But my phone is turned off during the night and she knows that."

"Yeah, you got a good point, but I thought we were closer than that."

"Jazz, I just don't know. Only time will tell." I don't want to say what is on the tip of my tongue. Instead, I keep my dark thoughts to myself as we wait for Buddy to come out of Sammie's room. The waiting is the hardest part. Trying to get comfortable in an uncomfortable and unfamiliar room runs a close second, and the third is not giving way to the fear that is struggling to choke me.

"I think now would be a good time to pray." Leah crosses the room and we join hands with heads bowed. Buddy joins us when he comes back into the room and we welcome his strong hands into our fold. We are interrupted by the doctor.

"Sammie is stable. There is nothing that you can do here for her tonight. We will call you if anything changes." I don't want to leave, but I am starving and too tired to pay attention.

"I'm not going anywhere. You two go 'head and I'll call you when she wakes up." Buddy is trying his best to hold it together.

"Yeah, Jazz, we can come back in the morning."

"Leah, do you wanna go and get some breakfast?"

"Yeah, I could use a bite to eat. I'll follow you."

"Buddy, do you want us to bring you something?"

"No, I'm fine. I'll call you if anything changes or Tyson shows up."

# Leah

I call Craig as I drive the few short blocks to Waffle House.

"Hey, baby, everything okay?"

"Still no change with Sammie, but I guess no news can be considered good news. Jazz and I are going to get something to eat. She's a wreck, so I want to spend a little more time with her."

"Take your time, sweetheart. The kids are fine."

"I love you."

"I love you too." I don't know what I did in life to deserve such a good man, but I constantly thank God for him each and every day. I lock the car and join Jazz at the door to the restaurant.

"I'm so hungry, I could eat raw horse meat right about now."

"Damn, that's hungry. I prefer my meat cooked."

"Girl, I'm just playing. I like my shit well done."

"Me too." We order the all-star breakfast and settle back with our coffee.

"So how have things been going with Craig?"

"Girl, I can't even complain."

"He's one of a kind."

"Look, Jazz, this might not be the best time, but I can't keep this information to myself much longer. Craig and I got married." Noticing the ring, Jazz lets out a high-pitched squeal.

260 TINA BROOKS MCKINNEY

"Oh, Leah, I'm so happy for you. Why didn't you say anything? This ring is off the chain." She reaches across the table to get a closer look.

"Thanks, Jazz. I've barely had a chance to get used to it myself. Our lives have been high drama ever since we did the do."

"Did ya'll do it when you went away last weekend?"

"Yeah. It wasn't the way he'd planned it, but he said the ring was burning a hole in his pocket. He was acting strangely and I was getting worried that he wanted out of the relationship. Next thing I know, we are in front of the wedding chapel."

"Wow, how romantic. So what did your mother say?"

"Mom is on cloud nine. We are going to have a reception as soon as things start to calm down."

"Girl, I knew that man was the truth from the moment I laid eyes on him. I wish you both the best of luck."

"Thanks Jazz, I wasn't going to say anything while Sammie is so ill. She just has to make it through this. I can't lose another friend."

"I know that's right. Sammie's biggest problem is that she's spent her entire life worrying about what people think of her. She's never felt free to be who she really is and keeps trying to reinvent herself to make someone else happy. That's why I like Buddy so much, because he allows her to be herself."

"Then what happened?"

"I can only guess. We had that cookout and it didn't go as nicely as I'd planned. My aunt made this comment about her mother, which kinda started things off on the wrong foot, but it got better. My aunt can be a pain in the ass, especially when she's drinking. She took a jab at me when she mentioned Buddy and that pissed me off too."

"Jab at you? I don't understand."

"Buddy and I used to kick it. We never got intimate, but that's not because he didn't want to. He used to follow me around and my aunt remembered him. So she insinuated that Sammie stole Buddy like her mother stole my father."

"Damn."

"Yeah, she kind of threw us all under the bus making it seem like I can't keep a man and Sammie was just like her mother, trying to steal one. I almost let that old bat have it right in the kisser. I tell you the truth, Leah. I've never been so ashamed of my family as I was at that moment."

"That's deep. But you know how old folks are; you can't control what comes out their mouths. It's like kids say the damnest things; old folks take it a step further."

"Ain't that the truth? If Sammie wasn't so hurt by her candor, it might have been funny."

"So do you think it was enough to push Sammie over the edge?"

"I hope not, but I really don't know. Sammie is her own worst enemy at times. She has this self-destructive behavior that kicks in when things are going good."

"You noticed that too? I thought it was just me. It's like she can't stand for things to go right and she just has to stick her hand in it."

"Exactly." She looked so distraught I felt that I had to say what was on my mind.

"Look, Jazz, I want to say something and I'm afraid that you might take it the wrong way."

"Go ahead, girl."

"You know I love you and Sammie to death, but now I'm concerned about both of you. Sammie is lucky as hell to have found

262 TINA BROOKS MCKINNEY

you when she needed you, but you can't save her from every
bump and bruise in life. She's grown through your love and it's
time she stands on her own two feet, for better or worse."

Many emotions play across Jazz's face—anger being one of
them. For a moment I thought I'd overstepped my bounds, but
a weary smile wins out in the end. Tears of acceptance appear as
she grabs my hands across the table.

"Thank you. I needed to hear that. Ever since I met Sammie,
I've felt responsible for her. Her life was so much different from
mine, and I took it upon myself to right the wrongs that were
done to her."

"But, Jazz, can't you see that you can't fix what you didn't break?
You're doing a disservice to yourself by trying. What about your
goals and aspirations?"

"Girl, it's not that bad. I'm okay."

"Okay, humor me. Name one thing that you've always wanted
to do and haven't gotten around to." I put down my fork and
give her my full attention. This is the first time that Jazz and I
are actually talking to each other one to one.

"Be a mother."

I think she's kidding until I look in her eyes. "You're serious,
aren't you?"

She nods her head. To say she caught me by surprise would
be an understatement. Jazz doesn't seem like the change-the-
diaper-in-the-middle-of-the-night type.

"I love kids and since I can't have my own, I wanna do the next
best thing."

"I didn't know you can't have children. I just assumed it was
your choice."

"Naw, it isn't a choice on my part at all. I didn't know it, but my ex left me a little something to remember him by and as a result, I can't have kids. Motherfucker almost killed me. I'm just glad I went to the doctors when I did."

"Damn, girl, that's deep. Did you confront your ex?"

"Yeah, but what's done is done. That's why he's paying me out the ass to keep quiet about that, and the fact that I caught him dick deep in my next-door neighbor's ass. If word gets out that he is HIV positive, his practice will be over."

"He gave you AIDS?" My heart feels like it has dropped into my shoes as fresh tears well in my eyes. I cannot take another friend being at death's door.

"So far no. I get tested every six months to be sure. The realization that he was sleeping with a man was enough to scare the hell out of me about having kids until I knew for sure. But his stank ass gave me an STD and I had to have a hysterectomy."

"Wow. He was sleeping with a man? Oh my God, that's some Jerry Springer shit."

"I know, right? For a long time, I couldn't talk about it but I'm cool now. I've been thinking about adopting, but I keep having second thoughts."

"Why? To me it's simple; either you want kids or you don't."

"Spoken like a true mother. Leah, I've never been around kids like that. I play with your kids, but at the end of the day they go home with you. What I really need is to be around them just to see if I am actually cut out for the job."

"Well, that's easy to solve; you could start spending time at Craig's center. He has all the kids you need and I'm sure he could use the help."

"Actually, that's what I was thinking, but I didn't know how to bring it up. Do you think Craig would let me?"

"Hell, yeah, do you want me to call him right now?"

"No, not right now. You can talk to him later. Tonight's been hard enough without going into mo' drama. Let's just eat and see if we can get any rest tonight. I plan on being back at the hospital at the crack of dawn." We pay the check and head to our cars, each lost in our own thoughts. I give Jazz a long hug and a kiss on the cheek.

"Make sure you call me if there's any change, or if you need me. I have to go back to work in the morning."

"I hear ya. Oh, how's your ex taking your marriage?"

"I haven't told him yet. I haven't spoken to him since the fire."

"Fire, what fire?"

"That's a long story and I need to get home. I'll call you later and fill you in on the details."

"Make sure you do. This sounds like it's going to be good."

"Trust me, it is. That fool finally started paying child support and watching the kids. He thinks we're getting back together."

"Now, where in the world did he get that idea from?" We both laugh as we get in our respective cars.

# Kentee

"Leah is not going to have any choice but to see me today. I'm going to sit at her job until she comes out. I'm sick of waiting for her to return my calls and I want to see my children."

Speaking to my reflection in the mirror, I am trying to bolster up some confidence that I'm not really feeling. I feel sorry for Tarcia, but until I find out the circumstances of the fire and why she stabbed me, that bitch is on *hold*. Life is tough enough without having to deal with crazy pussy, and to me, that is all Tarcia is. I never had the feelings for her that I have for Leah. I just thought I did.

Part of the problem was that I was unwilling to accept that I could father a child with a mental disability. That was the beginning of the end, but when it is all said and done, Leah has more class in her pinky toe than Tarcia has in her entire body. Tarcia is strictly ghetto and for once, I am ashamed of my own damn self for leaving my lady for a ho.

I remain resolved to win my baby back and reclaim my family. Glancing at the clock, I decide to make a trip to the mall my first stop before camping out at her job. My neck is still sore, so I swallow two more pain pills.

"I hope this shit doesn't make me sleepy. That's all I need right now is to fall asleep and wreck my car." I carefully choose what to wear. I want to be sexy cool for my baby. I know it is going to take more than a two-karat engagement ring and some flowers to woo her back into my life, but I am prepared to use the children to my advantage as well. Once I've proposed I know I can find my way back in the house and into her bed.

A little voice in the back of my mind speaks up. *What about Daddy Daycare? Don't you think he's hitting that?*

"Hell fucking no! That's my shit. She wouldn't give it away no matter how bad I fucked up." I try to shake that annoying voice right out of my head. In fact, I shake my head so hard, I develop a headache. Briefly, I consider taking another pain pill but change my mind. Hopefully, the fresh air will cleanse my thoughts and ease the pain.

Grabbing my keys, I set my alarm and jump in the car. Again that nagging voice whispers to me. *You know Leah is going to let your ass have it for taking the kids to Tarcia's. How ya gonna handle that, player?*

"Shut the fuck up. Ain't nobody ask you a damn thang." I gun the engine and jump on 285 headed to The Shane Company. After all, diamonds are a girl's best friend. Leah's first ring wouldn't even compare to the ring I plan on buying her this time. I turn up the radio and try to think pleasant thoughts as I fight the afternoon traffic.

"Don't these motherfuckers have jobs?" I say, slamming my hand down on the steering wheel, willing them to get out of my way. I turn widely into the mall parking lot and hastily look for a parking spot. Again that voice speaks up. *Dude, do you think Leah is stupid? Ain't it a little late for a ring? I'll bet she been hanging out with that Craig guy and that's why she hasn't been home every time you do a drive-by. Are you sure he ain't hitting your pussy?*

"Ugh, shut up, damn it!" I yell. I turn to see if anyone is paying attention to me. Heads turn to face me, but quickly turn away when our eyes meet. I can see eyes stealing glances at me as I stumble through the mall. The pain pills are affecting my equilibrium.

*I have got to get myself together. When she sees this ring she is going to cream her panties and start begging me to give her this dick. Leah always loved this dick and the way I put it down. That much I am sure of.*

An hour later, with the ring safely in my pocket, I drive to Leah's job. I am acting mainly out of fear. I am afraid of what will happen when Leah finds out I left the kids with Tarcia. I cannot tell her that I am slinging drugs and need to reup. I don't want her to find out that I am doing drugs again for fear that she won't allow me to spend time with the kids. I also don't want to mess up any chances of us getting back together. The ring is burning a hole in my pocket and I cannot wait to give it to her.

I am still stunned that Tarcia actually stabbed me. I thought I had that heifer under control, but obviously I was wrong. I should have left that young pussy alone, but my dick has a mind of its own. Don't get me wrong. The shit was good when it was good, but on the back end, I paid a healthy price. The pain in my neck is not worth the pleasure of my dick.

I knew Tarcia was straight-up 'hood when I met her, but she had a booty that went on for days and I just could not resist it. In hindsight, I should have done things differently and remained true to my wife, but shit happens. Now it was up to me to pick up the pieces of our lives and make lemonade out of the lemons I have.

Sweat is pouring from my forehead as I wait in the car. I don't know if it is because of the medication or just plain fear that Leah is going to ignore my ass, or worse than that, clock me upside the uninjured side of my face. I am hoping she will be sympathetic to my injury and show me some love. I don't see Leah's car, but I am not leaving until I show her how much I love her. I didn't count on her boyfriend picking her up from work and it takes me a moment to regroup when I see her getting in his car.

He is not her type. He is a *GQ* wannabe and seems too suave for her. Left with no choice, I follow them. I am prepared to wait until he leaves to present my ring to her. I almost crash into his car when he leans over and kisses her. She is obviously talking and pays no attention to me tailing them. That is my woman and he has no right to put his lips on her. The fact that she is smiling and shit doesn't sit too well with me either.

Something isn't right; they ride right past the center and they don't stop. *Where is he taking her and where the hell are my kids?* I have no choice but to follow them. This shit isn't cool at all. I fight the urge to dial her number because I know she won't answer when she sees my number on her caller ID.

My worst fear is recognized when they pull into a circular driveway. He eases his car into the garage and I lose sight of my wife. *Shit, what do I do now?*

# Tarcia

Finally, I am allowed to talk to a public defender. After being detained for two weeks without the benefit of a single phone call, I am being released on a technicality. They are not going to press charges against me for assaulting an officer as I originally feared. Feeling better than I have since this whole mess started, I walk out of DeKalb County Jail a free woman. They wanted to blame a black man for hitting his wife, but I was defending myself against her.

Regretfully, I say good-bye to Chauncey, but we are going to stay in touch because we still have unfinished business to handle. He gives me a little pink pleather pouch with some instructions to read, but I dare not open it until I am safely out of the jail. It feels good to be in my own clothes again even though they are splattered with dried blood. That jailhouse garb leaves a lot to be desired. The fact that I didn't have anyplace to go and no money to get there doesn't hit me until I get outside.

I haven't felt this alone since my mother passed away. Suppressing a shudder, I walk to the nearest intersection, which is Memorial Drive. I knew I would find a phone there and with any luck, my cousin would accept my collect call. I hadn't talked to her, or anyone else other than Chauncey for that matter, in over two weeks.

I am nervous about placing the call. I'm not ready to hear my cousin tell me she told me so, but since I have no other family in Georgia I don't have any choice but to call her. Kentee, of course, is out of the question, at least until I find out where his head is.

I wait for what seems like an eternity for the call to go through. I start talking the second I hear her voice and do not catch her greeting.

"So what's up, Lorena?"

"Huh?"

"Lorena Bobbitt. Last I heard you were cutting up some shit." She is laughing at my expense.

"Oh, you've got jokes."

"Lighten up, cuz. What else am I to say to you? You've been AWOL for two weeks; the least you could have done was call me."

"I was in jail."

"Stop lying."

"Trust me, I wouldn't lie about something like that. They wouldn't let me call anyone."

"So where you at now? I thought you were somewhere having make-up sex. I didn't know they locked you up."

"I'm standing on Memorial Drive near the jail. Can you come pick me up?"

"Sure, I've got to be at work by four but I'll swing by and get you."

"Thanks, cuz." I hang up the phone. Questions swirl through my mind, but I am so tired I don't have the energy to ask them. I will wait until after I've taken a bath before I try to find out what has been happening while I was locked up. At least my cousin had enough tact not to try to chastise me over the phone.

The little pouch that Chauncey gave me is itching against my skin. I had tucked it into the waistband of my pants. I still don't know exactly what it contains, but he made me promise to wait until I get settled before I open it. He called it a gris-gris bag. I recall his parting words to me as he leaned in close and whispered in my ear.

"*Don't play* with what you don't understand. This magic is potent, so don't open it until you are sure you intend to have this man Kentee in your life. Cleanse yourself. I've written down everything you need to do. Follow my instructions to the letter and tell no one of the gris-gris you have received. Do you understand?"

I nodded, not trusting my voice to answer. He was scaring me. "I've put you on my list of visitors. Come see me in a week and bring the stuff I asked for in the letter. Remember, trust no one." I am awakened from my trance-like state by the honking of a horn. Lasonji is laying on the horn and waving at me impatiently to get in the car. Traffic is stopped behind her and Memorial Drive is not the place to start a backup.

"Damn, girl, are you going to get in the car or hold up the pole?"

"My bad. I wasn't paying attention."

"No shit. You were in a zone." Relieved to be off the street, I get in her car. She looks me up and down and shakes her head.

"Please don't say I told you so. I've had a rough time."

"I won't. I was worried about you. I got back to your apartment right after they took you away. The neighbors said you freaked out and attacked Kentee, but I didn't know it was serious enough that they kept you in jail all this time."

"Hold up, you weren't looking for me? What's up with that? I could've been dead."

"True, but you could've been off minding your business and

expecting me to mind mines. Did Kentee press charges against you?"

"No, my lawyer said he didn't, but in cases like this it's up to the arresting officer to decide what to do with you. I probably would have been released sooner if I hadn't assaulted an officer." I rest my head against the window. I am so tired and happy to finally be able to let my guard down.

"You did what?" Lasonji hits the brakes so fast I almost bump my head on the dash. I hadn't buckled up, but I quickly secure my seatbelt after that.

"It's a long story and I promise to fill you in but I need to take a bath and change my clothes if I have any left."

"Okay, I won't give you the third degree right now. The fire destroyed the kitchen and the living and dining rooms. I was able to get all of our clothes and some of the furniture out of the bedrooms. I had to throw away both mattresses because they smelled of smoke. I also managed to get an apartment right down the street, so you can bunk with me for a change."

"You did all of this in two weeks?"

"I didn't have much choice. I didn't want to waste all my money staying in a hotel and I'd planned on getting an apartment anyway. The fire just sped up the process."

"Damn. My, have the tables turned." Here I am again with my life in the toilet.

"Do you want to go get your car first, because I have to be at work in a few hours and I don't want you to be stranded if you don't have to be."

"Shit, I need my car, but I need a bath more. I can't stand the smell of blood and it's just going straight to my nose right about now. Can I take a quick shower and still get to my car?"

"Yeah, but we'll have to hurry."

I like her apartment community immediately. If the inside looks as nice as the outside, I know I will enjoy staying with her.

"Hey, nice place."

"Thanks. I'm month to month right now. I really want to buy something soon, but I didn't want to rush into a house purchase that I would later regret."

"Dayum, cuz. You got it like that?"

"What? Just because I crashed with you, you thought I was broke?"

"Naw, I didn't think you were broke. I just never expected you to land on your feet so fast."

"So I guess that means you didn't have a contingency plan. Did you at least have insurance on your apartment?" I don't bother to answer as I follow her up the stairs.

"The bathroom is down the hall. I put your clothes in bags, but I haven't washed them yet. I'll give you a pair of sweats to wear until you can figure out what you got. Some towels are in the linen closet."

I follow the hallway, unbuttoning my shirt as I go. The gris-gris started to heat up as soon as I walked into the apartment and I can't wait to get it off of me. Before it was itching, but now it is actually burning me. Grabbing a towel, I shut the door and immediately strip. I don't look at myself in the mirror until I am completely naked.

I am shocked by my appearance. I look as if I have aged five years. I have bags under my eyes and my cheeks appear sunken. I lean closer to the mirror looking for answers. Lasonji's voice comes through the door.

"I put the clothes on the bed to the left. Let's try to get out of here in the next fifteen minutes, okay?"

"Okay." Tearing myself away from the mirror, I turn on the

water. The shower is refreshing, and I have to stop myself from getting carried away. I turn off the water and quickly dry off. Rushing from the bathroom, I quickly put on the clothes Lasonji has laid out for me. She has my bedroom furniture and I am pleased to see my purse on the nightstand. I put the gris-gris in the nightstand drawer. I wouldn't have time to deal with it until I get back to the apartment anyway.

Swinging my purse over my shoulder, I meet Lasonji in the hallway. "Alright, I'm ready."

"Thanks, it ain't much, but it will do for now." She could have rubbed it in my face and I am grateful she didn't. I've worked most of my adult life and I barely have a pot to piss in or a window to throw it out of. Lasonji hands me a key and I slide it on my keychain. I like my humble pie served hot and right now I am feeling a little cold.

We drive to my place in silence because I really don't know what to say. I mean, I have no plan or backup plan. Now, not only am I out of a job, I have no place that I can call my own.

"I don't get off until midnight. There's some leftover pasta salad in the refrigerator if you want it and feel free to help yourself to anything you need. We have a washer and dryer, so you can wash your clothes. Sorry I couldn't do it for you."

"You've done enough already."

"I left the phone number on the kitchen counter. I looked for your cell phone, but I couldn't find it."

"I had it with me, but the battery died. I'm just glad you were able to get my purse."

"You were lucky. Your apartment got the most smoke damage but the apartment downstairs suffered water damage and they weren't able to recover much of their belongings, if anything."

"Did they say what caused the fire?" I knew but I was wondering if anyone was pointing the finger at Kentee's child.

"I didn't stick around to ask. Folks were kinda upset so I just grabbed what I could and got the hell on."

"Can't say I blame them. I'm still pissed off my damn self." When we arrive at my apartment, the windows on the front of the building are boarded up and I want to cry just looking at it. My hand stalls before opening the door.

"Are you going to be alright?"

"Yeah, it's just strange looking at this in the light of day. I'll see you later, and thanks again."

"Shit, that's what family is for." She kisses me on the cheek as I give her a hug. I'm not used to accepting kindness even if it is from my family.

# Kentee

I turn my phone off cause the last thing I need is for that crazy-ass Tarcia to call while I am trying to win back my wife. I had not planned on begging for a second chance in front of ole dude but I am willing to do whatever I have to do to get my family back.

I hate that I am gonna lose my fuck partner, but I am tired of Tarcia's shit and want the stability that Leah provided. She is such a good woman, I have a hard time believing that I fucked up so bad with her. That was never my intent. Sucking up all the pride I can muster, I knock on the door. Craig answers and by the look on his face, he seems to be expecting me.

"Hold on a second." He closes the door in my face without inviting me in. A few seconds later, Leah comes out and she looks beautiful. I have to stop myself from pulling her into my arms and never letting her go.

"What are you doing here?" She hisses at me as if I've lost my damn mind.

"I had to see you and since you would not return my phone calls, I followed you from work."

"Did it ever occur to you that I didn't want to take your phone calls?"

"Leah, cut the shit, I've got a right to see my children and know where they are."

"Don't you come over to my house talking about your rights after what you put our children through!" Her voice is shrill and rising. I knew she was going to be mad, but I wasn't prepared for this she-devil before me. She is so mad, I completely miss what she says.

"I know I fucked up, but I can explain."

"Save it, Kentee. You knew the rules when I left the children with you. The fact that you ignored them is the only thing I care about." Sensing this spiraling out of control, I pull my ace in the hole out of my pocket, wanting to shock her with a little bling-bling. I open the top, anticipating that she will smother me with kisses and tears. Boy, am I wrong. She laughs.

"What's that for?" She is laughing hysterically.

"Uh, it's for you. I want us to try this again and this time, I promise I'll get it right. Tarcia and I are through and I just want my family back."

The door is snatched open and ole dude comes out to see if everything is okay. He places his arm around my wife and I want to slug him. "Is everything okay, sweetheart?"

She doesn't answer him, she just points to my ring like I'd pulled it out of a box of Cracker Jacks. That's when I notice the rings she is wearing. She is not only wearing an engagement ring, she has the wedding ring to match. I feel like someone has their hands around my lungs and is squeezing the air out of them. Surely she can't be married; this has to be some kind of sick joke.

"Craig and I are married."

Not only am I feeling like an ass, I look like one as well. If it wasn't such a punk thing to do, I would faint. Why didn't I just wait to spring the ring on her? At least I would have kept some of my dignity, but that phat-ass ring she is sporting makes mine look like a chip.

"Oh, I see. I guess you didn't think it was important enough to tell me about."

"Frankly, Kentee, what I do is really none of your business. Now if you'll excuse me, we have some other things that we need to be attending to." They turn as a couple to go inside, leaving my dumb ass with my mouth hanging open.

"What about the kids?"

She turns back to me as Craig goes in the house. "What about them?"

"When can I see them?"

"When you arrange through the courts to have supervised visitation. You will not put my babies at risk again." She turns and closes the door in my face. Damn, what could I say? I brought this shit all on myself. I want to knock on the door and demand to see my children, but I don't want them to see me like this. I feel as if the carpet has just been pulled from under my feet, landing me on my ass.

Losing Leah was never really an option to me. Because she allowed me to get away with my dirt before, I assumed she would let me get away with it again and again. Now, I've lost any chance of winning her back. Craig looked as if he was there to stay. And what exactly does *supervised visitation* mean? I don't have the money to hire a lawyer, but I am not ready to give up on my children. Defeated, I walk back to my car. Tears run unchecked down my face. What am I going to do now?

*I told you she was giving up the pussy.* That voice is back in my head, only louder. I don't bother to tell it to shut up because this time, it is right.

## Tarcia

**F**ishing my phone from my purse, I plug it in to charge. I'd thought Kentee would have at least called to check on me, but I don't have any new messages. Nine times out of ten, he is sniffing behind Leah's ass and isn't thinking about me.

I quickly leave the parking lot and the bad memories it holds for me. I check my wallet and lucky for me I still have money in it, so I stop at McDonald's for a Quarter Pounder with cheese. After eating prison food for the past few weeks, I am in need of a real grease fix and no one does it better than Mickey D's.

After eating, I drive back to Lasonji's to see how much of my life she was able to salvage. Since the bag still smells of smoke, I don't dump it on the bed. Surprisingly, much of my clothing is there. After putting the first load in the washer, I retrieve my instructions from Chauncey. He'd written:

*"Put the gris-gris that I gave you in a secret place that no one will find. You cannot—and I repeat, you cannot—use it right now. Place it inside two socks, one black, one white, in that order, and store in a dark place. Remember, if it's discovered or used before its time, the power will be destroyed.*

*Are you alone? If not, do not go further. You must be very focused when you deal in Magick. If your thoughts are unclear, you will get* mixed results, so concentrate. We are going to start with a simple money spell. Follow my instructions to the letter and remain focused. I can't say this to you enough.

You will need a blank deposit slip, honey, a green candle, a toenail clipper, sugar, sage, and a few strands of your hair from a brush—not a comb—and a black cup. Hopefully you have all these items at home but you will have to do some shopping later as you learn more.

Mix a pinch each of sugar and sage together, using a burnt end of a toothpick to stir. Add a teaspoon of honey to make a paste. Write the amount of money you would like to receive on the deposit slip. Don't be greedy. Add hair and toenail to paste and spread it over the deposit slip. Light the candle and burn the deposit slip in a black cup until only the ashes remain. Wipe ashes over your breasts. Do not bathe for twenty-four hours.

The hardest part of Magick is patience. The fastest way to kill a spell is through obsession and impatience. Money is not going to float out of the sky, so don't expect it. Come see me in four days.

Chauncey

Damn, his handwriting is tight. If I didn't know he was gay, this handwriting would have clued me in. People don't take the time to write like that anymore. Despite feeling utterly ridiculous while performing the spell, I do everything Chauncey told me to do. Luckily, Lasonji had everything I needed, including the green candle, which I will replace when I go to the store. While I wait to put in my second load, I make a laundry list of things that I need to do, which includes going back to my old apartment and checking the mail.

I don't feel comfortable in Lasonji's apartment when she isn't here. I feel like I am being nosey as I peep around. I didn't pay much attention to the décor when I first arrived, but now that I have some time on my hands I am able to inspect things more closely. She has furnished the entire apartment, including a new bedroom suite for herself. Briefly, I wonder what happened to my old set, but I have enough on my plate without worrying about trivial shit.

After a cursory inspection, I check the floors and walls for weird markings. I know I am being hypocritical by accepting Chauncey's use of black magic while frowning on my cousin's use of it. It should be the other way around since I know very little of Chauncey and Lasonji is blood. But I can't help it. I intend to keep that part of my life out of the limelight and if things go the way I've planned, she will never find out. Finding no evidence of Magick, I grab my keys off the table next to the door. I want to check the mail and stop by the post office to put in a change of address. With any luck, an unemployment check is waiting on me and possibly some responses to the resumes I'd sent out. Since the tables have turned and I am now living with my cousin, I want to get a job in the worst way, so I can escape.

I am trying to keep from calling Kentee. But the reality is, with the exception of Lasonji, I don't have anyone else that I talk to. Prior to being locked up, I never missed the company of another woman, but I got spoiled by the late-night talks with Chauncey.

Despite our obvious differences, I am looking forward to Chauncey's getting out and being able to develop a real friendship for a change. Besides, he gave me some pretty good advice regarding men that I can't wait to put into motion.

I manage to slip into my apartment building and collect my mail without running into any of my neighbors. I'm so relieved that I don't check it until I get to the gas station around the corner. Unfortunately, there are no answers to my job search, but I do have two checks from unemployment.

Filling up my tank, I quickly finish my errands and head back home. I am anxious to at least try some agencies to get a job. The chump change from unemployment will keep me with food and gas for at least a little while. There is also a letter from the apartment management office. This one is making me nervous, but it will have to wait until I get home.

# Leah

"Well, that went well," Craig says as he stands behind me massaging my shoulders. His hands feel good and I roll my neck in appreciation of his strong touch.

"Hmm," I murmur. Craig leads me over to the sofa and pulls me onto his lap.

"Tell me how you are feeling." Instinctively, I tense up because I'm not used to sharing my innermost thoughts, but his gentle but firm pressure on my neck and back soothes my muscles.

"Honestly, I don't know how I feel. I mean, I'm glad that he knows that it's over. I've wanted to tell him for some time, but didn't want to fight with him. So in that respect, I'm glad it's over."

His hands pause for a few seconds as he releases a heavy sigh. "Do you still have feelings for him?" Craig's voice was so low, I almost didn't hear him.

"Yeah, I do." His hands stop moving altogether and I can feel him holding his breath. "Pity."

"Pity? I don't understand."

"There are few things in life that you get for free. The love of a child is one of them. You don't have to work for it, it's given freely and you have to be almost subhuman to fuck that up." Craig's arms tighten around me, pulling me closer to his chest.

"Ah, I can see that."

"Kayla will probably always love her dad because she remembers when he was attentive and showed genuine interest in her, but the twins didn't have that kind of love from him. He used them as pawns to get to me."

"Funny, I thought I was the only one who saw it that way."

"I guess we didn't really talk about this before. Did you really think Kentee had fooled me?"

"Well, *fooled* isn't the word I would chose, more like *blinded*."

"*Blinded*? Now I don't understand."

"Well...I know how important it was to you that their father be in the children's life. I thought you would sacrifice yourself for the sake of your children."

Turning to face my husband, I throw my arms around his neck. "Oh sweetheart, from the moment I met you, I fell in love. The happiest day of my life was when you said you loved me too. I did what I had to for the sake of the kids, but I would never ever turn my back on a gift from God and that is the way I think of you."

Craig's eyes water, but his eyes tell me how happy I've made him. "Woman, if you don't get up now, we'll never get those kids of ours to bed."

"I know that's right. I'll start dinner if you help with homework."

"Deal, and after we finish with the kids, I've got a few things to show you myself."

"I'll bet you do." I switch off to the kitchen secure in the love of my man. It is truly a wonderful feeling.

# Kentee

I feel like I am standing in a field full of shit and the stench of reality is burning the hairs in my nose. I can't blame anyone but myself. As much as I want to hate Leah for moving on with her life, I can't. It was time for a real reality check and not one painted with rose-colored glasses.

I drive home in a semi-daze, barely aware of the traffic and the changing lights. I want to end the pain, but I know that until I straighten out the mess that I've made of my life, I will continue on the same vicious path. It isn't often that I allow myself to be totally honest, but I am going to do it today. My life depends on it.

For the first time in months, I go to my apartment instead of crashing wherever my body fell out. Although it isn't much, it is mine and it is the only place that I can go to really be alone. I rented the apartment when I realized life with Tarcia wasn't going to work. Basically, she was a good woman although a little rough around the edges. All she ever wanted was someone to love her unconditionally, and I used her.

The ring I bought Leah feels like a lead weight as I pull it out of my pocket and place it on my dresser.

*Well, I guess she told your ass.* Looking into the mirror, I don't like the man whom I see. My eyes reflect the pain of knowing that

Leah is sleeping with another man. I feel violated just thinking of her allowing some other man into my space. I shed each item of clothing that I am wearing. I don't ever want to see this outfit again because it would only serve to remind me of what a total ass I made of myself.

Throwing the jeans and shirt into the trash, I walk around the apartment naked, pausing to turn on some music. I pour myself a shot of Remy Martin. I'm not ready to talk with a lawyer, but I vow to do it because despite my actions, I really do want a relationship with my children.

Flexing my neck, I wince in pain. Although it is healing nicely, this is yet another reminder of how I've fucked up my life. In retrospect, I don't blame Tarcia for stabbing me. If the shoe was on the other foot, I would have hurt me too. When I got to her house, the only thing I was thinking of was saving my own black ass. For that, I owe her an apology. Without giving myself a chance to change my mind, I call her cell, hoping she will pick up but not really expecting her to.

"Hello?" I don't detect the anger I expect to hear in her voice.

"Hey, Tarcia, it's me, Kentee. Just checking to make sure you're okay."

"I'm fine, thanks for calling."

"Wait, don't hang up."

"What?" Attitude is sprouting wings and I am determined to nip it in the bud.

"I owe you an apology. I've treated you very badly and I want to say I'm sorry."

"Look, Kentee, I'm not up for your games, okay?"

"Tarcia, I'm not playing with you. I mean every word. I know I've been shady in the past, but this time, I'm being real. You had every right to stab me and lucky for me, your aim was whack." I chuckle, but she doesn't laugh with me.

"Well, alright then." I could tell she was about to hang up.

"Look, I know you ain't trusting me right about now and I can't say I blame you, but for once I ain't running game. Can we get together to talk?"

"I don't know about that. I ain't trying to go back to jail."

"Jokes, I guess I deserve that one. But seriously, can we meet at Starbucks over coffee? If you don't like what I'm saying, you can bounce."

"Uh…I have a lot of things that I have to do."

"Please, I promise I won't keep you long." I hadn't originally planned on seeing Tarcia again, but something tells me that it is the right thing to do. If she sees me, I am convinced she will believe me.

"When?"

"Now. Where are you? Do you want me to pick you up?"

"No, I'll drive. I'm in Stone Mountain."

"There's a Starbucks on Highway Seventy-Eight, I can be there in an hour."

"Okay, but I ain't staying long."

"Cool. Thanks." I hang up the phone, happy at least to be given the chance to make amends. I dress quickly while I still have the courage. Facing my mistakes is not one of my strong suits unless I have an ulterior motive. For once, my apologies will not be sugar-coated with flowers and gifts. This time, my intentions are good.

## *Tarcia*

I cannot believe what just occurred. The entire time I was in jail, all I could think of was Kentee. I couldn't wait to get out so I could speak with him and now that I have, I don't feel a thing. Sure, I am going to meet with him, but I'm not holding onto any expectations. I only want to hear what he has to say so I can move on with my life.

I bump my hair, but otherwise I do not bother to beautify myself. Lucky for me, the black eye is gone as well as the other evidence of my jailhouse abuse. I feel as if I have done enough for Kentee; now he will have to take me as I am. I drive to the coffee shop with mixed emotions. I'm not going to say that I don't still love Kentee, but I am having my doubts as to whether I am in love with him. Chauncey was right about one thing — I need to get my life in order and the job starts and ends with me.

Kentee is already inside when I arrive. I am hesitant to approach him, especially after I see the large bandage on his neck. Despite all the pain he caused me, I really didn't mean to hurt him.

"Hi, thanks for coming."

I don't reply. I just take a seat.

"Can I get you something? I'm having a Caramel Frappuccino."

"That sounds good." He rises from the table to get my drink.

I can't help but to steal a look at his tight ass. My indifference aside, Kentee is still a fine-looking man, especially without the bullshit and swagger.

"You look good," he says as he sits back down, handing me my drink. I shrug my shoulders; his comment doesn't need a reply. I am anxious to get the reason for the face-to-face meeting.

"Kentee, I have a lot of things to do, so if you don't mind, can we cut to the chase?"

"Uh…yeah. Sorry about that. I was trying to decide where to begin." Again, I don't respond.

"Look, I asked you here to apologize for all the shit I put you through. I made a mess out of both our lives and I'm sorry." I am starting to get upset. I didn't interrupt my day to hear this same old shit. I can tell he means what he is saying, but it is too little too late as far as I am concerned.

"Okay, you said it. Thanks for the drink." I get up to leave.

"Wait, I'm not finished. Why you keep trying to rush off? You got a hot date or something?"

"For your information, I just got out of jail this morning and I'm trying to put the pieces of my life back together."

"Are you shittin' me? That was over two weeks ago."

"I don't need you to remind me. I was there."

"Oh, my bad. I just didn't know. I thought they would release you immediately."

"So I guess that means you didn't check on me." That realization hurts me more than anything. Regardless of how mad I was at him, I still worried about him. This admission is like a slap in the face. Rising again, I attempt to get away from the table before I allow him to see how much he's hurt me.

"Tarcia, please don't go. I know I hurt you. Can you just give me thirty minutes?"

Resigned, I hold up my watch. I will give him the time, but no more.

"When we first got together, I was hurting. Not physically, but mentally and spiritually. My marriage was going downhill and I wasn't getting the attention that I needed at home."

"Yeah, that would be the marriage that you failed to mention, right?" He shakes his head. Again I want to leave as my old wounds open but I am determined to give him his thirty minutes and not a minute more.

"You're right, but it's deeper than that. I didn't embrace fatherhood as I should have and was even jealous of my children. When we found out about Mya's disability, I denied both of them and started stepping out in my marriage. How could I admit to you I was married, but deny my children? So I lied and it was eating me up inside."

"Humph, could've fooled me." The comment slips out before I have a chance to stop it.

"I deserved that, but hear me out. I'm trying to do the right thing." I nod my head.

"When you got pregnant, I had to make a decision. Either run again or do the right thing, which I thought at the time was to marry you. I should have been a man, admitted to being married and waited until the divorce was final, but I didn't. I didn't want to lose you so I concocted that story about Leah lying about the divorce. I wanted you to hate her so you wouldn't question the lies I told you. But she is innocent in this."

*Oh, so now he is going to defend that bitch on my dime? Oh, hell to the fucking no! Every time I give this nigga an inch he takes a country mile. Well, I am through with that shit once and for all. He can kiss my natural black ass.*

In my haste to get up, I knock over my chair. Kentee bolts from his seat, grabbing my arm. Misunderstanding his intention, I swing at him, clocking him upside the head. The blow stuns him, and hurts the hell out of my arm, but he gets my point.

"I didn't come here to discuss your wife."

"Neither did I. I wish I could tell you it was just about you and me but that would be a lie. Could you please sit down and let me finish?" I want to bolt because I have a feeling that I will be hearing more things that I don't want to hear. But against my better judgment, I sit.

"Thank you. As I was saying, she is innocent and so were you, up to a point."

"What's that supposed to mean?"

"I know you lied about the baby." Busted. I have two choices, either shut up or deny it. When I don't deny it, he continues.

"Once that cat was out of the bag, I used Leah to control both of you. I figured that as long as you hated each other, there was little chance of me getting caught trying to have my cake and eat it too." He stops talking, forcing me to look at him. My eyes hold many questions to which only he holds the answers, so I allow him to continue.

"Imagine my surprise when I found out you two were working at the same company. Life is funny that way. It has a way of forcing you to accept things even though you don't want to. I used to see Leah when I stopped by your job and I'll admit I started to regret ever leaving. By then, you were sick of my shit anyway and all we did was argue. So I started staying out all night. I wanted you to think I was with her and when she came in with a smile on her face, I wanted you to think I put it there."

I am amazed because his plan worked perfectly. I fell for the whole plan—hook, line, and sinker. He played us both and if he'd kept his mouth shut, he would have gotten away with it.

"So one day I followed her. I found out where she lived and I got to see my kids. With the exception of Kayla, they were strangers to me but what hurt me the most was seeing the way this dude from the school was looking at my ex-wife. I believed my own hype and thought I could have you both. So I start spending time with my kids and you resented that. Little things began to add up and I was falling behind financially, with the child support and shit. I wanted to go home just to keep some of my check in my pocket."

Wow, I can feel his sincerity. How come he never opened up to me like this before? I would have accepted it better than all the lies and deceit. I mean, I wasn't without sin either. In the beginning I was using him too, and unfortunately I fell in love with him. So where does that leave us now?

"Thank you for sharing."

"Are you being sarcastic?"

"No, I'm not. I really mean it. Just think how different things would have been if we'd just been honest with each other."

"Ain't that the truth?"

I waited for him to go on but it seemed like he was finished. I glance at my watch and realize he has used his allotted time. Noticing my stare, he gathers our cups. When he gets back to the table I asked the question that has been worrying me.

"So what now? Are you going back to your wife?" I was standing at this point, ready to walk out with him. I felt relieved and slightly annoyed that it took this long for us to finally talk.

"Don't know. Going back ain't an option. She got married." I sit back down. There was no way I was going to leave until I had every last detail.

"Say what?"

"Yeah, she married that guy who runs the school. Told me I

couldn't see my kids unless it was under court supervision. I sure have made a mess, haven't I?"

He ain't even lied. As much as I wanted Leah out of his life, I couldn't stand to see him hurting. Somehow, I fight the urge to hold him because by his own omission, he brought this shit on himself.

"Wow, I guess I played a role in this since they were with me when the fire started."

"Thanks, but I won't let you share the blame. Once again, I wasn't being responsible. I'm just happy you allowed me the opportunity to explain it to you. Honestly, I feel much better just admitting to my mistakes."

"Then maybe there's some merit in the saying 'The truth will set you free.'"

He walks me to my car and holds the door open for me. I'm not sure how to end this little tell-all conversation, so I let him make the first move. He kisses me on the cheek.

"Can I still call you?"

"I'd like that." I start my car and drive away. He is still standing in the parking lot when I look in my rearview mirror. His confessions leave me with no one left to hate. Imagine that.

"I can't wait to tell Chauncey this."

# *Jasmine*

Today is the day they are going to take my sister off the medication that has been keeping her in a coma for the past month. They removed the respirator earlier in the week and we were all surprised when she began to breathe on her own. Now she is facing the final test of whether or not she wants to wake up.

Her brain has shown no activity for quite some time and it is anyone's guess as to what will happen once the medication has worn off.

Buddy and I have been taking turns staying with Sammie, each of us afraid that she would wake up alone and decide to give up the fight. He took the morning shift while I stayed with her at night. Buddy, bless his heart, has dropped at least ten pounds and his eyes have what appears to be permanent circles under them. If I had any doubts about the depth of his love for my sister, they are gone now.

Tyson came and spent a few days with us, but he has a family that needs him, so he could not stay. He has grown into a fine young man and I am proud to call him my nephew. The look on his face when he first laid eyes on me was classic and if not for the gravity of the situation, it would have been funny. He vowed to stay in contact with me and true to his word, calls every other day to check on me and his mother.

I started doing exercises with Sammie the day she was admitted to the hospital. The doctor said that if she regains consciousness, she will have to undergo therapy to get her body toned up. These exercises will help with her recovery so I spend about two hours a day pumping her arms and legs. Buddy doesn't mention it, but I am sure he has been doing the same thing. Through it all, Sammie does not seem to notice.

Sometimes the four walls get to me and during these times I sit in the waiting room. The interaction with other family members helps to alleviate some of the boredom. I have been a fixture at the hospital for so long, they have given up on trying to make me go home. In fact, I think they are beginning to like having me around. I do everything for Sammie except for administering medicine so they have more time to attend to other things. In fact, I am seriously considering going back to school for nursing.

I am on my second cup of coffee when Buddy comes in the room.

"What are you doing here?" This is the only time that he gets to sleep and I am worried about him.

"I just left the club and thought I'd stop by to see if there was any change."

"Buddy, you should be sleeping. If those circles under your eyes get any darker, folks are going to start calling you Panda."

"Ha, ha. That is so funny."

"I'm sorry, Buddy, but you do need to start taking better care of yourself."

"Look who's talking. You spend as much time in this camp as I do."

"Yeah, but I ain't holding down a full-time job. At least I do go home and try to get some rest."

"I get rest, but I wanted to be here just in case..." I know exactly what he means. They gave Sammie the last dose of medicine at four o'clock. The doctor didn't tell us when we could expect her to start responding, so tonight is particularly tense.

"I'm glad you came. When she wakes up, I want her to see your face." He smiles at me and edges his chair closer to the bed. "Do you want me to get you some coffee? I just put on a fresh pot in the nursing station."

"Damn, you taking over in this piece?" We laugh and it feels good.

"Naw, it ain't like that, but those ladies know that I'm not a nice person without my cup of java and if they have to look at my ass all night, they would want me to be nice."

"I know that's right. I'd hate to see you stab somebody up in here with one of those needles."

"Well, I wouldn't be that mean, but I'd run a close second." We sit in silence for a few more minutes.

"Are you sure you're going to be able to handle this?" I ask him.

"I'll be okay. I just want her to wake up, man."

"It's not going to be pretty, that's why I asked them to do it at night. We don't know if she is in any pain, so she may go into shock when her body starts to react to not getting the drugs."

"Seriously, I don't know how I'm going to handle it. We'll just have to see. I just know it would've been worse not knowing."

He has a point. I might have to leave the room myself, but I had to be here. The plan was to stop all medication and, if she woke, to give her just enough to mask the pain until they can find out what her capabilities are. My biggest fear is that she will be brain dead. I can deal with her not walking or talking, but it will kill me if she has to live the rest of her life as a vegetable.

I go to get us coffee, stretching my back in the process.

"Hey, girl, any change?" asks Alita, one of the nurses with whom I had struck up a friendship. She is a down-to-earth sista who pulls no punches and tells it like it really is. She is the one to tell me honestly what to expect if Sammie comes around.

"Naw, not yet." I don't know whether to be happy or sad about it.

"Try not to worry too much. She's in the best hands."

"Hey, I hear ya. From your mouth to God's ears." We shoot the breeze for a few more minutes until she has to answer a flashing light.

"Duty calls, but if you need me, holla."

"Thanks." I manage to get back to Sammie's room without spilling a drop of coffee out of either cup. I use my back to push open the door while handing off the cup to Buddy. I can tell from the look on his face there has been no change.

We settle into a comfortable silence, born from years of knowing each other's habits. He is lying back in his chair with his feet up on the bed, me trying to get as comfortable as I can in the other chair. Although I could have stretched out on the other bed, I want to be on the ready if something happens.

I'm not sure at what point I fell asleep, but I can tell you with absolute certainty when I woke up. It is three forty-five in the morning and all hell is breaking loose. Sammie is bucking off the bed as if she is being fed a live electrical current. Every limb of her body is twitching and jerking. The IV bottle suspended over her bed is threatening to topple with each movement.

Snatched from my dreams, I try to make sense out of what I am seeing. Buddy is trying his best to hold Sammie down, but she is challenging his strength. I don't have to ask him what is happening—I know.

"Did you ring in yet?"

"I can't get to it." The buzzer has gotten tangled in the sheets and while we can see the cord, we cannot get it from underneath Sammie.

"Fuck it." I snatch open her door and yell as loud as I can.

"We need some help in here, code blue." I had heard the term enough during my days and nights at the hospital. I just never thought I would be calling it for my sister.

Still leaning out the door, I snap commands to Buddy.

"Talk to her, Buddy. She can hear you. Don't let her go!"

"I said I need help, damn it." Nurses emerge from rooms; the crash cart is rolling as the hospital comes alive. I hold the door, open partly because I am afraid to see what is going on, but mostly to monitor their progress. They were taking too long. Tears are streaming down my face and I make no attempt to wipe them. Behind me, I can hear Buddy urging Sammie to live.

She stops bucking and my heart skips a few beats.

"Oh no," I yell. Hands pull me out of the room. Blindly, I allow myself to be led down the hall to the waiting room. Buddy is there holding me. I feel so cold and empty. Even though I knew this could happen, I am not prepared for the reality.

"Oh, sweet Jesus, no."

"She's in God's hands now." *What the hell is he talking about? I don't want to hear that shit. That's my sister.* I search Buddy's face. His eyes, once shrunken and small, are now wild and fixed and his face is pale. We cling to each other, each lost in our own misery. I can't tell which of us is shaking more.

"It isn't supposed to be this way. It isn't…" I can't finish my sentence; my cries prevent it. For the second time in my life, someone I love is ripped from my arms. It hurts so badly.

# *Kentee*

Things went a lot better than I'd anticipated. I was expecting her to start clowning, especially when she realized that I'm interested in pursuing a relationship with her. I am just happy that we will be able to remain friends. This is something that I would never have imagined would be possible with Tarcia since she is an all-or-nothing type of person.

"Maybe she had a life-altering experience in jail like I did." The thought of some butch rolling up on Tarcia sends a shiver down my spine.

"Naw, that didn't happen 'cause Tarcia would have lost her damn mind and whooped a heifer's ass." I can see that picture a lot more clearly. In fact, Tarcia probably butched up just to endure the two weeks she was locked up. I owe her for that because if it weren't for me, she wouldn't have been there. Not to mention the fact that she no longer has a place she can call her own.

This new Tarcia is an enigma. She isn't needy, belligerent, or hostile. In fact, she didn't even bother to tell me where she is living or offer me her new number. *Could it be that she has moved on as well and isn't telling me? Hell, Leah blindsided me, so why not Tarcia?*

*Should I ask her? What if she asks to move in with me? Are you ready for that, player?"*

I shake my head, trying to clear out the unwanted voices chattering inside.

*What you need, player, is some tits and ass to get your mind off your problems.*

I don't want to listen to that voice because it is the same voice that got me in trouble time and time again. Accepting the stupidity of my ways isn't an easy pill to swallow. For so long I believed that I was in complete control of my life, but in reality I was a fool. My heart is heavy. I'm not sure what changes I am going to make, but something has to give because this shit isn't working.

# *Tarcia*

I sit at the kitchen table, determined to talk to Lasonji today if it kills me. Even though we share an apartment, I never get to see her and I want to make sure that she isn't spending an inordinate amount of time away from home because of me. Since she works at night and I now work during the day doing different jobs for Chauncey, we are like two ships passing. On the weekends I usually have the place to myself and as much as I enjoy the privacy, it is starting to unnerve me. So instead of going to bed at a reasonable hour so I can be bright eyed and bushy tailed in the morning, I wait up for her.

I don't get nervous until I hear her key in the door. I am going to tell her I am moving out and for some reason I am scared to do it. I mean, I appreciate her being there for me in my time of need, but I'm ready to stand on my own which is something I've never done. Wiping my moistened palms on my pants, I wait until she flips on the light before I speak.

"Hey."

Lasonji practically jumps on the table.

"Damn. Why the hell you sitting in the damn dark? You scared the shit out of me."

"My bad. I guess I dozed off. I was waiting up for you."

"No shit." Slamming her purse on the table, she yanks open the door to the refrigerator, peering inside as if she is looking for something that just isn't there.

"Wow, you in a bad mood or something?"

"No, I just don't like to be scared at one o'clock in the morning."

"Dag, I said I was sorry." I immediately regret waiting up. Pushing in my chair, I decide to wait to talk to her when she is in a better mood. She stops me as I am leaving the kitchen.

"Wait, don't go." She sits down at the table, releasing a long sigh. Her intense gaze scours all words from my brain and I feel like I am standing before her naked. Stumbling to the nearest chair, I grab it for support. Her stare is draining and strangely erotic. The brown of her eyes are flecked with green and I can't tear my own eyes away. Never before have I experienced such a magnetic pull from a woman. This scares the hell out of me because I actually want to kiss her, and not just a "hey cuz" kind of kiss either. I want a full-bodied, passionate kiss complete with tongues dancing and hands groping. I grow dizzy just thinking about it. Now my eyes are glued to her lips. They are sensuous and I want nothing more than to trace them with my own. Stunned by my reaction to her, I want to get as far away as possible before I do something stupid that I will regret later.

"It's okay. I can talk to you this weekend. That catnap took more out of me than I thought." Abruptly, I spin around, needing to get the hell out of the room.

"What's the matter with you? You look as if you saw a ghost."

*She isn't even lying. How can I explain what I saw in her eyes? I can actually see us entwined on the floor and the intense desire is searing a path from my pussy up. I want her so badly, I can taste her. In my mind, I do and my body tingles…*

"Tarcia, I thought you wanted to talk."

Her voice jolts me back to reality. Shaking my head, trying to clear the elixir from my mind, I am baffled by the intensity of the emotions flowing through me. I struggle for something to say that would make any sense.

"Wow, what time is it, anyway?"

"It's one-thirty. Perhaps you should go to bed. You're not looking well at all."

Keeping my eyes on the table to avoid getting caught up in her spell once more, I grab my purse and a balled-up napkin I was fidgeting with before she came home. In my haste, I drop my purse, causing the contents to roll onto the floor.

"Shit." Letting go of the napkin, I gather my personal belongings.

"What the hell is this?"

I have no idea what she is talking about, but I don't want to look in her direction to find out lest I be caught in her spell once more.

"What?"

"This." She is shaking the napkin in my face, as it contains pornographic details of the images I'd just envisioned..

"Oh that? I was just doodling, that's all. Ain't nothing to get your panties in a knot about."

"Where did you see this before?"

"Huh?"

"Damn it, Tarcia. Where did you get this?"

"I told you I drew it."

Spinning on her heels, Lasonji leaves the room mumbling. Forgetting my purse, I start to follow her, but the second she clears the door I can't remember why I would want to. In fact, I have a hard time remembering why I waited up for her in the first place. Stifling a yawn, I go to my room and am about to drift off to sleep when Lasonji switches on my overhead light.

She is holding a small book in her hands that I do not recognize.

"Have you been going through my things?"

"Huh?" I feel like I have pea soup in my brain and her words are not making any sense. Squinting at the alarm clock, I try to make out the time. I've forgotten our previous conversation and I cannot understand why she is in my room so early in the morning.

Lasonji punches me in the arm hard enough to scatter all the dust that has settled in my head.

"What the hell you hit me for?"

"I asked you a question."

"And I was fucking asleep."

"You were just in the fucking kitchen looking like a space cadet."

"No I wasn't."

"Yes you were."

"Fool, you betta stop trippin'. Now would you please shut off my light so I can get to sleep?" I pull up the covers and close my eyes. I am struggling not to get an attitude with her because after all, I am living in her home, but she will not go away. I can feel her staring at me even with my eyes shut.

"What?" I yell, forgetting all attempts to be cool and collected.

"Have you ever seen this before?" She pushes the book so close to my eyes that I have to rise up to see it.

"What the hell is that?"

"You drew it."

"No I didn't."

"Tarcia, you told me you did."

She shoves a napkin with a crude replica of the drawing in my face, but I don't recognize it either. She is starting to freak my ass out again. When it becomes clear that she is very serious I get out of bed.

"Okay, I'm up now. What's this all about?"

Lasonji just stares at me without saying anything for a few minutes. The silence is getting to me.

"You don't remember sitting at the kitchen table talking to me?"

"No."

"Or drawing this picture?"

"No, I can't draw a straight line."

"This is crazy."

"What?"

"When I got home from work, you were sitting in the kitchen in the dark. When I turned on the light you were looking all weird and shit, and when I questioned you, you dropped this napkin. You told me you drew it."

"You're serious, aren't you?"

"About as serious as a heart attack."

"What does it mean?"

"I'm not sure."

"You got any of that green tea? I think it's going to be a long night."

# Tarcia

If memory could be contained in a lightning bolt, one just struck me as I enter the kitchen. My purse is on the floor, my makeup and Life Savers are scattered around it. Vague images bombard my mind. While the drawing now seems familiar, I cannot remember where I'd seen it before tonight.

As I'm picking up my stuff, I start talking.

"I remember waiting for you. I wanted to tell you I would be moving in a few weeks and I didn't want to just leave you a note."

"Did I do something?"

"How could you do something? We never see each other."

"Then why are you leaving?"

"It's time."

I am glad she didn't ask me what it was time for because I honestly don't know. I remember urgently wanting to talk to her about moving, but I can't remember why because our situation is ideal. We are splitting the rent without the normal chaos that comes with two women trying to live under the same roof. So why did I want to leave? I am thinking so hard, I am getting a headache. So rather than dwelling in the past, I change the subject.

"Whatcha been up to? I haven't seen you in about a month; where the hell you been?"

"Working, trying to take care of a little business. What's going on in your world?" She is obviously still thinking about the drawing, but once again it's lost its importance to me.

"Believe it or not, things have been good for a change."

"That's good to hear. We've been passing like ships in the night, I almost forgot you were staying here."

"Who you telling? If it wasn't for the occasional cup in the sink, I'd swear that I am here by myself. You hiding a new man or something?"

"Why does it always have to be about a man with you?"

"Damn, cuz, I didn't mean to strike a nerve, my bad."

"You didn't strike a nerve. I've been back and forth to New Orleans trying to fix up my house."

"Why? You moving back?" The hair on my neck bristles as I brace myself for her answer. I mean, I care and all, but my hands grip my cup hard waiting for her reply.

"To be honest, I don't know. There is grant money available to rebuild, so I'm taking advantage of it. Especially since Spike Lee is rumored to be doing a documentary on the actual events that occurred, I gotta do it."

Relieved, I sit back in my chair.

"Are we going to bullshit each other all night or are you ready to talk to me?"

"I don't know what else to tell you, but that paper is giving me the creeps."

"Ha, you did it." She balls up the paper and throws it in the trash. Frankly, I wanted to burn it, but I feel better now that it is out of sight.

"Listen, it's late. I need to get to bed."

"All right. I'm going to do some research in the morning and see if anything funny shows up."

"Okay, see ya in the morning."

"Oh, how's Kentee?"

I stop dead in my tracks, wondering where that came from. I didn't even think she remembered his name since we hadn't discussed him in quite some time.

"Oh, I guess he's fine."

"Are you two still together?"

"We're still friends, if that's what you mean, but we haven't made any commitments for the future. Why?"

"I was just curious. It's been a minute since we talked so I am trying to catch up."

Muttering good night, I go to my room, but sleep eludes me. I spend the rest of the night tossing and turning with my thoughts flitting from one idea to the next. I cannot get the picture out of my mind, so it is a no-brainer that I would dream about it. But when I awaken, I can't make heads or tails of the dreams. The other thing that confuses the hell out of me is my total lack of feeling toward Kentee. That by itself should send off alarm bells in my head, but I am too tired to think. I can't wait to talk to Chauncey about this latest development. He has become my friend and confidant. I'm looking forward to his early release from jail in the coming weeks.

# *Tarcia*

I sit in the waiting room of DeKalb County Jail for the longest thirty minutes of my life. It isn't enough that I had to be subjected to a pat-down search by an overzealous jailor, I have to sit in the same room with the guy who tried to rape me several months ago. I am disappointed with the penal system for not firing the pervert in the first place, but I have to admit I enjoy seeing his disfigurement. He wears a patch on his left eye and from the way he holds the newspaper so close to his right eye, I could tell it is impaired as well. Serves that fucker right! For three months, he had me scared each time I came to visit the only person who cared about me. That shit is over now.

The first time I came to visit Chauncey and realized who the guard was, I was scared shitless that he would recognize me. However, after several visits, I realize he can't see warts on his own ass, so visiting Chauncey isn't as traumatic as it was in the beginning. The worst part about it is the waiting. If you arrive between shifts, you might have to go to the desk several times before you are allowed to see your inmate. One time, I waited for over three hours only to be told lockdown was in effect and no visitors were allowed.

Finally, I hear my name being called. My gaze shoots to the

guard to see if he recognizes my name, but he doesn't look away from the paper he is struggling to read. Chauncey is led in a few minutes later.

"Hey, chile."

"'Bout time, I've been sitting here for thirty minutes."

"I feel ya, but just remember at the end of the day, you can walk out the door."

"Damn, you got a point. How's it going?"

"Slowly I've been released, but these motherfuckers are holding up my paperwork. I swear, if it wouldn't land me a one-way ticket back to jail, I'd blow this bitch up when I get out."

"I know that's right. Be patient. It's almost over."

"You still going to let me shack with you when they let me go?"

"Yeah, I told my cousin last night that I was going to start looking for my own place."

"Was she upset?"

"Naw, she's cool. She was just surprised because it ain't like I'm in her way or nothing. We hardly ever see each other."

"Did you tell her about me?"

"No, she ain't ready for you."

"What's that supposed to mean?"

"Don't get your panties all twisted. Lasonji is just different, is all. If we weren't related we probably wouldn't even speak to each other."

"Oh, okay. I thought you were going to say she doesn't like jailbirds or something like that." I wave away his comments because I really want to tell him about the drawing.

"Something real strange happened last night."

"Oh yeah?"

"My cousin said I went into a trancelike state and she said I was speaking to her, but I can't remember anything I said. She showed me something that I was drawing, but I don't remember doing it either."

"Show it to me." He leans forward in his chair, pressing his face near the glass.

"I don't have it. She took it last night and when I got up this morning she was gone."

"Well, what was it?" He is still perched on the edge of his chair.

"I don't know. I stayed up half the night thinking about it and today, I can't even tell you what it looked like."

"Then it must not have been important." Chauncey sits back in his chair and begins to examine his nails.

"She seems to think it is. She looked scared when she saw it."

"But you said yourself that she is weird so why you letting that bother you?" Suddenly, the drawing isn't important anymore and I begin to feel foolish for even bringing it up in the first place. Aside from the burning desire to talk to Chauncey about the picture, I don't have anything else left to say.

"So how's that fine Kentee?"

"Oh, he's fine."

"I know that, I saw his picture. Have you seen him again since that time you had coffee with him?"

"Come to think of it, no. I talk to him over the phone, but we haven't connected in person."

"What's up with that?"

"I don't know. Tell you the truth, I haven't even thought about him since the last time I was here. Maybe I'm finally over him."

"You think he's kicking it with someone else?"

"Beats the shit out of me." I am feeling uncomfortable discussing Kentee with Chauncey. I know that he is cool, but today it just doesn't feel right. Since I got out of jail, I had been sending three or four letters to Chauncey a week so he knows every little detail about my relationship with Kentee. I even shared his dick size, something I would not have bragged about to another girlfriend. But Chauncey is more like a big sister and a good luck charm all rolled into one man.

Ever since I met him, my life has changed for the better. I have a good job with benefits, money in my pocket and I'm not living from check to check. In fact, it is Chauncey who told me about renter's insurance. If he hadn't reminded me about that policy I would have never thought to seek a claim for the items I lost in the fire. So the way I see it, I owe Chauncey big time and letting him stay with me when he gets released from jail is relatively small by comparison.

"Damn, are you just going to sit there and stare or are you going to speak to me? You know I only get thirty minutes."

"My bad. I was daydreaming."

"No shit."

"So what else has been going on? You didn't mess with that spell I gave you, did you?"

"No, I put it in the closet just like you told me to."

"Good, 'cause if you had tried using it at your cousin's house, he would have broken down the door trying to get at you." I was about to tell him I wasn't interested in that anymore, but the guard stopped all further conversation.

"Hurry up and sign that lease. I'll be out in a couple of days." Chauncey yells this to me over his shoulder as he is being led from the room. Everyone including the guard looks at me and I quickly leave the room feeling as if I am standing naked the whole time. I don't know what it is, but something about the whole jail scene always leaves me feeling downright dirty and I cannot wait to get home to take a shower. I rush out of the building with my eyes glued to the floor. I am moving so fast, you would think I am being chased, but that's just how I feel.

*I sure hope he gets out of there soon 'cause I don't think I will be making too many more trips to that bitch.* I turn my phone on. I'd left it in the car rather than having to run it through the security in the jail. They don't allow camera phones, as if I would be trying to take pictures up in there to send home to my family. What a joke. I guess they have their reasons, but I can't figure out what they are.

Putting the car into reverse, I check both ways before backing up, but am interrupted by my cell phone. I put the car back into park because DeKalb County has just implemented a new law that prohibits driving and talking on the phone. I almost feel like it is a test to see if they can get me back on lockdown.

"Hello?"

"Hey, Tarcia, it's Kentee. What's up?"

"Not much." *Why is he calling me now? I haven't heard from him in weeks and all of a sudden here he is. Did I speak him into existence?*

"Oh, well, I've been thinking 'bout you and I just wanted to check in on you."

"Oh, I'm fine." There are a few seconds of uncomfortable silence.

"So what are you up to? Sounds like you're in the car."

"Yeah, I had a few errands to run. In fact, I'm apartment hunting." *Why the hell did I tell him that? Shit, all I want to do when I leave Chauncey is go home to take a bath.*

"Oh yeah, can I come?"

"Sure." *Whoa, heifer, what the hell are you saying?*

"Where should I meet you?"

"How about I meet you at Starbucks again? I'm not too far from there."

"Cool, I'm on my way." Perplexed, I disconnect the call. It is as if my mouth has a mind of its own and isn't consulting me for anything. Sure, I want to find an apartment, but there is no real urgency. Chauncey has been saying he is going to get out in a few days for the last few weeks. Plus, I haven't decided where I want to live. I sounded like I had a plan over the phone, but if I have one, it is news to me. I start to call him right back, but he called from a private number. I have two choices: go to Starbucks as planned or stand him up. Putting the car back into gear, I proceed to Starbucks on auto pilot.

# Jasmine

"Mom, I don't need you to drive me to the airport. Hell, you'd get lost and I'd worry myself to death about you getting home alone. I have a cab coming and that will be just fine."

"Humph, what kind of way is that for you to travel? You've never caught a cab in your life."

"How do you know?"

"Don't you get smart with me, missy. I can still beat the behind. I don't care how old you get."

"I'm sorry, Mom, I wasn't trying to get smart. But it's for the best that I catch a cab. I don't want to leave my car at the airport for two weeks, and there is no one else available to drive me."

"Oh, so now I'm no one?" She is working herself up to a good mad and I know I have to say something to diffuse her anger soon or there really will be hell to pay the captain. Grabbing her hands in mine, I lead her to the couch to sit next to me.

"Mom, the last two and a half months have been hell on me. I need to get away and regroup and decide just what it is I want to do with the rest of my life. You yourself said I need a break, so I'm taking it."

"But you're going halfway around the world. You could have taken a break in Florida. They have beaches there."

"I know, but I need to do this. Can't you understand?"

With a defeated slump to her shoulders, Mom nods her head. Tears hang from the corners of her eyes and I wipe them away. Leaning forward, I kiss her first on the forehead, then on each cheek. She used to do this to me when I was a little girl and it always made me feel better.

The impatient sound of a car horn prompts me to jump up and grab my bags. "I left the name of the hotel by the phone. I'll call as soon as I get situated. Who knows, with any luck, I might bring home a Latino husband."

"You do and I'll kill you." Her voice is gruff, but she is smiling.

"You know to call me if anything changes."

"Yes, baby, have fun and be careful."

"I will, Momma. Grand Caymans, here I come. Lawd knows, I hope you're ready for me." I laugh all the way to the cab, feeling as giddy as a teenager. The driver rushes around to open the door and lifts my suitcases into the trunk. I skim my mental checklist but can't think of anything that I left behind. If I did leave something, it's too late now. There is no way I am going to risk missing my flight and with the heightened security at the airport, there is no such thing as arriving too early.

"Hartsfield-Jackson, please." I lean my head back on the seat, willing every muscle in my body to relax. My plans for the next two weeks consist of food, drink, sun, and fun and not necessarily in that order. I saw pictures of the hotel I am staying at in a travel magazine during the many nights I spent in the hospital with Sammie. I prayed I would get to go with her, but that isn't possible right now.

Sammie is on a long road to recovery, but she will live; that is the important part. For that I am thankful. I was so sure that I was going to lose her and I thank God each day for sparing her life. Her prognosis is good. She will have to have physical therapy to walk and talk again, but from the preliminary reports she's been blessed. Although I was reluctant to leave her now, Buddy convinced me I would be the next one up on that bed if I don't take some time to myself. Ergo, I planned this little trip to the Caymans by myself. I am going to order up some tall dick or two with a side of latex as my first meal of the day when I get to my hotel. And since my hotel is right on the Seven Mile Beach, I am sure I can pick up some other sustenance along the way.

My perspective changed when I almost lost my sister. I feel like I am being given a second chance to make some changes in my own life. For one thing, I am no longer tormented by the ticking of my biological clock. I thought I needed children to give my life purpose, but that is not necessarily true. My biggest problem is that when I love I give so much of myself away that I never have any left for myself. I did that in my marriage and when the marriage failed it almost destroyed me, and I was doing it with Sammie. Recognizing that I do not have to control everything that goes on in my life has lifted a tremendous weight off my shoulders, and I am determined to keep it off.

# Chauncey

Spells of manipulation are difficult enough, but it becomes particularly dicey when you're trying to control several people at the same time. My daily incantations keep the guards from releasing me from jail before I have complete control of my destiny on the outside. That is the easy part because I can immediately see the effects of my spell when the guards bring me my meals. Controlling Tarcia is also easy because she is a simple-minded bitch who doesn't know her ass from a hole in the ground. Her cousin, however, presents more of a challenge because she is familiar with the tricks of the trade.

Her influence is keeping me in this shit hole and I have just about lost my patience with the whole damn thing. Tarcia can't recall how many visits she's actually made to the jail, but she remembers the nightly phone calls she accepted in which she revealed in vivid detail just how well endowed Kentee is. I cannot wait to have that jimmy for myself. In fact, she shared so many details, it's taking all of my powers as a master priestess to remain steadfast in my determination to stay in jail until the last pieces of the puzzle are in place. I'm not been concerned about Kentee's preference for pussy because I've been controlling his destiny too with the blood that Tarcia gave me. I don't use it to mess with his libido. I use it to control his fantasies. Instead of pussy-popping, he dreams of ass slapping, balls meeting balls, dick-flopping, and lip-locking. My dick is getting hard just thinking about how sweet it is going to be.

I engineered the call Kentee made to Tarcia. It is very important that he remain connected to her for my plan to work. I have funneled most of my assets into her account and I need Kentee to make sure that Tarcia doesn't do something stupid with that money. She is so naïve, it is hard to believe that she has made it this far without someone like me in her life. After I am freed, I will discard her like a used paper towel. Of course, she will have to disappear once we get settled into our new place. Perhaps she will return to New Orleans, back to the very roots she tried to deny, with no memory of her life in Atlanta. Giving Tarcia the *katra* was a big mistake, one that I hope will not come back and bite me in the ass. She was supposed to burn it along with the contents of the bag I gave her for Kentee.

When I first met Tarcia, I honestly wanted to help her. I was bored and she provided a diversion from my daily routine. However, I fell in love with her man as she shared details that she wouldn't normally share with her female friends for the very same reason. She makes him sound so enticing, I just have to have him for myself. I told her casting spells isn't for the weak at heart, but that silly bitch doesn't know what she wants. Serves her right for trusting a fucking convict anyway.

# Lasonji

Tarcia's crude drawing is driving me nuts. It is clearly part of a *gris*, but I can't tell where it is directed. She isn't dating anymore to my knowledge, so what is she doing with it? I destroyed the napkin, but it was a copy—of that much I am sure. Where is the original? She'd told me she doesn't believe, but too many things are happening for that to be true. I no longer believe that Kentee is working his own magic on Tarcia. Frankly, he is not that clever, but I do believe that he is a part of the puzzle. Since Tarcia has no other friends, he has to be the link. Whatever it is I am up against, I'm not powerful enough to stop it; that much is clear to me. She has stepped into some deep shit this time, and I will do all I can to pull her out if I can without drowning my damn self.

# *Tarcia*

O nce again, Kentee beat me to the coffee house. He is starting to scare me because punctuality was never one of his strong points, especially if there isn't something in it for him.

"Okay, who are you and what have you done to Kentee?"

"Huh?" He is reading the newspaper when I approach him. This is another first. Usually if it wasn't a tit-and-ass magazine, he wasn't reading it.

"You're acting like a stranger. What's up with that?" I sit down across from him, playing with my keys to keep from looking into his eyes.

"What? I just want to spend some time with you. Is that a crime?"

"No. Is that the classified section?"

"Yeah, where are you looking to move?"

"I'm not set on any particular place. I just know I want out of DeKalb County."

"What about Rockdale or Covington? They aren't too far from city life."

"Okay, I'm game. Let's go."

"Have you thought about renting a house?"

"No, I'm sure I can't afford that. Plus, I don't want to be cutting no grass and shit."

"Look at this ad: *'For rent—three-bedroom ranch, two bathrooms, two-car garage, fenced yard, must see $750 month/$750 deposit.'*"

"Wow, that's the going rate for most apartments. Let's check this one out."

He calls the number listed in the ad and gets the directions. We go out to the parking lot and, without asking if I want to drive my own car, he opens the door to his car for me and I climb in.

"So are you seeing anybody?"

"To be honest, I've been so busy with work I haven't had time to look for another man."

"Yeah, me too."

I start laughing at the irony of it all.

"Hey, what's so funny?"

"Us. If someone would have told me that we would wind up as friends I would have called them a bold-faced liar. I just knew you were going to become my baby's daddy."

"Dag, I know what you mean. But I like this new twist to our relationship. Perhaps that's where we failed in the first place. We were so busy taking it to the physical, we didn't develop the emotional."

"Oh, Lawd, you tryin' to get deep on a sista."

"I'm serious, Tarcia. We skipped all the preliminaries and got disqualified." We arrive at the house before I can answer him, but he is right. However, I'm not going to tell him that.

The house is nice, right on a cul-de-sac in what appears to be a quiet neighborhood. Since it is vacant, we are able to peek in the windows. From what we can see and smell, even from the outside, it is newly painted. Without going inside, I decide to take it. It is more space than I actually need but it is perfect for my budget and it feels just like home.

"Do you like it?" We spin around as this older white lady approaches us, dangling keys in her hand. Before I can respond Kentee answers.

"Can we see inside?"

"Of course." She leads us through the house and it is perfect. While I am no Susie Homemaker, I can't beat the price with a stick.

"Where do I sign?"

"You will have to fill out a credit application, and if you qualify, when do you want to move in?"

"Yesterday."

"That soon, huh?"

"Yes."

"Okay. Here is the application. It will take a few days to process and I'll be back in touch."

"Oh, can't I fill it out now? I'll pay a rush fee if that will help move the process along, and I'm willing to pay the first six months in advance." Kentee looks at me like I've lost my mind.

"Well…that's not the normal procedure but since you like it so much, I can call the application in while you wait."

"Thanks." I rush over to the counter, quickly fill out the application, and give her a check for the credit application fee. Kentee pulls my arm and ushers me off to the side of the living room.

"Aren't you rushing this? I mean, we haven't even looked at the other houses I circled."

"This is the one, Kentee. I feel it."

"Uh, okay. So when did you become such a big baller?"

"Recent development. I'll tell ya about it later. I just want her to say yes." We wait for half an hour before I am given the keys. Things go so smoothly, it is like someone is orchestrating it.

"Hey, how about I take you to dinner to celebrate?"

"That would be great. I got to call my cousin first, so I'll meet you in the car." I don't want to talk to Lasonji around Kentee because I still feel like she doesn't like him very much and there is no telling what she will say. She answers on the first ring. I quickly tell her about the house and even though she appears to be happy, there is something funny in her voice.

"Look, I'm going out to dinner to celebrate. If you're home, I'll pop my head in."

"Oh, by the way, some guy named Chauncey said to give him a call. You got his number?"

"Huh? No, I don't have a number for him. Did he leave one?" I dial the number in a state of shock. I know Chauncey has mad privileges at the jail, but I didn't realize that he has a phone.

When Chauncey answers, at first I am afraid it is a guard, but I can tell it is Chauncey by his sista-girl response.

"Chile, where you at? My ass is cold. Can you come pick a sista up?"

"Chauncey? Pick you up? Where are you?"

"I'm a free woman. They just gave me my papers and I need a place to crash."

"Oh wow, damn. I'm about to go to dinner. Can I hit you back?" Before I can get the words out my mouth good, I hear an echo in my head that makes my blood run cold. *Pick me up.*

"Chauncey, I'll be right there. See you in about fifteen minutes."

"Good, and bring Kentee."

*How does he know I am with Kentee?*

# Chauncey

I wouldn't change my life for all the tea in China. In fact, if it went any better I wouldn't be able to stand myself. There are two surprising aspects of my life that I didn't plan. One is that Tarcia is still in it. I'd planned on using her to get to Kentee, but it wasn't as difficult as I had envisioned. Sure, he balked when I stuck my dick in his ass, but he's with the program now. The other surprise was finding out that pussy isn't all that bad and that I love sucking female boobies. Man tits are one thing, but it goes to an entire different level when you get to hold them in your hands as you suck them. Kentee taught me that. When I lick his tits I use the flat of my tongue, however, I suck her boobs using my entire mouth to twirl the nipple. I enjoy it so much, I don't even get jealous when he suckles for what feels like hours. I just take the one that's left and have at it. I've even gotten so bold as to stick my finger in her cunt while he sucks her off. He would catch her coming and going and I reap the benefits as I wear out his ass.

For now, I draw the line at eating pussy. I don't believe that hype and raw fish ain't for me. So I let Kentee do the honors while I suck his dick or she sucks mine. Either way, all of us are getting something out the deal. Will I ever eat pussy? I can't say.

I've kissed Kentee after he has partaken, so in a sense, I guess the big test will be when she starts to drip in my mouth and if I have the ability to get her there.

To the outside world, I don't exist. People don't see me entering and exiting the house. Kentee and Tarcia don't speak of me. They can't, but when those doors close, it's on.

Until then, we are one big happy family, open to new possibilities. Care to join us?

## THE END

# About the Author

A native of Baltimore, Maryland currently residing in the Atlanta suburbs, Tina wears many hats, as she balances her time between that of wife, mother, talk-show hostess/interviewer. Tina was first introduced to readers across the country by her debut novel, *All That Drama*, in 2004, and its sequel, *Lawd, Mo' Drama*, in March 2007. Tina also hosts a weekly internet radio show called "Real Talk with Tina McKinney" at www.blogtalkradio.com/tinabrooksmckinney. Visit www.tinamckinney.com or www.myspace.com/tinamckinney.

IF YOU ENJOYED "FOOL, STOP TRIPPIN'," GET STARTED
ON THE BACK STORY WITH THIS EXCERPT FROM

# all that drama

BY TINA BROOKS MCKINNEY

AVAILABLE FROM STREBOR BOOKS

## chapter 4

Sammie married the first man that asked. At the tender age of eighteen, he took her from her parents' house and moved her halfway across the country to California. His name was Jessie Alexander and he was six years her senior. Jessie took Sammie to California because he wanted to mold her into a supermodel. She stood 6'2" and her beauty was unequaled. She looked like an Egyptian Queen and her movements were as sleek as a jaguar's. Jessie loved showing her off. His aspirations for her were motivated by his greed for money. Jessie was a hair designer by trade so Sammie was like a giant black Barbie doll to him. He did her hair, her makeup and even chose her clothes. He also scheduled numerous appointments with various modeling agencies trying to break into the fashion industry.

Despite his best efforts, Sammie never received those high-paying jobs mostly because her heart wasn't into modeling. She just went through the motions to keep Jessie happy.

Jessie was a pretty boy. He had light green eyes and clear caramel-colored skin. His eyes were slightly slanted and he had very long eye-lashes to which he secretly applied mascara. His hair was longer than that of most women, and he wore it either in a bob or a ponytail. He was conceited, arrogant and egotistical. He was unaffected by the looks he received from his daring hairstyles. Most people thought that he was gay because he was a hairdresser and because of the way that he carried himself. He stood about 6'2" and was rail thin, weighing perhaps 155 pounds soaking wet.

Jessie was frustrated that Sammie was not making the money that he believed she could make. He had invested a small fortune building up her portfolio on one hand and exploiting her on the other.

During the day Jessie promoted her beauty and at night he exploited her body. On her twenty-first birthday, Jessie found a small strip club in a remote section of town that catered to an unsavory clientele.

"Jessie, why are we celebrating my birthday here?" Sammie inquired, not quite comfortable with all the women in various stages of undress.

"Uh, I just thought it would be different, that's all," he mumbled in response.

Sammie tried her best not to look at the women but everywhere she looked all she saw were tits and ass. A waitress came within shouting distance and Sammie stopped her.

"May I have a gin and tonic, please?" Sammie ordered, while looking at Jessie for approval. Not that she really needed his approval to have a drink; she just needed to know if they could afford it. Jessie nodded his consent.

"Look at her," he said, pointing to a lightskinned woman on the stage. She had bent over at the waist and was sucking her own pussy. She alternated between fondling her breast and sucking herself, which was driving the men wild.

Sammie glanced in her direction and quickly averted her eyes.

"What about her?" she inquired, studying the tablecloth as if seeking answers to life's most difficult questions.

"She can't hold a candle to you, baby," he said. Sammie fully looked up at him for the first time since entering the bar. He called her "baby" and it had been some time since he had done that. She looked to the stage to see if she could see what Jessie had seen.

"Look, she can't even move like you. She looks all stiff and unnatural!" he said. The waitress placed Sammie's drink on the table and she quickly drained the glass. She signaled for another refill. Jessie did not even notice that the waitress had been there since his eyes were glued to the stage and it had his full attention.

Jessie held up a bill and the woman on the stage came over to the table. She did a special little dance in front of Jessie and Sammie turned red. She could not stand to watch the woman but it was even worse watching Jessie as he slobbered all over himself. He tucked the bill in the front of her g-string and the woman went back to center stage. He turned his attention back to Sammie with a *what do you think* look in his eyes, obviously expecting a response from her without asking.

"She's all right," Sammie said, not knowing what else to say to describe the other woman.

"She could learn a lot from you," Jessie said.

"Is that a compliment?" Sammie asked, not sure how to take his remark.

"Yeah, if you don't know nothing else, you sure know how to shake that ass," Jessie said, eyeing her midsection.

She no longer felt like she was being complimented. Jessie continued to ignore her for the rest of the night.

Over the next few months, Jessie continued to take Sammie to the strip clubs at least three nights a week. He never told her their destination until they pulled up in front of the dimly lit bars. Sammie eventually learned to tolerate it. However, she still felt uncomfortable openly staring at the women. She tried to imagine them with clothes in a fashion show but could not get past the tits and ass on display.

One night they arrived at Paradise. The club was real crowded when they got there but a table had been reserved for them in the front row, close enough to the stage for Jessie to get his hands on any of the dancers if he wanted to and did. Sammie saw the same dancer that she had seen the first night Jessie had brought her to the club. She was talking with the manager. They were both looking in her direction and she began to sense an uncomfortable feeling in the pit of her stomach again. Sammie knew the woman's first name was Kim but that was the extent of her knowledge.

She looked over at Jessie and he had a shit-eating grin plastered on his face that usually meant he was up to no good.

"I want you to do this for me," he said. His voice was gentle but it had an underlying tone that said, *if you don't, bitch, there will be hell to pay.*

"Do what?" Sammie asked, leaning closer so she did not misunderstand or misinterpret what he was saying. She also wanted to get out of the eyesight of Kim and the manager. The hair at the back of her neck began to stand up as she noticed the maniacal look in Jessie's eyes.

"You know damn well what," he snapped. "Don't pretend like you don't know why I have been bringing your ass here. You're not that stupid," he jeered.

His evil side surfaced and Sammie swallowed a knot of fear that formed in her throat and threatened to close off her airway. She knew what he wanted but she was unwilling to give it to him.

"Please, Jessie, not that," she pleaded.

"Shut up! You're sniveling," he shouted back. "We need the money, plain and simple."

"But we can make it some other way. I'll get a full-time job," she declared.

"Doing what? Your dumb ass didn't finish high school! You ain't making shit with those modeling gigs I managed to get you either," he announced.

"Jessie, I have never done this type of stuff before. I can't," she said as tears welled up in the corners of her eyes. Just then Sammie noticed Kim making her way to their table.

"Bitch, you better not embarrass me in front of Kim. You're going to dance and you better make it good," he growled at Sammie, slamming his hand against the table to emphasize his point. The force of the blow caused Sammie to jump.

"Are you ready for the spotlight?" Kim asked, grabbing Sammie's hands and propelling her out of her seat. She winked at Jessie as he patted her on her partially clad behind.

"What the fuck?" Sammie interjected, looking to Jessie for understanding of what was expected of her. What she was getting loud and clear was that Kim and Jessie had developed some kind of relationship.

"I, uh," Sammie stuttered still confused.

"Don't be shy, girl," Kim said. "We all acted like this the first time. Jessie tells me you're a natural and born for the stage! For tonight, you can borrow some of my things but after that, you will be expected to bring your own." She turned and pushed Sammie towards the door. One final look at Jessie's stern face told Sammie that she had no choice in this matter. He did not smile as she walked away. His face was frozen like a block of ice, wearing a menacing sneer that was meant solely for her.

Kim led Sammie into the back dressing room. She cried inwardly. She knew she had little to no choice in this matter if she didn't want to receive an ass whipping from Jessie when she got home. It was evident that he had arranged this before they arrived at the club.

"Don't worry, honey," Kim said, trying to console her. "The first time is always the worst. Just pretend that you are home alone with Jessie and no one else is in the room. He told me how hot you make him when you dance for him," Kim went on.

"Jessie told you that?" Sammie asked in a state of shock. First of all, she had not danced for him since they first moved to California and second, now days he acted bored. She wanted to ask her just how well she knew Jessie but thought better of it.

"You have a great manager," she said with a broad grin. "I wish I had someone like him to look after me."

"Manager?" Sammie choked. "Is that what he told you he was to me?" Sammie asked, unable to contain the fire she felt upon hearing her own husband refer to himself as only her manager.

"Yeah, sugar. Count yourself lucky," she said with the utmost sincerity. "Some of us are not blessed with good management."

*If she only knew*, Sammie thought to herself. She wanted to correct Kim on the true nature of their relationship but she was not ready for the big beat-down that would ultimately follow if she did.